POPPIES

Whether in her serious literary novels, her children's books, or the lighter romances written under the pseudonym Susan Scarlett, Noel Streatfeild wrote about what she knew, and put to good use the experiences of her early home life and career. So from her vicarage upbringing we have *Parson's Nine*, *Under the Rainbow*, and *The Bell Family.* From her work in munitions at the Woolwich Arsenal in World War I we gain *Murder While You Work.* From her social work in Deptford came *Tops and Bottoms,* and her extensive war work in Civil Defence and the WVS went into *I Ordered a Table for Six, Saplings* and *When the Siren Wailed.* There was even a short spell of modelling which she used in *Clothes-Pegs.* And then there was the theatre, where her ten year acting career embraced many branches of the profession. Chorus girls and concert parties (*It Pays to be Good, Poppies for England*), pantomime, with its troupe of children, (*Wintle's Wonders*), ballet training (*Ballet Shoes, Pirouette*), a touring Shakespeare company and her eventual disillusionment with the profession (*The Wicharts*) - all of these found their way into her books. She had a long and distinguished literary career with 90 books, the Carnegie Medal and an O.B.E. to her credit.

BY THE SAME AUTHOR

Clothes-Pegs
Sally-Ann
The Man in the Dark
Ten Way Street
Peter and Paul
Babbacombe's
Under the Rainbow
Summer Pudding
Murder While You Work
Pirouette
Love in a Mist

POPPIES FOR ENGLAND

SUSAN SCARLETT

Greyladies

Published by
Greyladies
an imprint of The Old Children's Bookshelf
175 Canongate, Edinburgh EH8 8BN

This edition first published 2008

ISBN 978-0-9559413-1-3

Set in Sylfaen / Perpetua
Printed and bound by Biddles, Kings Lynn, Norfolk

Preface

An interest in the theatre and the performance arts runs throughout Noel Streatfeild's work, including several of the 12 novels she wrote under the alliterative pseudonym 'Susan Scarlett'. She was inclined to dismiss these novels as little more than light romances, but they were well received when they were published, with favourable reviews from the critics. For example, the reviewer in the *Daily Sketch* said of the first of these novels, *Clothes-Pegs* (1939), 'It is not only original in theme but sparkling in style. Susan Scarlett is an accomplished writer who need have no fear as to her future.'

Reading the Susan Scarlett novels today one can see many of the themes that were to crop up again time and again in Streatfeild's children's books – the father whose shop goes smash or struggles to survive (*Sally-Ann* and *White Boots*), the orphan making her own way in the world (*Ten Way Street* and *Thursday's Child*), the discovery of the world of the film studio (*Love in a Mist* and *The Painted Garden*). Then there is the use of language that time and again evokes one of the better-known books. The Mayne family in *The Man in the Dark* refer to their father's wealthy patients as "The Jams" because they are the people who put jam on their bread. The characters, especially perhaps the younger children and the family servants, are characters who we have met already in Streatfeild's better-known books. And there is the familiar interest in clothes, from Lorna's faded green velvet dress which leads her to go shoplifting in *Clothes-Pegs* to the pink plastic shorts and top worn by plump Betty in *Poppies for England* – so very reminiscent of the black plastic outfits worn by *Gemma and Sisters*.

Susan Scarlett books are a veritable goldmine for any reader wanting to enter more fully into her world, yet she suppressed mention of them. The first post-war edition of *Authors and Writers Who's Who and Reference Guide* contains an entry on Streatfeild, but there is no mention of her work as Susan Scarlett. In her Bodley Head Monograph on Streatfeild published in 1961, Barbara Ker Wilson notes 'All the time she has been writing her children's books, Noel Streatfeild has also continued to increase her reputation as an adult novelist. She has written sixteen adult novels'. That bibliography not only omits all mention of the Susan Scarlett books but also a number of such minor publications as the 12 Baby books, *The Picture Story Book of Britain* (1951) and *Christmas with the Chrystals* (1959).

According to her biographer, Angela Bull, in *Noel Streatfeild* (Collins, 1984) Streatfeild dismissed the Scarlett novels: "she rightly considered them to be very much inferior to her serious novels. They were romantic pot-boilers, of a type which Noel had deplored before financial necessity drove her into writing them." In a talk given in Manchester in September 1937 Streatfeild said: 'I don't myself care for books which come under the heading of "a strong romance". I don't believe in idylls of that ilk.' They are considerably happier in tone than her adult literary novels, which at best take a dark view of human nature.

Life and Works

Noel Streatfeild was born in Frant, Sussex, on Christmas Eve in 1895, the second child of the Revd William Streatfeild and his wife Janet. A vicarage child, she grew up in Amberley, St Leonards and Eastbourne. As an adult Streatfeild drew continuously on her vicarage background, not only in her semi-autobiographical *A Vicarage Family* (1963) but also in her work for BBC Radio's Children's Hour later published as *The Bell Family* (1954) and *New Town* (1960) and in her novels for adults. Her second book to be published, *Parson's Nine* (1932), and her Susan Scarlett novel *Under the Rainbow* (1941) share as hero a clergyman who may have resembled William Streatfeild in character.

During the First World War, Streatfeild worked in munitions at Woolwich Arsenal; an experience she made use of in *Murder While You Work* (1944) and in her first novel, *The Whicharts* (1931). In *Murder While You Work*, the heroine, Judy Rest, a former VAD, is on her way to work in munitions at Biglands, Pinlock. She falls in love with the Hon. Nicholas Parsons (the girls in the first few Scarlett novels tend to fall in love with titled men). In *The Whicharts*, the Brigadier settles £500 a year on his mistress Rose and saddles her with bringing up his three illegitimate daughters. He dies and, short of money, she goes to work in a munitions factory.

In 1919 Streatfeild joined the Academy of Dramatic Art (later RADA) in London. She worked as an ingénue in repertory, shows of the kind described in *Poppies for England*, and pantomime. Throughout her writing career,

Streatfeild made excellent use of the nitty-gritty information she picked up from her own experience. In the 1920s Noel worked as a model. In *Clothes-Pegs* (1939) she details precisely the clothes a professional model would need to buy: 'A small satin suspender belt. Step-ins. As sheer as you can buy. Brassiere, backless'. In both that book and in *Away from the Vicarage* (1965), she describes how the models 'would sit in their underclothes eating sticky buns waiting for various groups of buyers' and be given glasses of port to keep them going. In *Sally-Ann* (1939), the romance of a beauty specialist who buys a second-hand couture frock, she exclaims, 'What a difference clothes made. This deceptively plain frock swept her away from the girl who went to work every morning.'

No one claims that Streatfeild was more than a moderately successful actress, but it gave her the background she needed to make her books real. When, in *Poppies for England*, Streatfeild has Alfred explain how to apply a professional make-up, there can be no doubt she knows what she is talking about: "Streak your whole face with number nine. Show him which is number nine, Dan." "Now, rub that smooth all over as if it was your own skin. See you don't get a mask, that means take the paint well down to your neck. Show him how not to get a mask, Dan." *Poppies* focuses on how to run a concert party in a holiday camp – the need to get permission to perform various songs, the struggle to get the necessary clothing coupons to make costumes, and information about how much a performer with Dulcie's background should be paid. The happiness with which young Betty plunges into the activities of a Junior Camper – 'table tennis and physical training and skating and hikes and treasure hunts' reminds one vividly of Hilary's enjoyment of the holiday camp in *Wintle's Wonders* (1957) – as does the fact that the camp's theatre orchestra is conducted by Pinkie Pinkerton. In *Poppies for England*, the spoilt heroine is called Dulcie (another echo from *Wintle's Wonders*), and the camp entertainment is run by Pinkie Barrow.

As an actress, Streatfeild toured South Africa, Rhodesia, New Zealand and Australia. These experiences did not creep into her Susan Scarlett books, which are firmly set in England. Her father died in 1929, and Streatfeild returned home and took up a career as a writer. She wrote plays for adults and children, somewhat grim novels, including *The Whicharts*, where three sisters, who uncannily resemble the Fossil sisters, become actresses and dancers, *Tops and Bottoms* (1933) set in the world of the music hall, and *It Pays to Be Good* (1936) tracing the rise of Flossie Elk from the squalor of Madama Elise's Dancing Academy to stardom and marriage to wealthy Lord Menton. In the same year she published her classic work, *Ballet Shoes*.

In 1939, Streatfeild was commissioned to write *Clothes-Pegs*, the first of her 12 Susan Scarlett novels for Hodder and Stoughton. The novels were serialised by various women's magazines owned by Amalgamated Press, and the steady income promised by the books was a godsend. In *Away from the Vicarage*, she refers to her 'dress allowance of fifty pounds a year' and the fact that she found her parents extraordinary about money ('Victoria could not believe that they thought she had saved anything out of her salary of three pounds a week, knowing it not only had to keep her but pay for stage shoes and other accessories.').

Throughout the war years Streatfeild focused on her adult and Scarlett novels, producing little to match her pre-war trio of *Ballet Shoes* (1936), *Tennis Shoes* (1937) and *The Circus is Coming* (1938) for which last she deservedly won the Carnegie Medal. *The House in Cornwall* appeared in 1940 and *The Children of Primrose Lane* in 1941 but nothing of lasting merit until the publication of *Curtain Up* in 1944 and *Party Frock* in 1946. These, like *Poppies*, reflect the physical difficulties of putting on a show in war torn England. During the war, Streatfeild kept writing but also trained as an air raid warden and worked in the Women's Voluntary Service, running a canteen service in Deptford. Her flat opposite the Natural History Museum in London was bombed in 1941.

In summer 1947 Streatfeild visited the film studios of Hollywood and witnessed the making of the film of *The Secret Garden*, with Margaret O'Brien as Mary Lennox. This experience led not only to *The Painted Garden* (1949) but also to her final Scarlett novel, *Love in a Mist* and the Rose of England Films Incorporated studios described in that book.

Streatfeild went on to write many books, some of which were broadcast on radio and television, including her last truly great novel, the story of four conventional children set free in Ireland during *The Growing Summer* (1966). She wrote three slightly fictionalised autobiographies and drew on her Edwardian childhood in *Thursday's Child*, *Far-to-Go* and *Gran-Nannie* (both 1976). As a child I remember visiting the Puffin Club's exhibition in London and queuing up to see her. When she wrote 'Bless you, Joy' in my new autograph book, I felt she meant it. In 1983 she became an OBE. She died three years later on 11 September 1986 in London.

Susan Scarlett

Noel Streatfeild adopted the name Susan Scarlett as a good way of earning money, and one's impression is that she thought of her Hodder & Stoughton novels as little more than pot-boilers. But there is more to them than that. Her other books for adults – *A Shepherdess of Sheep* (1934), *I Ordered a Table for Six* (1942), *Saplings* (1945) and the rest – are at times poignant, but in the main they present a bleak tragic view of society. It is almost as if by adopting a cloak of anonymity, Streatfeild/Scarlett allowed herself to indulge in romantic fantasies. The woman reader could pick up the latest Susan Scarlett secure in the knowledge that nothing very unpleasant would happen along the way and all would end in a happy peal of wedding bells.

As Barbara Ker Wilson notes, 'children feature quite largely in her adult novels', and this is true of the first Scarlett novel, *Clothes-Pegs* (1939). It is the story of Annabel who stitches in a high-class dressmaker's shop, and Lord David de Bett, 'as rich as Rothschild'. Annabel is chosen to be a model and casts aside her 'wool vest and buff artificial silk knickers with elastics at the knees'. Shop-lifting, shrimps for tea and the fact that his close friend has fallen in love with Annabel's colleague who has a father in Wormwood Scrubs, draw them together.

Both *Clothes-Pegs* and her next book, *Sally-Ann* (1939), pander to escapism. Annabel and Ann are from homes where money is short, the daughters go out to work and showing a respectable face to the world is very important. Both fall in love with titled men – Ann's is Sir Timothy Munster, son of a soap manufacturer. Ann is thrown into the aristocratic world when she becomes a substitute bridesmaid at a society wedding and meets Timothy. He takes her to the Ivy. Marie Tempest, Dodie Smith, John Gielgud, Jessie Matthews and Sonnie Hale are there. 'Ann felt dizzy. Such a plethora of fame.' Does this reflect Streatfeild's own sparkling experience of London in the 1930s? The story is brought down to life when they go for a walk on the sands and find a policeman by the body of 'a young man, dressed in nothing but his pants.' And it ends with social reform as Ann plans that after the wedding she will introduce lockers into the Munster factories and let people decide when they want to go on holiday.

Peter and Paul was published in 1940 and is the story of vicarage twins, plain Pauline and pretty Petronella, who go to work in a dressmaking business owned by Lady Bliss's nephew David and run by the widowed Hon. Moira Renton. (Her marriage was not a success and 'He fell over Beachy Head.') Petronella is meant for better things and secures a career in Hollywood late in the book. Family jargon abounds – 'I-swear-by-us-being-twins-never-to-say-what-I-shall-now-hear-so-help-me-God.' recalling both the Fossil sisters and Harriet's family from *White Boots.*

Published in 1940, *Ten Way Street* is set in the world of the theatre. Orphan Beverley Shaw becomes governess to the three difficult children of actress Margot Dale. The turns of phrase describing the children are pure Streatfeild. When David is ordered to spend a day in bed with nothing but milk he comments, 'You're a very nasty woman. Anyone decent wouldn't try starving a person out.' Margot is more of an egoist than the Dulcie of *Poppies*. She is portrayed as an actress of outstanding presence, somewhat like the grandmother in *Curtain Up* in her theatricality. Beverley's romance with the biological chemist is almost incidental to the story of the actress and her family.

Babbacombe's (1941) sees a return to shop work and life in a big department store. The romance between Beth, the Junior in 'Gowns', and David, son of the firm, is pleasant enough, but the spice in the story comes from the outrageous behaviour of Beth's cousin Dulcie, a lift girl at Babbacombe's with decidedly cheap values. All three of Streatfeild's Dulcies, in *Poppies*, *Wintle's Wonders* and *Babbacombe's*, are self-centred creatures, but only the Dulcie of *Poppies* is fortunate enough to find a man who knows the worst about her and loves her still.

A concert by 'the Southerners' plays a pivotal role in the rehabilitation of James Longford, *The Man in the Dark* (1940), who has not left the house since he was blinded in a motor race six years before. The book received good reviews: Philip Page in the *Daily Mail* wrote 'Not for many moons have I read a novel so charming, so alive. I congratulate her on her delicious book.'

Amateur dramatics bring two lovers together in *Under the Rainbow*, a love story set in Sussex. 17-year-old Chloe and schoolmaster Michael play the leads in Arnold Ridley's

The Ghost Train, although the major story concerns vicar Martin Richards and the two women in his life. *Summer Pudding* (1943) is a country romance ending in a series of misunderstandings that result in a quick succession of engagements and happy endings for all. A darker work is *Murder While You Work* (1944), Streatfeild's crime novel, in which the murderer polishes off various members of her husband's family – including the dog! – using a glass syringe and sedative in the soup.

First published in March 1947, *Poppies for England* is the story of a concert party and concerns the attempted reformation of slightly spoilt Dulcie Corner by her father. The importance of songs in capturing the public's imagination, as in *Tops and Bottoms* (1933), plays its part. *Pirouette* (1948) is Susan Scarlett's ballet story focusing on the fortunes of dancers who fall in love with each other's brothers. The detail about the hard-working life of the dancer does not overwhelm the story.

A gap of three years followed before the appearance of *Love in a Mist* (1951) the final Susan Scarlett story. This is the story of three sisters-in-law, their children and the family matriarch 'Mum-Tring'. As in *The Painted Garden*, there is considerable detail about the day-to-day routine of a film studio as young Paul unexpectedly becomes an actor.

The Susan Scarlett romantic novels were designed to lift their woman readers out of the difficult times of the Second World War and its aftermath, to enable Noel Streatfeild to earn some money, and to establish herself as a professional full-time writer. They succeed on all three counts.

Joy Wotton

POPPIES FOR ENGLAND

It was twelve-fifteen. The kitchen clock was always fast, but Alice had heard the mid-day hooter at the margarine factory. She gave her stew a prod with a fork. "Bother these carrots! Always disobliging."

Alice Corner was an attractive woman. She looked all her forty-two years, but she had kept her figure, and taken what care she could of her skin, and her hair was smooth and glossy. The last years had been hard on her and had left a legacy of lines, but they gave her face character. She had a quiet voice, but there was firmness behind it. What Alice said was listened to.

There was a sound of running feet down the stairs. Dulcie Corner rushed into the kitchen.

"Goodness, Mum! The table isn't laid. You know I must have dinner sharp at twelve-thirty when there's a matinée."

Alice looked at Dulcie. She never could look at Dulcie without a shiver of pride running down her spine. However had she and John given birth to anything as beautiful as Dulcie? Her own hair, even before it faded, was honoured by being called mid-brown, mid-mud her brothers used to say. John was what you might describe as sandy. How then had Dulcie that moonlight fair hair, falling in waves to her shoulders, so fair that on the stage it looked silver? How had Dulcie come by those enormous blue eyes surrounded, of all unlikely things, by coal black lashes? Why had Dulcie a skin like a rose petal? Her own face freckled in the summer and chapped in the winter, and she had a nose that any change of climate was apt to turn pink. John was inclined to go brown and stop that way all through the winter. He was not so brown now, he had never picked up his colour properly since the prison camp; his skin, even when she had married him, and he had been very young then, had never been anything near a rose petal. More like a dried-up autumn leaf, as she had always told him when he kissed her. The other children had not come by any of these glories. Young Dickie was not bad-looking, tall, straight and manly, but he had a shocking skin for spots. Of course, all boys of his age were bound to have a spot or two, but Dickie looked like an old strawberry when the seeds were sticking out. Betty was a nice little roundabout with quite pretty hair, if you did not mind hair being straight, mid-brown, of course, but good lights in it the day it was washed; her colouring was not bad if you liked a high colour. People often mentioned Betty's high colour. Alice was not sure if it was mentioned in admiration or sympathy. "Extraordinary high colour that child has." "Never saw a child with such red cheeks." Of course, at fourteen you had all the faults; quite likely Betty would fine down, and with make-up she could do something about her colouring, but whatever she did she would not be Dulcie. From the cradle Dulcie had never known a plain day. As a baby people had stopped in the street saying, "Ooh, what a lovely child!" As a toddler she had won three beauty prizes, and by the time she went to school men were turning round to look after her. Dulcie was a responsibility, but a responsibility in which Alice gloried. Still, however much you may glory in your daughter, you can't have her laying down the law to her mother.

"Well, you're ready, aren't you? How about you laying the table yourself?"

Dulcie's eyes became dreamy. Dulcie's dreamy look was well known in the family. It meant that she was planning how to get out of something she did not want to do.

"I would, Mum, but I want to give my hair another brush."

Alice had never had the faintest hope that Dulcie would lay the table. The suggestion had only been thrown out to show who was lord of the kitchen. She nodded resignedly.

"All right, dear. Give Betty a call."

When Betty moved it was as if horses were stampeding. The kitchen ceiling shook and a piece of plaster, loosened by the bombing, fell on to the kitchen table, and the stairs creaked as she bounded down. Alice heard the sideboard cupboard thrown open, the plate basket put down with such a crash that the spoons and forks jingled; even placing the mustard, pepper and salt pots was marked by three separate thumps. Quite unconsciously Alice braced herself against the moment when the kitchen door would be flung open and Betty bounce in for the hot plates.

To be almost fifteen is an awkward age for anybody. For Betty it was a particularly awkward age. She bulged wherever it was possible to bulge. Coupons, or rather the lack of them, made it necessary to dress her in what was about rather than what suited her. What was about was a school gym tunic. Never an attractive garment, on Betty it was at least three inches shorter behind than in front, for it caught up on what her brother called her tail-piece, and no amount of pulling ever kept it in place. She was cruel on her stockings, and so, against her will, Alice kept her in socks. Betty had not the legs for socks; her calves bulged over them. Not that Betty cared; she had an incurably gay disposition. To her life was a riot of fun from the time she got up in the morning to the time she went to bed at night. Nobody who came near Betty could help getting fond of her. To be close to such an intensity of enjoyment gave pleasure to existence. Moreover, Betty really liked being useful. It did not matter to her who asked for help; she at once responded. It was not always a fortunate responding, as when she gave away her only pair of gym shoes to another girl at school. "But, Mum, she hadn't got any fit to wear, and she had a chance of winning the long jump. I hadn't a chance of winning anything, so it was stupid me having good shoes." Alice had said no more but had gone round to the girl's parents and fetched the shoes back. Since Betty could talk she had done a good deal of fetching back.

Betty put her arm round Alice's waist with such violence that she almost threw her off her feet.

"What's for dinner, Mum?" She leant forward and sniffed. "Stew. Oh, goody, goody!" She took the plates from Alice. "You know, Mum, I don't think there is any food I absolutely adore more than any other, but if I had just one thing that I might eat and nothing else, I think I should choose stew."

Alice refrained from reminding Betty that she had made the same remark yesterday about cod. Instead she asked:

"Dad in?"

"No. But Dickie is." Betty lowered her voice. "I'm afraid he isn't getting into that show. I watched him come up the road, and he had a bent-in-the-middle look."

Alice sighed.

"Oh, dear, I am sorry; he'll be disappointed."

Betty paused by the door.

"He's the wrong age, you know, Mum. Seventeen's awkward. He isn't a man and he isn't a boy. You all shouted me down the other night, but I was quite right when I said that what he ought to take to was animals. Nobody could see what he looked like as the front legs of a horse, and all that tap-dancing he does would come in very useful. The front legs are expected to dance beautifully."

"Take the plates in. I'm just bringing the stew, and for goodness sake don't tell Dickie he ought to apply for the front legs of a horse. A person who's tried for a dancing part in a revue and not got it won't be pleased at the suggestion." Alice stopped, her head lifted, her voice took on a warmth of which she was unconscious. "There's Dad. When you've put down the plates, Betty, give him a kiss, he likes one of us to be around when he comes in."

The family sat down to dinner. It was still quite funny to Alice not to be sitting at the head of the table. For five years she had sat at the head of the table. When John was first taken prisoner she had put Betty close to her so that she could move her plate if she was eating carelessly. Queer to think that when John went away Betty had been only nine. Queer, now she came to think of it, how she had got through those years. Fortunately, with three children, there was always a lot to do, otherwise she might have become an invalid with worry. Not that she was the invalid sort, it made her feel silly to sit down in the middle of the day, let alone lie in bed, but sometimes, in those five years, what with not sleeping and one thing and another, she had properly had to drag herself about. That's what came of marrying the man you loved. When he was away you only felt half there. She watched John helping the stew. He had been back some months now and yet she sometimes wondered if he was quite back. It was difficult; she and the three children had such a wealth of things they shared, it was hard not to get talking and cut him out of a conversation. Silly, wartime jokes. That time Dulcie got under the table when the flying bomb hit the end of the street, and that time she had stood in a queue for two hours to buy strawberries, only to find that she was in the wrong queue and had fetched up at that peculiar chemist who had such odd things in his window that she always looked the other way when she passed, and that time when the house was blasted and they stayed for a week with the Binns, and that time when the Binns lost their windows and part of the roof and stayed nearly four months with them. It was particularly noticeable the experiences the family had had, which John could not share, when the Binns were about. There they would sit, Muriel Binns and herself on the sofa with their sewing, and Nella Binns and Dulcie gossiping about their dancing school, Dan Binns, when he wasn't making sheep's eyes at Dulcie, talking to Dickie about the days when they were messengers for the A.R.P., and Betty breaking in on everybody's conversation with, "Oh, don't you remember?" Sitting at the other end of the room would be John with Alfred Binns. They had their jokes, too. Called themselves S'arnt and Corporal. They talked sometimes about their prison camp and the shows they had got up, and, of course, everybody listened and was interested, but it was two worlds, you couldn't get away from that. Two worlds with five years coming down like a fireproof curtain in the theatre cutting off the actors from the audience.

John seemed fairly cheerful. Alice was glad of that. He wasn't always very happy in himself these days. Of course, like all theatricals, he hated being out of work. It was bad luck that show he had got into when he came home having so short a run. He liked being in a theatre. Quite a different man when he passed through the stage door. Lucky, in a way, though it was mean to say so, that Alfred Binns hadn't got a job, they were company for each other in the evenings. All the same, somebody had got to get a job soon or they would be in queer street, and that was a fact. Of course, Dulcie was earning good money, extraordinary what they paid actors these days, but it was a job to get two pounds a week out of her. Couldn't wonder, really, a girl of that age wanted fun, you'd only be twenty-one once.

"Will you help me first, Dad?" said Dulcie. "I've a matinée."

John looked at the clock.

"You don't need to be in till half-past one. It's only half-past twelve."

Dulcie wriggled her shoulders with a faint frown between her eyes.

"I like to start early, you never know. If I ever did have to go on for Rose Reilly I shall want extra time, but you bet I never will. That miserable girl would go on if she was in her coffin."

John passed a plate of stew to Betty.

"That's for your mother."

Alice sighed and looked at Dulcie out of the corner of her eye. It was a pity she and her father did not get on better. John could not realize that she was not the sixteen-year-old he had left when he went to France. He was not tactful with the child. He brought out the worst in her. She could be difficult at times, no one knew that better than her mother, but when a girl was as lovely as Dulcie and had every boy for miles running after her, you had to expect them to be difficult, they got spoilt and no wonder. Betty leant on the table.

"If you ever got such marvellous notices as Rose Reilly got you wouldn't stay off, would you, Dulcie? I remember one paper said, 'Genius is an overworked word, but little Miss Reilly has it'."

Dulcie swept a curl off her shoulder.

"Because Rose Reilly's good that isn't to say I wouldn't be. Besides, she isn't always good. If you danced behind her in the chorus like I do you'd know that. I heard that old F .J. said to her the other night that she was lousy."

John passed Dulcie her stew.

"You eat that and don't talk so much, and don't let me hear you calling your manager 'old F. J.' He's Mr. Higgs to you."

Dulcie daintily picked up her knife and fork.

"Everybody calls him old F. J., so why shouldn't I?"

"Because it isn't fitting. Because other people talk in a familiar way there's no reason why you should."

Alice felt it was time to interrupt.

"Where've you been this morning Dickie, dear? You're very silent."

Dickie was at the awkward age. He had grown fast and his wrists stuck out beyond the sleeves of his coat. It seemed to him that he was clumsier than most boys of his age. Not that seventeen was a boy; it was a man really, only men didn't treat you as if you were grown up. Because he was growing so fast and was not used to his big body, and because of his disfiguring spots, he was self-conscious and blushed easily. He blushed now. He turned to his father.

"I didn't get it, Dad. The agent said it was all fixed yesterday. There's a fellow back from the Air Force they'd given that little bit to."

Betty looked at him sympathetically.

"That's because of your spots."

John gave Betty's knuckles a rap with his fork.

"Don't you be personal." He smiled at Dickie. "Don't you worry, old man, I told you you were a bit young. Besides, though it's hard on you beginners, it's right that they should give the jobs to the ex-service men."

Dickie did not look much comforted.

"I know, Dad, but it's time I was working. If only I could get a start. I'm sick of saying I've had no experience except as a Redskin in *Peter Pan* and an elf two Christmasses in a kids' play. It wasn't that I particularly wanted this part, it's not much of a show and twice nightly and all that, but the dancing was all right and it would have been a beginning. I asked the agent if there was any chance of a chorus job in London, but everything's running so long, none of the big musical shows are coming off and the agent said if they did there'd probably be a new show by the same management and they'd engage the same people."

The family were all served. John helped himself.

"I know, old man, that's the worst of our profession. Things are difficult to-day. A theatrical boom cuts two ways. It's grand if you're in a run, like Dulcie here, but if you're out it's hard to hear of anything."

Dickie remembered he had a message.

"I say, Dad, I forgot, I saw Uncle Alfred. He says would you ring him after dinner. It's important." John's eyes lit with interest.

"Heard of something?"

"Don't think so. He didn't say anything about that. He asked if you were doing anything this afternoon."

"Right. I was going over in any case. I'll pop round after dinner and have a word with him."

Alice looked across at her husband. He looked as if he had news of some sort. He had been to see somebody this morning, but it would be quite likely that he would tell Alfred Binns before he would tell her. John and Alfie had been so used to having no one else to discuss things with they had got in the way of running to each other. She and Muriel Binns had both noticed it. She must find a way to get him alone before he went out. It was bad that he should get out of the way of talking things over with her. A man needed to talk things over with his wife, especially after five years. It was one of the ways of bringing him back.

Dulcie got up as soon as she had finished her meal.

"Well, so long, everybody. I might be out to supper to-night, Mum. It's either to-day or tomorrow, I'm not sure which."

Alice looked worried.

"Oh, dear, and I'd managed to get a little bit of oxtail. I don't want to cook it unless you're coming in, could you telephone?"

Dulcie went to the mirror over the mantelpiece and put on some lipstick.

"I will if I can. There's only the one telephone at the stage door. Everybody's always using it."

John tried to hide his annoyance, but it came through what he was saying.

"Look here, young woman, there's no difficulty in your going out to a public call-box. Must be one somewhere near the theatre."

Dulcie looked out of the window.

"Well, I might do that if it doesn't rain."

John lost his temper.

"You'll telephone or you'll get no supper. I won't have your mother stopping up till all hours cooking meals for you that you don't come in to eat."

Dulcie went to the door. She looked, Alice thought, absurdly young and too pretty to be true. She did not know how John found it in his heart to snap at her.

"All right. All right. Keep your hair on." Dulcie grinned at the assembled family. "I thought I heard there was a peace on, but I must have been mistaken."

* * *

Betty usually helped her mother wash up, but today Alice did not want her. She gave the child an affectionate smile that was meant to carry with it a hint.

"You run along, Betty dear. I'd like Dad to help me to-day."

Hints were wasted on Betty. She sprang to her father's defence.

"Poor old Dad. Why on earth should he? I don't mind, Dad, honestly I don't, and you want to go and see Uncle Alfred, don't you?"

John did want to see Alfred. He did not want a heart-to-heart with Alice. But he was as conscious as she was of the iron curtain which was between them. Strange how hard it was to get back. Easy enough to get back bodily, and easy enough to fall into the old way of doing things and an appearance of ease with the family. What was missing was the old understanding. Why, back in thirty-nine, he and Alice could spend a day without speaking and know exactly what was in each other's minds. Every step that either of them took they discussed together; anything else had been unthinkable; and here he was slipping off just to avoid talking things over. He jerked his thumb at the door.

"You hop along, young Betty. Give me the tea-cloth."

Alice felt her heart beating a little quicker than normal. Silly. Fancy being shy with John. But there it was. It was difficult these days to talk to him. Not a difficulty you could put your finger on, something intangible. This time she must be brave, she must insist on his talking. She took her hands out of the sink, dried them and swung round to face him.

"Well?"

He smiled back at her. A non-committal, anxious smile.

"Well what?"

"What are you going to tell Alfred Binns?" John was cornered.

"I've got a chance of a job."

Not one sign of what it meant to Alice to have to force a thing like that out of him crossed her face. She said lightly:

"John! How splendid! Whose management?"

John fidgeted with the tea-cloth.

"Frobisher."

There was a scared look in her eyes.

"A try-out for London?"

"No. It's a tour."

Her voice dropped to a whisper.

"How long?"

He was looking at his feet.

"Twenty weeks for certain, and another twenty if it's a success."

Alice picked up a plate as if to wash it, but instead, without seeing it, she twisted it round in her fingers.

"You can't take this tour, John, and you know it."

"I've got to get a job. What are we going to live on?"

"Not on tour. You've been a prisoner since nineteen-forty, you are still almost a stranger to your own children, and sometimes, I think, a stranger even to me. If you go away for twenty weeks, forty if things go right, you smash up this home for good. Not that it won't be here, not that I shall have stopped loving you, but the years do things, you grow apart, you can't help it."

"You could come on tour with me."

"What's to happen to the children? Can't leave young Dulcie in charge here." She saw agreement on his face and hastened to fly to the defence of her darling. "She's a good girl and got a head on her shoulders, but it's too much for her at her age."

"You married me when you were younger than Dulcie."

"I know, but I was a different type, and I wasn't on the stage."

John gave her a nudge with his knuckles.

"Well, get on with the washing up, we've time to discuss it. I haven't got to give my answer until to-morrow. The money's good."

Alice did not move at once.

"You know it would be a mistake, don't you? If you didn't, you'd have said yes, right away."

He nodded.

"You've done a wonderful job keeping the home together and all that, but I think it's time I took a hand now. Young Dickie needs a bit of help and Dulcie . . ."

Alice put the plates into the sink.

"You're always picking on Dulcie."

"No, I'm not, but you've spoilt her, and that's a fact. When I went away she was a pretty little kid, going off every day to that dancing school with Nella Binns. She fancied herself, and who could blame her? But she was a nice kid, though I do say it of my own daughter, always willing to give you a hand, there was something good and straightforward about her. Now she's spoilt. She thinks herself too grand for her home, and she's too pleased with herself. It's fine she's got into F. J.'s management . . ."

Alice smiled at him over her shoulder.

"I thought we'd got to call him Mr. Higgs."

"I didn't tell Dulcie so, but I've known him for years, but what I was going to say is that it's fine she's got this job, but if I had my way, I'd see her slogging round the country. Too long in the chorus never did any girl any good, specially the type of young Dulcie."

Alice piled the plates up on the drying-board.

"Well, if you think that Dulcie needs you, why are you going away?"

"Nothing else has cropped up, and we do need the money."

"Not that badly, we don't, we've your gratuity, and come to that, I'd rather go out charring than have you away for another twenty weeks."

John was silent, drying the plates and stacking them in the rack. At last he said:

"I'll have a word with Alfie. He feels as you do. He told me Muriel'd murder him if he had to go away again. All the same, old girl, I'm not promising anything. It does something to you sitting around day after day. You say I shall break things up if I go away again, but I tell you I'll break things up if I stop here on the dole. Five years a prisoner is a long time. You get into the habit of being unemployed. I don't want it to grow on me."

Alice said no more. It was true Alfie Binns didn't want to tour. He had said so often. But even if Alfie had not been on her side, there was nothing more she could say. She had put her case and John had listened. The fate of the family must hang on that.

* * *

The Binns family, too, were washing up. Alfred was a little man with the puckered face of the professional comic. If it was possible to squeeze a laugh out of anything, Alfred was the one to squeeze it. To wash up he had rolled a handkerchief into a tiny semblance of a cook's cap and had balanced it on his head, and he had stuck another handkerchief into the top of his trousers as an apron. Muriel Binns was a wonderful audience for her husband. She had been a well-developed redhead when he married her and was now a plump, hennaed head. There was nothing, as she always said, that she enjoyed more than a good laugh, and she had the gift of finding something to laugh about in the dreariest situation. She must have seen Alfred in a fancy hat thousands of times, but she went now into paroxysms of laughter.

"Oh, Alfie, you are a caution."

Nella Binns knew that her father's drying would get no further than a cap and apron, so she was unobtrusively doing the work. Since babyhood the Binns children had been brought up to laugh at their father's jokes. "Do it again, Alfie. I don't think little Nella can have seen it the first time, or she'd have been sure to laugh." Both Nella and her brother Dan thought their father very funny, but they were not given to laughing out loud. Any sound of laughter they had made would have been drowned in a roar from their mother, so they contented themselves with inward chuckles. Nella, at twenty-one, had still a childish, undeveloped look. She had dark hair, parted in the centre, which fell with a slight curl to her shoulders, a wide, innocent brow, and good grey eyes. She was a little thing, only five foot three high, a ha'porth of nothing, her father called her, and slim in proportion. She was instinctively graceful, and she could not put a plate in the rack or hang a cup on a nail without her body falling into a good line, but either because she was small, or because she was so retiring, few people noticed Nella. Only the head teacher at the dancing school at which Dulcie and Nella had both been trained, and which they still attended, appreciated Nella.

"We ought to do something with Nella Binns. She really is a dancer. The only first-class classical dancer we've ever had," she had said to the principal. Then Nella was sent to auditions. Nella had attended practically every audition where the chorus were required to dance on their points since she was fifteen and she had never been engaged. The principal of the school gave up hoping. Nella got an ever-deeper inferiority complex, even the dancing instructress was discouraged. "Talent there all right, it's the girl who's wrong, she simply cannot put herself over."

The Binns' son, Dan, was putting away the plates in the basket. At seventeen he did not look much more than fourteen; like Nella he took after his father in that he was small. Unlike Nella, he was full of bounding ambition. He had something more than a gift for juggling and worked at it for hours on end. He had not yet made a professional appearance, but that was not because he had not been offered one. Locally no charity entertainment was complete without Daniel Binns, the Boy Wonder Juggler, and more than once he had been brought to the attention of a music-hall manager, but he had refused so far to accept an engagement. "When I start I'm going to be the tops. I'm nearly ready, but not quite. When I want an engagement I'll ask for it." Alfred and Muriel looked upon their son with the awed admiration of the merely talented for the genius.

Alfred Binns gave up all pretence of washing up the moment John walked in. They were so used to being together they wasted no time on greetings. Alfie led the way into the sitting-room.

"Any luck this morning, S'arnt?"

John sat down and filled his pipe, and explained about the tour. Alfie, as was a habit of his, listened with his head on one side. At the end he asked:

"Taking it?"

John puffed away at his pipe.

"I don't know, Corp, and that's a fact. You and I have both been away too long. It's a mistake to go away again, but what am I to do?"

Alfred was a quick mover. He nipped across the room and sat on the table by John. He lowered his voice confidentially.

"This morning I ran into Pinkie Barrow. You remember he was in our *stalag* till they moved him." John nodded. "Well, it seems his father is the Barrow who runs these holiday camps. They didn't get going much last year because the land was still mostly requisitioned, but they're going big this summer. Pinkie says his father has handed the entertainment side over to him. He needs concert parties."

John raised his head.

"The sort of thing we put on in the camp?"

Alfred pursed his face till it looked as wrinkled as a walnut.

"Better than that, S'arnt. The very same show you and me ran in the camp. Remember that revue we wrote, *Here's Fun*? He says that, altered a bit and cleaned up, is just the stuff he's looking for. I told him I'd have a talk to you and let him know."

John puffed at his pipe a moment or two in silence.

"We haven't got much of a property to sell there. They weren't our songs."

Alfred waggled a finger in front of his nose.

"You haven't got it, boy, you haven't got it. We put on *Here's Fun*, we act in *Here's Fun*, we put our family into *Here's Fun*, and if Alfie Binns isn't wrong, we have a bit of fun ourselves."

John sat bolt upright. There was a light in his eyes.

"Well, that's an idea. Let's see, what've we got? There's you and me for the comics."

Alfred nodded.

"My old trouble and strife, she's put on a bit of what-have-you round the middle, she says it's the war bread, I tell her I'm waiting to find out if it's an American, still she can still doll herself up to look all right, and she's singin' better than ever."

John nodded. Many nights since he had been home he had been soothed by Muriel Binns' singing.

"Your Nella do anything?"

Alfred made a face.

"Not got the push or drive. Dances all right, could support a number, do some little bits, you know, but I tell you who will be useful, and that's my Dan, with that juggling." The two men looked at the roof from which was coming the rhythmic rap of billiard-balls. Alfred spoke with the warmth of a light comedian for a maestro. "Five billiard-balls at a time, he uses. Four between his fingers and the extra one. Makes them hop around as if they were a lot of performing fleas. What about your Dickie?"

John was looking positively excited.

"It's the very thing for the boy. He hasn't a job. What he needs is experience and confidence. We can use him in all sorts of ways and he's a beautiful dancer."

"Betty."

John laughed.

"I think we must put Alice down as wardrobe mistress and Betty as assistant. If only she could sing a bit we'd have her on as a young Tessie O'Shea, but there's no talent there. She's learning the accordion but I don't think she's got very far with it."

Alfred was approaching the point of what he had to say. He gave John a quick, rather nervous look.

"Everything tickety-boo except that we've not got a leading lady." The two men gazed at each other. There was no need to speak. Alfie went on, "Born for it. Just put her photograph in the foyer, and you'd need St. John's

Ambulance to carry away the men."

John murmured.

"Do her good, too. Nothing like concert party work. Background of half the stars on the stage today."

They looked at each other again. Then Alfred said:

"Would she?"

John scooped some threads of tobacco into the bowl of his pipe.

"I don't know if she'd want to, but I do know the whole thing hangs and falls on her. A girl of her type would cost a lot and reduce our profits considerably. We'll have to put our gratuities in to dress the show as it is. Besides, Alice wouldn't leave Dulcie alone in London, and that means Betty would have to stop, and that means the home's broken up."

Alfred was pleading.

"Can't you do something? It's a wonderful chance for all of us. Keep together, nice holiday by the sea. I'm to let Pinkie know to-night."

John got up.

"All right. I'll go round to the theatre and see her."

* * *

John was half-way to the Royal Windsor Theatre, where Dulcie was working, when an idea struck him. He climbed off the bus and went to a telephone box. He rang up the secretary of F. J. Higgs. Would Mr. Higgs be in his office this afternoon? And would Mr. Higgs see John Corner? No, it was not about a job; it was a bit of a favour he wanted to ask him. There was a pause and then the secretary came back to the telephone. Mr. Higgs would be in, and if John would turn up she was to squeeze him in between appointments. John felt in his pocket, found two more pennies and dialled the stage door of the Royal Windsor Theatre. He spoke to the door-keeper. Would he send up a message to Miss Dulcie Corner? Would he say that her father would be round to take her out for a meal before the evening performance.

F. J. Higgs had started life in a circus. He had learned to walk by propelling an enormous rubber ball round the ring. His father had been a not too good clown and his mother a fairly good bareback rider. F. J., from the time he could walk, had been forced to make himself useful about the circus, a not too good clown, and a fairly good bareback rider were better worth their keep when their contract included an obliging small boy who would help with the horses, sell programmes and carry messages, and, later, as he grew older and stronger, assist with the build-up and pull-down. F. J. had been a sharp child, and by using his eyes and his ears had, by the time he was twelve, learnt practically all there was to know about running a circus. He had experimented in all lines of circus business himself and discovered that he was not made for it. He was thirteen when he saw his first musical comedy and decided that it was badly produced, badly lit, badly dressed, and lacking in punch. He went to his father. "I'm going to get a job in a theatre, Dad. I want to learn the business right through. I'm going to produce musicals when I grow up." He had, too. Started as a call-boy, moved on to be assistant stage manager, stage manager, producer of shows for the road and, finally, of shows for London. He had been thirty when he had made his first London success and he was now sixty-nine. In those thirty-nine years his name on a play-bill meant the last word in glamour and gloss. Everybody did not like an F. J. Higgs' production, but nobody had ever denied that he knew his business. He was sitting at his desk when John came in. He twinkled through his horn-rimmed glasses and ran a hand over what was left of his grey hair.

"Welcome home. Sent out some music to you through the Red Cross. Did you get it?"

John nodded.

"Yes, thanks. It went into a show called *Here's Fun.*"

"Well, what do you want? My secretary says you said it wasn't a job. Just as well. Nothing to offer anybody. Present show's likely to run another year from the look of things."

John drew a chair forward and explained about Alfred's plan. At the end F. J. opened a drawer and took out a box of cigars. He pushed them across the table.

"Have a cigar?"

John took one and sniffed it with obvious pleasure. It was clear that a cigar was a treat. F. J. studied him thoughtfully.

"Lot of work putting on your own show. Board of Trade'll drive you mad over these coupons. Why don't you try for something on your own?"

John laid down the match with which he had been piercing his cigar.

"I've been five years a prisoner. My wife seems to think that if I go on tour now there's a risk I'll break up the home for good. There's a limit to how long a family can live apart."

F. J. nodded understandingly. He did not bother to say what both he and John knew, that John was not the class of comedian to star in the West End. He had taken over comedy parts in F. J.'s shows on the road many times, and very adequate he had been, but he was not the London type. F. J. took off his glasses and laid them on his desk.

"So you want young Dulcie."

John nodded.

"I want to have her under my eye. My wife's done a wonderful job while I've been away, but I'm not very pleased with Dulcie. She was a nice, obliging, unaffected kid in nineteen thirty-nine, she's a mass of affectation now. Thinks of nothing but dolling herself up, never gives her mother a hand. I know the real Dulcie's there and only wants bringing out, besides, a season in a concert party would do her a world of good."

F. J.'s eyes twinkled.

"Pretty girls, certainly girls as pretty as Dulcie, are very apt to become affected young ladies thinking of nothing but dolling themselves up, whether their fathers are there to watch their growing pains or not." His face grew more serious. "I'm not sure about Dulcie. When I had her with me first I thought her very promising. My stage manager reports he's not so sure of her now. I don't mean she couldn't go on if Rose Reilly was off, which heaven forbid, but she'd only be just adequate. I don't know what Dulcie's got in her. She's a nice little dancer, nice little singer, and one of the prettiest girls I've ever had in my shows, but is there any more there? Are we ever going to have her out of the chorus?"

"Concert party work ought to bring out anything there is."

F. J. scowled thoughtfully at his spectacles.

"Don't half want much, do you? Upset the chorus routine, take away my understudy, still, I was always one to believe in the rough road to stardom. You take Dulcie, see what you can make of her. If you think she's any good I'll come down and see her myself."

John stood up.

"Will you tell her, or shall I?"

F. J. laughed.

"You do your own dirty work. I can see young Dulcie's face when you tell her you are taking her out of the West End for a concert party in a holiday camp." Then his face sobered again. "Sit down a minute, I've thought of something. When you were telling me just now about this show, you said that you and Alfred Binns were the comedians, that the Binns have a son who's doing a bit of juggling, that your boy could work with Dulcie and do a bit of dancing on his own, and that the Binns have a girl who could fill in for the sketches and so on, and that Binns' wife sings. What you didn't tell me was who's the pianist."

John looked at F. J. with dismay.

"Pianist! Course, Alfie and I only had a short time to talk, we never got around to that."

"Pretty important thing to get around to. In a concert party the pianist is never off the stage."

"No. I suppose we'd better advertise."

"You needn't. I've a purpose in asking. I've a young fellow

called Tom Pollard. He was sent to me by a chap in the navy. He joined up as an ordinary seaman, knows nothing about himself, came from an orphanage. One day, when he should have been cleaning out the wardroom somebody heard him at the piano. Of course, there was discipline, and he had to be ticked off, but the man who heard him, the very one who sent him to me, is a musical fellow, so he took an interest. He got Pollard to the piano for a concert or something, then heard him playing a tune he didn't know and found he was a composer. I've had him under contract for a year. He plays at rehearsals and that kind of thing, but what I'm nursing him for is that I think I've found an Irving Berlin. I hope to get some songs out of him for my next show. The trouble at the moment is that he's awkward. Writes a song, starts to hit you, and then kills it by refusing to repeat a refrain or whatever it is. He doesn't seem able to feel what the public want." F. J. leant forward. "Now what I propose is that I'll lend you Tom Pollard. I'm paying his salary so you've nothing to bother about there, and in return you've got to make him write and try out every number he writes. Let him sit on the stage, playing his own stuff, and if he's got an ounce of theatre in him, he'll know when he's got 'em cold and when he hasn't." He pressed a bell. "I'll get him in. You'd like to see him."

John's first impression of Tom Pollard was how extraordinarily well he must have looked as an ordinary seaman. He had brown curly hair and dark eyes and, in spite of his slenderness, gave the impression of immense muscular strength. He was over six foot tall, but there was nothing ungainly about him. John felt a surge of excitement. Snakes! With this Greek god at the piano and Dulcie dancing and singing, they ought to pull an audience in.

F. J. told Tom of the proposition. Tom thought of the matter for a moment before he answered. It was clear that to him everything was judged in terms of music.

"Might be a good idea, sir, I should like a chance of trying my stuff out on an audience." He grinned at John. "Once will be enough if it doesn't go. Have you got any singers?"

John explained about Muriel Binns. F. J. laughed.

"There's also Corner's daughter. You must have noticed her at rehearsals. She's the very blonde blonde who wears the black evening dress in the finale."

Tom shook his head.

"I'm afraid I've never noticed the girls, sir." F. J. was appalled.

"Good God! Well, I've got another appointment. You two had better go and have a talk outside." He looked at John and jerked a finger at Tom. "Never noticed the girls. Here have I got a set of beauties that all London is fighting to have a look at, and he's at the piano within touching distance of the lot of them, and says he never noticed them. Shouldn't wonder if that's what isn't wrong with his music. For goodness sake, Corner, educate him at your holiday camp."

John and Tom walked into the outer office. John said:

"I'm picking up my daughter for a meal between the shows. I suppose you couldn't join us? I'd like you to meet her. You'll be doing a good deal of work together."

Tom had taken a piece of paper from his pocket and was

scribbling notes on the back of it.

"Here's fun is rather a nice phrase. I must work out an opening number." John repeated his invitation. Tom unwillingly dragged his eyes from his paper. "I've got to see somebody as soon as the curtain comes down, but it won't take long. Where are you taking your daughter?"

"That little place called 'The Rose Bush'. It's quiet. I know that nobody has time to take off their make-up now that the evening shows begin at half-past six or thereabouts, but I can never get used to grease paint in the street. It was unheard of before the war."

Tom nodded.

" 'The Rose Bush.' All right. I'll be along." He was back at his paper again scribbling hard. "Here's fun. Here's fun."

* * *

Dulcie was not pleased at her father's choice of "The Rose Bush".

"It's such a drab place, Dad. You don't often take me out, you might take me somewhere nice."

In spite of her heavy make-up Dulcie was looking so enchanting that John could not be cross with her. He tucked her arm into his.

"Come on, and don't grumble. I've got a lovely young man coming to meet you."

"Who?"

John hugged her hand to his side.

"I shan't tell you yet. Do you remember that summer we went to Bournemouth and I'd bought a new frock for you, and I told you I had a surprise for you at home, we walked along the front and you kept saying, 'What is it, Dad? Do tell me, Dad?' "

Shaftesbury Avenue was crowded. They were jostled at every step but neither John nor Dulcie was conscious of it. They were back on Bournemouth sea front. There was a smell of sea and pine needles in their nostrils. It was nineteen thirty-eight and Dulcie was fifteen. "What is it, Dad? What have you got for me? Do tell me." In those moments of memory they were nearer to each other than they had been since John came home.

"What young man, Dad?"

John laughed.

"No, you wait, but I promise you he's good-looking."

He steered her round the corner and into "The Rose Bush". They sat at a table in a corner. John had a glass of beer and Dulcie a gin and lime. He ordered fried fish and chips for both. He felt nervous. He did not under-rate what he was asking of Dulcie. He put the whole matter before her.

"Your mother feels we can't break up the home again and your Uncle Alfie has got this offer, but, of course, we need a leading lady."

Dulcie was gazing at her father in amazement.

"Me?"

John nodded.

"I'm hoping you'll be a star one day. There's nothing like concert-party work for training a star."

The colour was creeping up Dulcie's cheeks. It showed even through her make-up.

"You've got a nerve. Ever since I started training I dreamed of getting into one of F. J's shows. When I got my first chance in his chorus I said to myself, 'This is just one foot on the bottom rung of the ladder, now go on, climb.' I did all right in that show, though I never got out of the chorus. In the next one I was tried for a little number, you remember, I wrote to you about it." John nodded. In his memory he saw the gravelled yard and the barbed wire, and the grey field uniform of the German who delivered the post; he saw Dulcie's rather round, unformed handwriting. "It's a gorgeous number, half sung and half spoken. It's about a girl warden on duty at the telephone and her boy in the navy. I very nearly got it. Nobody can understand why they chose Rose Reilly, she's not a bit pretty. We're rather glad she's got it, really, we thought she was a bit plain for an F. J. chorus." Dulcie was still speaking. "And then, of course, in this show, I got the understudying of all Rose's bits. You can't think I'd throw all that up in order to go to some lousy theatre in a holiday camp. Anyway, F. J. wouldn't let me."

John felt that this was not the moment to remind Dulcie that he had told her not to call her manager F. J., he knew what he had to tell her would hurt her pride. He spoke gently.

"I've been to see him. He will let you go. He agrees with me that the road through the concert party is often the road to the stars."

Dulcie got up. She was so angry she was shaking.

"Do you mean to tell me that you sneaked off to old F. J. behind my back. How dare you! I wish you were still in your prison camp. We were much happier before you came home."

John leant forward and caught her wrist. She tried to drag it away but he would not let go.

"Don't be angry, darling. I dare say you think it was a cad's trick, but I had to do it. It was no good our going ahead with this scheme unless I had Mr. Higgs' permission. Besides, I wanted you. I think what you've just said is very true. You do wish I'd never come back and you were happier without me, but that wasn't always the way. I can remember a time, and so can you, when a little girl cried because her father was leaving for the front. Another thing, I am proud of you. You've certainly got looks. I hope you've got talent, and I know you've got ambition. You look on this summer as the second step of that ladder you were talking about. You said you'd got one foot on the bottom rung when you joined F. J. Higgs. Well, I think you'll look back and say, 'I put two feet on the second rung the day I joined the 'Here's Fun Concert Party '."

Dulcie was still tugging at her wrist. There were tears in her eyes.

"I still don't believe it. Burying myself in some lousy seaside village."

"There's a young man coming with us, Tom Pollard."

Dulcie opened her eyes.

"Tom Pollard! But he's F. J.'s star discovery. He's supposed to be a genius."

John nodded.

"He's to write the songs and we're to try them out. As I said, F. J. Higgs believes the road through the concert party is the road to the stars."

Dulcie sat down abruptly. There was a calculating look in her eye. Tom Pollard's songs, Tom Pollard's interest. That put an altogether different complexion on the concert party. A voice behind them made them both jump. Tom Pollard said apologetically:

"I'm afraid I've been longer than I expected. I forgot the time. I was messing about with that opening chorus for you."

John, with a gesture, brought Dulcie into the conversation.

"This is my daughter."

Dulcie gazed up at Tom.

"How d'you do? I hear we're both going to be in the same concert party. I'm so looking forward to our working together."

* * *

The Corners and the Binns were so busy that Betty said, "We're like Waterloo Station on a bank holiday." John and Alfred were happier than they had been since they joined up. Their revue needed a lot of revising to change it into suitable material for family parties on a seaside holiday. As well there were arrangements to be made with Barrow's Luxury Holiday Camp. John and Alfred, acting as joint managers, had charge of everything. Both families waited on the completion of the script and the completion of the arrangements, and this gave the fathers a feeling of being very much needed. All day long they were asked questions as to how things were going; it was like the old days when nothing, however small, happened in their homes without their approval.

Coming back from an interview at the offices of Barrow's Holiday Camps John broached a subject to Alfred that was worrying him.

"Corp, what are we going to do about this money business? It's generous all right, I don't mean that, but how are we going to divide it?"

Alfred was surprised at the question.

"A pint of 'alf and 'alf."

"Can't do that. You're putting yourself, Muriel, Dan and Nella into the kitty. I'm putting myself, Dulcie and Dickie."

They were walking down Regent Street. In spite of the congested pavements Alfred stood stock still and gave an imitation of a parson preaching.

"Dearly beloved brethren, cast from your minds all thoughts of filthy lucre." John laughed and put his arm through Alfred's and pulled him along, for he was congesting the traffic. Alfred spoke seriously. "If you go on like that, S'arnt, I'll give you a rocket. I suppose Alice is to work free as wardrobe mistress, and we're going to forget that you're providing the star?" John opened his mouth to answer but Alfred would not let him speak. "It's not the slightest good your saying anything, a pint of 'alf and 'alf's fair and a pint of 'alf and 'alf it's going to be."

John did not argue any more. He had expected Alfred to say just that; he would have said the same thing in his place. It was not true that Alice ought to get the same salary as Muriel Binns because, as well as singing, Muriel was helping with the clothes, but half and half would be the easiest arrangement, and it was true he was providing the star. Talk of money brought John to another problem.

"Wonder what's fair to give Dulcie. She oughtn't to lose by coming here. Of course, she'll be living free at the holiday camp and won't have to give her mother a bit, like she does at home."

"I should ask her. What I've always said is, when it comes to talking money with a woman, give them what they ask and then they can't grumble. If Muriel tells me she wants a hat and I can see she means to have a hat, I give her exactly what she asks for, otherwise what happens? For as long as she wears that hat I hear, 'I've nothing fit to put on. I never did like that hat. I'm not the type for cheap hats'."

On the following Sunday John took Alfred's suggestion. He asked Dulcie to come with him for a walk. It was one of those days in the very early spring when there is a foretaste of what the proper spring will be like. The sky was blue and, against it the prunus blossom, shone radiantly pink. Dulcie had no hat, her hair blew around her head in a cloud, and every man and boy turned to look at her. John felt his heart warm with pride.

"I brought you out, darling, to talk about money, and business generally. We're going fifty-fifty with the Binns on the money and I wondered what you'd think was fair to yourself. You mustn't, of course, lose leaving F. J. Higgs, and you ought to have a rise seeing you're our leading lady. You'll be living free in the camp, so it'll be all yours. Would you think five pounds a week more than you were getting in London right?"

Dulcie was touched at the way he spoke. To hide that she was touched she answered almost roughly.

"I won't take more than you do. Then I suppose you'll take a salary for Mum as wardrobe mistress, and then there's Dickie."

"You're the lead."

"I'll take exactly what I'm getting in London. I said I'd come into the concert party as a family concern, and I'll stick to that."

John was terribly pleased with her, but the relationship between them made him shy of saying so.

"I'm afraid it isn't going to be very comfortable for you. Everybody lives in chalets at the camp. Very nice, too, according to the photos we've seen, but they're short of space, everybody needing a holiday, so you'll have to share with Nella and Betty."

Dulcie paused, pretending interest.

"Look, Dad, a daisy! If I could cover twelve with one foot it would be summer." She added casually, "Where's Tom going to sleep?"

"With Dickie and Dan. He doesn't mind, doesn't seem to mind anything as long as there's a piano somewhere."

Dulcie glanced at her father out of the corner of her eye.

"Nobody can be like that really, can they? I mean, all men like women in the end, don't they, like all girls grow up to like boys? I think he's shy. You see, he never had a mother."

John laughed.

"I can't help thinking he must have had one somewhere."
Dulcie flushed.

"You know what I mean. He was brought up in an orphanage."

John glanced at Dulcie. Ever since she had first toddled there had been boys round her. There had never been a dance but two or three had wanted to take her to it. Since she had been in F. J.'s show she had a crowd of young men who wanted to amuse her. She took admiration for granted and never seemed interested in one man more than another. It was queer to hear her talking about Tom Pollard like this. Could she be falling in love? In a way he hoped not. People in love made complications. Besides, young Pollard did not seem interested in girls. It was going to be the most contrary state of affairs if Dulcie did all the falling in love for once. He remembered the early days when he had first loved Alice and before he had known Alice cared for him. Lord, what a state he had been in! Poor little Dulcie! He hoped that if she had lost her heart, she would lose it to somebody who loved her in return. He took her hand and slid it inside his arm.

"I am looking forward to this summer. I've felt sometimes that I've lost the daughter I loved, and don't know the new daughter who has grown up in her place. This summer I hope I'll get a chance to get acquainted."

Dulcie wanted to answer. Wanted to say something nice, but she could not find words. She was in a muddled state of mind. There were rehearsals now most days for the numbers Tom had written for her. He would come to the house after breakfast and sit at the piano strumming, and she would try out her songs and the steps for her dances. Every day she expected that Tom would cease to be the detached composer and become an ordinary man; the sort of man that she was used to, who found excuses for holding her hand, and saved up to take her to the best restaurants, and every day she was disappointed. He did not seem to notice her any more than he noticed Nella or Betty. It was an extraordinary situation, and she minded. For the first time in her life it was she who wanted to find an excuse to hold his hand. She could have sung her songs from anywhere, but she found a reason to lean on the piano, and, now and again, over his shoulder. She had several times had to clasp her hands to keep herself from running her fingers through his hair. She excused herself to herself by thinking that it was such funny kind of hair, it shot away so crisply from his head it would be fun to stand his curls up when he took such trouble to lie them flat, but she knew that she was only making excuses. She wanted to touch his hair because it was his hair. When he got up and she saw all the slim length of him, and the muscles rippling under his skin, she felt quite giddy. How sickening it was that he was a pianist and not a dancer. How wonderful he would be to dance with.

John, disappointed at her silence, said:

"I suppose we ought to be turning round if we're not to be late for tea." Then, because he felt awkward with her, he asked politely, "Are you sorry that next week is your last week with F. J.?"

Dulcie turned her head away from him. She knew she had hurt him, but still the right words would not come.

"No. I shall be glad when proper rehearsals start. I think doing two things at once is rather a nuisance."

Terribly aware of the gap between them they walked home.

The rehearsals proper for *Here's Fun* began a week later. Alfred and John had succeeded in renting a stage in a local parish hall. They could not, of course, have it all day, but they had it for a good many hours a day, and at once the show began to take shape. Barrow's Holiday Camps were mostly used by families staying for one week. It was proposed that *Here's Fun* should be given nightly. The camp held, with staff, somewhere over three thousand people, but the theatre was small, holding about five hundred. It was proposed that there should be an evening performance every night and matinées when wet, and that for those who came in more than once there should be enough material for a slight change in the programme nightly. This meant the rehearsing of a great many numbers. As well the two houses hummed with activity. Pianos going, telephones ringing, materials and patterns all over the two dining-room tables. Even the outhouses were in use. Both families had a shed in which they kept bicycles and tools, now these were used as property shops. Alfred was a great believer in community singing. He liked verses of his songs hung where all the audience could read them.

"Nothing like having a song written out so they get to know it. Then back they go singing and whistling and we get a free advert."

Alice and Muriel had many heart-to-heart talks about the wardrobe. The great discussion was what their concert party dresses should be like. Alice, with Dulcie in her mind, was for putting the girls into something filmy.

Muriel saw her point, but had to put up a plea for herself.

"Dulcie would look lovely in a bath towel. You've also got to remember that I'm around; put me in something filmy and we're going to get a laugh. Talk about the battle of the bulge, it's nothing to what's going on round my waist."

Because Nella and Dulcie were both dancers Alice had in mind some ballet skirts. She appealed to the men for support.

"I'd like white things for you men and white dresses for the girls, with a mass of tarlatan petticoats underneath."

Muriel cast up her eyes.

"Tarlatan petticoats! I'll look like an advertisement for a tyre. Why not put us all into proper pierrot clothes? Black pompons and that. After all, this is a seaside show."

Alfred pretended to hide his face in shame.

"Your taste is shocking, old girl. This show is going to be very recherchey. No common pierrot clothes, something to catch the eye, that's what we want."

It was Nella who had the great idea. They were rehearsing in the Binns' dining-room. Tom Pollard had brought along a new chorus which they were trying out. During a rest, while Tom was running his hands up and down the keys, Alice said:

"If we don't get on with deciding what you're going to wear soon you won't be able to open because there won't be any clothes."

Alfred pretended to take off his coat.

"Come and see 'The Happy Nudes'."

Muriel shook a finger at him.

"Don't be coarse."

John sided with Alice.

"It's all very well for us to joke, we haven't got to make the clothes. We must decide on something. Muriel wants an ordinary pierrot kit in black and white, Alice thinks something a bit more classy, white for us, ballet things for the girls. Any other ideas?"

There had been plenty of ideas put forward from the beginning. Dulcie, to her father's surprise and her mother's pride, was curiously undemanding on the subject of her clothes. Alfred and John had applied for coupons, but they had not been granted anything like the number they had asked for, and Alice and Muriel had agreed that, except for superficial changes of costume, the person on whom the coupons should be spent was Dulcie. Dulcie was devoted to clothes, and was as excited as any other girl when planning her frocks and attending fittings, but she had not been dictatorial about what the concert party should wear. She had an often hidden, but strong streak of generosity in her nature. She looked at Muriel Binns and could not find it in her heart to insist on the frocks in which she, and, incidentally, Nella, would look charming, and poor old Aunt Muriel look comic.

"I do see Aunt Muriel's point, Mum; just picture that behind of hers in a ballet skirt."

It was a surprise that it should have been Nella who made the suggestion that was finally adopted. In the Binns family, with Muriel's bounce and personality, Alfred and his funny tricks, and Dan and his juggling, Nella was very apt to be forgotten. When she came out with an opinion it was almost as if a shadow spoke.

"Why don't we have a Harlequin effect?"

Alfred, to cover his amazement, pretended to be a deaf man. He cupped his ear in his hand and yelled:

"Aye? What's that?"

Muriel thought this screamingly funny and rocked with laughter, murmuring, "Harlequin! Oh, look at Alfie. What will the child say next?"

Dulcie had not attended classes with Nella for years without learning that when she cared to speak she had an opinion to be respected. Dulcie, though disliking herself for it, had succeeded in standing beside Tom at the rehearsal. Because all the family were clustered round the piano they pushed her against him. His shoulder touched her side. She was ashamed and puzzled at the pleasure it gave her. She was glad of something to take her mind from his nearness. Nella was at the far end of the piano leaning on its upright top, her chin resting on the woodwork.

"How do you mean Harlequin?" Dulcie asked her. Nella could always talk easily to Dulcie.

"A little different shape and a different colour for everybody."

Alfred clapped his hands together.

"The idiot child's got it."

Alice was at the table with Muriel looking at some patterns. She joined the ring round the piano.

"That's a very good idea, Nella. We might go two-and-two. We could dress you two comics in one colour and the three boys can pair off with the three girls."

Muriel held up a pattern.

"What I should like is this bright green. Show off my

colouring and take the eye away from my waist. Who'd like to wear green? Don't all speak at once."

Dickie flushed.

"I say, could I? I don't want a sissy colour."

Alice had a piece of paper in her hand. She wrote down "Bright green, Muriel and Dickie." She looked at Dulcie.

"What colour would you like?"

Dulcie considered.

"Yellow, I think."

Alice nodded.

"Nothing prettier. Daffodil yellow."

Muriel was full of enthusiasm.

"Lovely. Yellow for style, I always say. When Nella can have a nice baby blue."

"Not if she's pairing with me, she won't," said Dan. "Nobody's getting me up in baby blue."

Muriel turned to Tom.

"What about you wearing baby blue. You wouldn't mind, would you? Then Dan can wear the yellow."

Tom was not a smart dresser. His idea of perfect clothes was grey flannel trousers and a sports coat. It was all one to him what they dressed him in.

"Blue will suit me."

Alice started to write down, "Yellow, Dulcie and Dan," when Dulcie startled both herself and them. Whether it was Tom's quiet acceptance that he did not care what colour he wore, for she wanted him to say, "If Dulcie wears yellow so will I," or whether it was seeing in imagination Nella bracketed with Tom on Alice's paper, she had no idea, she just knew that she was losing her temper and that she was losing it badly.

"Tom's to be dressed in the same colour as myself."

Alfred was one for skimming round trouble where possible. He could not imagine why Tom had to be dressed the same as Dulcie. By no possibility could the pianist be considered the star of the show, still, if she felt strongly about it, something must be arranged.

"Why, old dear?"

Dulcie knew there was no answer, knew she was behaving like an idiot and looking a fool in front of Tom, but she was unable to control herself.

"Because I say so."

That was too much for John. Dulcie might be the leading lady, but she was also his daughter.

"Come off the high horse. You've heard Dan say he doesn't want to wear blue."

Dulcie was in one of those positions from which it is impossible to retreat. Everybody was looking at her, everybody had heard what she had said. She had to find an excuse for her seemingly idiotic behaviour. She picked on the unfortunate Dan.

"Dan's so much younger than me, he doesn't look more than fifteen."

Even in the happiest friendships there are some things which you cannot do. You cannot criticise a child before its parents. Muriel for once lost her good humour; Alfred wrinkled his face, but not to be funny.

Nella was as puzzled by Dulcie's behaviour as everybody else. She and Dulcie were friends, or at least had been before Dulcie joined F. J. Higgs. She had inherited from her father a wish for pleasantness and had inside herself a love of peace and quiet. As well she had not cared for her mother's suggestion that she should wear pale blue. She was only too apt, as she well knew, not to be noticed, in pale blue she might be mistaken for part of the scenery. She turned to Muriel.

"As a matter of fact, I don't want to wear blue. I want to wear scarlet. You wouldn't think that sissy, would you, Dan?"

There is nothing more annoying than to be given in to when you know that everybody thinks you have behaved very unreasonably. Dulcie could have cried she was so upset and mortified. If only she understood herself better. It was not like her to be so silly. However, she did not lack courage. She controlled her feelings and threw up her chin.

"All right then, we'll wear yellow. Yes, Tom?"

Tom did not appear to be listening. Alice filled in an awkward pause by saying brightly:

"That's settled. Nella and Dan scarlet. Dulcie and Tom yellow." She put a bracket round the names.

* * *

The effect of having the dresses fixed was that everybody was stimulated. In John there had always been a latent producer, and in his prisoner-of-war camp this had come to life. Now, with such lookers as Dulcie and Tom to deal with, he was fired with ambition. The Harlequinade idea stimulated Tom. Almost every day he arrived with fragments of new tunes. For Dulcie he had composed his two best numbers, "She Danced in Piccadilly" and "He Met Me at Waterloo." Not that Tom composed anything for anybody. He composed Dulcie's songs for somebody young, light of foot, and beautiful, and Dulcie happened to be all three. The trouble with Tom was that his talent came to him too easily. His head swam with melodies, and when he got a melody, in no time he found the words to fit it. The worry with him was that having heard a melody in his head and transferred it on to paper, it seemed almost impossible to get him to alter it. It was not that he meant to be disobliging, it was just that a particular tune was finished with and he was off on to something else. It tormented Dulcie. She was torn between her feeling for Tom and her ambition for herself. She hated to quarrel with Tom, but he spoilt so many of her numbers by a trick he had of repeating the dancing chorus in a slightly different way to the singing chorus, often to a very awkward beat. Dulcie was a pleasing dancer, light, graceful, but nothing more. She knew perfectly well what she could do best, and she wanted music to fit her dancing, but Tom either could not, or would not, write it.

"Tom, couldn't we have the dancing choruses at the same speed as the singing choruses? Look, I want to do this and hold the attitude, but I can't when you go so fast."

Tom barely glanced at her.

"I expect you can fix it." His fingers wandered up the keys. "I've got a bit of an idea. I wonder where your father is, I'd like him to hear it."

Dulcie restrained herself with difficulty.

"Do stick to my numbers, Tom. You've got plenty of time

for Dad later on. Do look what I want to do. If you watch me when I dance you'll see that I can't fit into your music."

Dulcie, in her black practice frock, looked exquisite. Anybody but Tom would have been only too thankful to stare at her, but Tom was miles away.

"A nursery rhyme thing. Your father thought we might all have funny verses to a different nursery rhyme tune. I'm rather taken with it. Listen."

Dulcie took a deep breath and managed a smile. She sat on the top of the piano.

"All right, play it to me."

While Tom played she watched his fingers running up and down the keys. Why was it attractive that hairs grew on a man's hands?

But her interest in Tom could not keep Dulcie in a good temper for ever. In the second week of rehearsals the show began to take shape. It was then Dulcie came in for a little criticism.

"What's wrong with the dance, Dulcie? It seems awkward somehow, as if you'd missed a step somewhere."

Dulcie hated criticism. Besides, wasn't she the leading lady?

"There's nothing wrong with my dancing. It's Tom's music."

Dickie, on the side of the stage, was trying out Dulcie's steps.

"You'll have to cut out that pause, Dulcie, you can't get it in on the beat."

Dulcie stamped her foot.

"Shut up, all of you. I'll do my dancing in my own way."

To Tom she said, "We'll go over it afterwards. You'll have to alter that dancing bit."

But after the rehearsal Tom proved as stubborn as ever.

"That's the way I wrote it, and that's the way it's going to be played."

Dulcie's eyes sparkled.

"It's because your music won't do as it is that F. J. wants you to come out with us."

Tom raised an eyebrow.

"What he told me was that he wanted me to see how my stuff went over with the public. He didn't say anything about altering every tune for every artist in the show."

Dulcie beat on the top of the piano with her fists.

"I'm not every artist. I'm the leading lady. I've got to put over your numbers. If I can't dance them they won't go down with the public."

Tom refused to be drawn into an argument.

"Let's wait till we get to the camp. If my numbers don't go then, I'll change them, but not before."

It was unfortunate for everybody that there should be this friction between Tom and Dulcie. The rest of the show was coming along swimmingly. The comedy numbers were going well. John and Alfred were wonderful foils for each other. John was a slow, big comedian with a warm grin who now and again scored off the little man. Alfred, with his screwed-up monkey face, and his ability to fall over anything in any position, was the right person for him to act with. In their prisoner-of-war camp they had written themselves two or three good song and patter numbers, many had to do with army life. In the holiday camp there were bound to be many demobbed men who would still enjoy army jokes, so they wrote up these numbers and Tom showed especial facility in accompanying them. They had sung their songs to well-known tunes, and he kept the basis of this idea and yet gave a freshness with his music.

"We aren't half lucky with Tom Pollard, S'arnt," Alfred would say, and John would nod.

"You've said it, Corp."

Tom was charm itself with Muriel. He liked playing old ballads. He agreed with her that the old favourites, "Little Grey Home in the West," and "Where My Caravan has Rested" were just her cup of tea. When playing other people's music he was, as Dulcie noticed, the perfect accompanist, following his artists with the utmost care. In the general numbers he was patience itself, going over and over his songs, repeating the opening chorus a dozen times if necessary, and literally teaching them their finale, "Good night, Campers". He became friends with Dickie. Dickie tap-danced to music of his own choosing, which Tom played; he accompanied Dickie's dancing beautifully, never taking his eyes off his feet, and never forgetting the pauses where steps were unaccompanied.

"He's grand," Dickie confided to Dan. "I bet we have fun when we're all three in that chalet."

Nevertheless, there was a tiny feeling of strain. It was imperative that Dulcie should be happy, and that Dulcie should be a success. If the campers did not like Dulcie the show would not go on. If Dulcie and Tom could not get on, arguments would go on all the summer. Disagreement in a company could get over to the audience. Nor were Tom's songs the only worry. Permission had been obtained from F. J. Higgs for Dulcie to do many of his numbers, especially the songs that had been made famous by Rose Reilly. Dulcie was all right, but that was all. John was a little disappointed. Alfred took the optimistic view.

"Not the type to rehearse well." 'By arrangement with F. J. Higgs' on the programme is half the battle. Even if Rose Reilly's songs don't suit her altogether, with Dulcie's looks and coming from that management, she's sure to go down."

John was not to be easily cheered.

"It's not only the numbers, it's the atmosphere I don't like. A show like ours depends on a happy family atmosphere. If we lose that we lose half our charm. There's a lot hangs on Dulcie."

* * *

The families left for Comstock-on-Sea on a Saturday in April. The night before was an orgy of shutting up and packing up in both houses.

"Thank goodness we decided against letting," Muriel gasped at Alfred, as she shut the last suitcase. "Seems kind of mean with such a housing shortage, but where we'd have put the rest of our stuff I don't know. Funny, we none of us seem to have a rag to our backs, but when it comes to going away we seem to have so many clothes that every suit-case is bursting and they're hanging out of the cupboards."

Alfred had not been made a corporal for nothing. When it came to the need for a leader he was there.

He had made a neat list of all that had to be done before the departure. There was Clemmie, the cat, to be remembered. The outhouse had been cleared for her reception, but the money for providing her with breakfast, dinner, lunch and tea had not been paid. Nella was down for this job. Nella, with her soft voice and gentle, shy ways, could be relied on to put things in the best light. Mrs. Jones across the way had agreed to see to the feeding of Clemmie, but she had murmured it was a lot of work.

"Quite true, too," Muriel had told her family, "nobody who hasn't kept a cat has any idea of the extra work it means. Still, we'll do the same for her Mr. Nubbins at Christmas if they want to get away."

Alfred briefed his children before they set out on these last-minute jobs.

"Up the road with you, Nella, the money's on the mantelpiece beside the packet of Tibbs, and the daffodil is in the pot in the hall. Say the daffodil's with our love and thanks, and don't forget to say your Mother'll be pleased to have Mr. Nubbins at Christmas if necessary."

"But don't press it," Muriel objected. "I never could abide a tom cat, and there's bound to be trouble with Clemmie. And don't forget the run through in the church hall at eight."

Nella disposed of, Alfred turned back to his list. "Remind the police station (Dan)." He looked at the ceiling from which, as usual, came the rhythmic click of Dan's billiard-balls. Dan might be a genius, but the Binns' household had no room for geniuses that night. Alfred went to the bottom of the stairs and raised his voice.

"Dan, Dan," he paused until the billiard-balls were silent. "Pop along to the sergeant at the police station and say to him, Mr. Binns' compliments and this is to remind him that the house will be empty as from to-morrow morning, nine-thirty."

Muriel joined her husband.

"And, Dan, tell the sergeant from me that if he lets a burglar break in while we're away, I won't sing at the police concert at Christmas, however much he asks me, and don't forget the run through at eight."

When the front door had closed on Dan, Alfred ticked the police station off his list and looked at Muriel.

"This is where I've got you down. 'Moth'."

Muriel groaned.

"We would be leaving the house in the moth season. I don't know what's come over moths in these last years. I suppose it's all this utility material, enlarges their glands or something, but they're twice the size and twice as savage."

Alfred ticked the word "Moth".

"When you've done it, it's done, as the stewardess said to the passenger."

Muriel was half-way up the stairs.

"I've never used this D.D.T. They say it can upset you. You come quick if I scream."

Alfred went to his task, the writing of labels. He had printed the words "Binns" and, in the corner, "Theatre"; he was too engrossed to reply.

There was less regimentation about the arrangements in the Corner family. Alice was so used to doing everything for herself that she had not left much over for her family.

John, accustomed to seeing to the welfare of the men under him, was not accustomed to having as much taken off his hands as Alice had removed. Of course, the children helped. Betty, thoroughly over-excited, rushed round asking what she could do next, and Dickie ran messages. There was no cat to be seen to in the Corner house, but there was Alice's garden. Alice was a great gardener, mostly vegetables nowadays, but enough flowers to make her heart rejoice. Because gardeners form a natural club, and because Alice was always willing to help other people, she had plenty of offers. She sent Dickie to remind her friends.

"Run along to Mr. Thomas in the next street and remind him we leave to-morrow, and that he's to have the daffs, and go to Mr. Lipman and tell him we're leaving to-morrow and not to forget I've got those lettuces under that bit of glass, and as you come back call in on Mr. Knocking, on the corner, and remind him to-night's our last night and he's going to look after my rose tree. And, Dickie, there'll be a bit of something to eat before the run through."

Now it was time to go Alice felt unwilling for the move. She was house-proud and, though she could sometimes slip up for the week-end, or the day, things would be bound to deteriorate without her eye on them, and she would miss her garden. John sensed how she was feeling.

"Sorry to leave it?"

It was like old times. With a warm wave of love sweeping over her, she laid her hand on his arm. It was almost the first time since he had come back he had felt what she was thinking. She gave his arm a slight squeeze.

"Not really. It's just that I haven't been away for six years and I've gone sort of broody. We women do, you know. I'll enjoy every minute of it once we're off."

Upstairs Dulcie was packing. She was a neat, methodical packer. Everything she intended to take she had laid out on the bed. In spite of coupons, Dulcie had never been short of pretty things. Friends in the American and Canadian Forces had helped out with stockings, and by hook or by crook she managed dainty underclothes. She made them herself and wore them very short; they took scarcely any material. Now they lay in neat piles on her bed, a collection, considering the times, of which any girl might be proud, but pride was the last thing that Dulcie was feeling. She was nervous and lacking in confidence. She was no fool and she was ambitious. On the surface not much lay behind this engagement, but in actual fact a lot did lie behind it. She was to put over all Rose Reilly's numbers from the last two shows. For so long she had told herself that she could do Rose Reilly's numbers as well, or better, than Rose Reilly that it hurt her to find out how difficult they were in actual fact. Listening to Rose Reilly it seemed so easy to get that little catch of pathos, but, now she was doing the songs, it seemed so easy to overdo it. Of course, playing in a family show you suffered from too much criticism. Her father and Alfred were not afraid to say, "Plugging it rather, aren't you?" They might be right or they might be wrong, but to them she was a little girl and they could say what they liked; that was the worst of acting with your own family. Then there was the trouble over Tom's numbers. Everybody was wild over them, especially over "She Danced in Piccadilly" and "He Met Me at Waterloo". It was perfectly true they did sound catchy and pretty, but they were bad to dance to. It was sickening how people would think it was Tom who was right all the time. Even Dickie, who ought to have been able to understand, was being stupid. Dickie's sort of dancing went fast and he could not see the need for holding attitudes. Of course, Nella would understand, but Dulcie could not bring herself to discuss her numbers with Nella. She was the star, and. it was humiliating to have to go to Nella and say, "Can you see what I'm doing wrong? Why I don't get this dance number right?"

Dulcie had the faults of her temperament. She was hypersensitive, she sensed disapproval that did not exist. But there was a little nervousness and she felt it. Actually no one was denying Dulcie's talent nor questioning their fortune in getting her as leading lady, but to Dulcie everybody was whispering about her behind her back, and their slight anxiety as to why she could not get her dances right was magnified into wails of disapproval. Above all was Tom. Why was Tom so stand-offish? Was it only that he had been brought up in an orphanage and then gone into the navy and wasn't used to girls? Or was it because there was somebody else? Theatre gossip had never suggested there was anyone else. He had been tremendously talked about by all the girls, how could he not be with those looks? But nobody knew very much about him. Dulcie felt as though she had dropped about seven years and was a gauche girl of fourteen. Dealing with men had been to her a simple affair. They admired her, they wanted to take her out, and a great many of them, having taken her out, hoped for kisses, and a few for much more. Dulcie had a natural fastidiousness which had kept her from harm. She had been well brought up, and never took expensive presents, and never suggested that she was going to be anything more than a pleasant companion, and she had been accepted as such and had a good time. Now, suddenly, she found herself up against a situation of which she had no experience, and she had no conception how to deal with it. What did you do with yourself when every waking hour you saw a person in your mind? Was it rather hateful to feel such a need to be near a man, and to be excited when he touched you? She had often heard conversations in the dressing-room about being in love, or at least about love affairs, but then it was a two-sided thing. The girl did only part of the loving, the man did more than half. Was there something queer about her that she should be in such a state about a man who was not fond of her?

Dulcie picked up an armful of her underwear and knelt beside a suit-case. "I don't believe it's queer of me. I believe it's Tom that's queer. I expect he's shy and needs sort of pushing along. There's a whole summer in front of us. I bet I get him interested before we've been at the camp long."

She got up and stood in front of her long mirror. She was wearing very short rose pink cami-knickers. Her bare feet were in blue furry slippers. Her face was flushed with stooping, and her hair needed combing, but there was nothing about her reflection to explain why any man shouldn't love her. She nodded at the girl in the glass.

"We'll make him care. This summer everything is going right. We'll be a success. F. J. will see us and star us, and

Tom . . ." Her thoughts broke off. She stood hugging herself and smiling at her reflection.

Tom's packing did not take long. He set off early for the parish hall for the evening run through. He travelled by bus. Two girls sat in front of him. They were talking about their holidays. By a strange coincidence they were going to the Comstock camp. One said, "My Dad says you ought to see the coast there when the poppies are in bloom." The second girl agreed. "Red for miles, I hear."

The phrase haunted Tom.

"You ought to see the coast there
When the poppies are in bloom."

When he got to the piano he began picking out a little tune. That was right. The east coast was poppy land. It would be a fine song for Barrow's camp later on, perhaps he could make it more than just a catchy tune. An airman had told him that the crimson streak of poppies was one of the loveliest things he knew coming home from a bomb raid. Might make a song for a man, really. To Tom there were no such things as limits to a cast. It never crossed his mind that the only men he had to deal with were two comedians, one dancer and one juggler. If he wrote a song for a baritone he took it for granted a baritone would sing it. He raised his head and visualized his baritone dressed in his flying kit and harness, perhaps a half-light, some red somewhere to suggest the poppies. It was then he saw Nella. Nella had not changed for the rehearsal as it was only a run through. She had on the kilted skirt and jersey in which she would travel to-morrow. She had a look at Alfred's list and knew that Clemmie's feeding arrangements were the last thing she was down to do, her packing was done; on her mission about Clemmie she had carried her dancing shoes; she had missed her daily bar practice that morning; she would get in a bit before the rehearsal. She had been surprised to find Tom at the piano, as she had supposed he was packing. Still, he did not matter. She had put on her shoes, taken off her coat and, using the back of the bench as a bar, was going through her pliés. Then suddenly her ear was caught by what Tom was playing. Such a queer, haunting little tune. She left the bar and invented a small dance. She had no idea what Tom was thinking about. She was thinking of a breeze coming in from the sea.

Tom's hands slid off the piano.

"This isn't meant to be danced to."

Nella paused on one toe, the other stretched out in front of her.

"It felt dancey-ish to me."

Tom considered her reply.

"Then I've got it wrong somewhere."

"Why?"

"It's an airman coming home after a flight, and seeing the coast red with poppies. In the summer all that part of the coast where we're going is starred with poppies."

Nella came over to the piano. He saw for the first time that her eyes were grey and unusually honest.

"I don't think you'd better write that sort of song. We've nobody to sing it. Unless it's for two airmen harmonising. Dad and Uncle John could do that."

Tom played the tune again.

"It's for a solo baritone."

Nella leant forward, her brown hair falling on to the top of the piano.

"If you don't mind my making a suggestion I think you'll find it'll be much nicer for you if you'd try and remember what we can all do."

Tom looked surprised.

"I do. Spend all day writing music for everybody." Nella fixed him firmly with her eyes.

"No, you don't. You think you do. Quite a lot of things you write we haven't done because we can't, and then, you know, you're being very silly about Dulcie. If Dulcie isn't a success the show won't be a success and then we'll all be back in London."

Tom found it very difficult not to attend when Nella fixed him with her eyes like that. He scowled at her.

"What's the matter with what I do for Dulcie?"

"Take 'She Danced in Piccadilly.' There's that little bit that goes very quickly." In tune Nella hummed a few bars. "What she wants to do is this. She can't because the beat's wrong and she's told you so."

"She should invent something to my beat. You could, couldn't you?"

Nella nodded.

"Yes, but it won't fit the sort of dance Dulcie wants to do."

Because they were talking about it Tom began to play "She Danced in Piccadilly." Nella traced out some steps. She was not thinking of herself, she was thinking of Dulcie.

Tom watched her. He had not noticed her before. There was very little work for her to do in the show. She came on for ensembles, and she had some tiny bits in the sketches, but nothing more. He knew nothing about dancing, but all the artist in him was satisfied as he watched her. No thought out charm, no artifice, just perfect movements, so easy they were like a seagull flying. It annoyed him when she stopped.

"You see, that's the place. If only the music slowed there Dulcie could do this." She raised her leg in an arabesque and stooped to the floor, her right arm and her left leg forming a perfect line. "As it is she has to do some little steps and they aren't half as effective."

Tom wanted Nella to go on dancing. For the first time he saw what the argument was about. He tried out the refrain a different way, slowing his music. Nella picked up the dance, not as Dulcie was doing it, but as Dulcie wished it to be done. She was exquisite, she made Tom catch his breath.

Nella leant against the wall resting. It was nearly eight, the family would be here at any minute. Tom said

"Why don't you dance in the show?"

Nella looked surprised.

"Any dancing there is, Dulcie does."

"But you're the better dancer."

She looked down at her small body and thought dispassionately of her brown hair and grey eyes.

"You need personality as well as being able to dance. People don't notice me."

"What rot!"

"It isn't. I'm what Dad calls a white mark on a white wall.

I'd be all right in a ballet, but the sort of school Dulcie and I went to doesn't put its girls into ballet. It's for musical shows, revues and things. You see, I can't sing. You must sing as well as dance in that sort of work. When I was sixteen I went to heaps of auditions, but I never got an engagement."

Tom struck a chord or two.

"Let's hear you. What'll you sing?"

She came towards the piano laughing.

"I'll have to stand very close to you, Mum says my singing is as difficult to hear as a bat squeaking." She leant against the piano. "The only place I ever sing is in my bath."

He looked at her, small, brown and childish. Without his being aware of it his voice had softened.

"What do you sing in your bath?"

She smiled at herself.

"You'll laugh. Old songs. I'm fondest of 'Mighty Like a Rose'."

Very softly he played the opening bars. It was all so friendly and informal that Nella forgot to be shy. In a tiny but very true voice she sang:

"Sweetest little fellow,
Everybody knows,
Don't know what to call him,
But he's mighty like a rose."

Tom had allowed his life to be arranged for him. The war years had filled his head with tunes which he had never written down. The interest of his musical officer had provided a piano and, later, the introduction to F. J. Higgs. Nothing that had happened to him had been done by himself. Someone had put him in an orphanage, someone had seen to his musical education, someone had arranged for him to join the navy, someone had found him a musical engagement. He had drifted along, neither happy nor unhappy, with only his music to spur him. He knew F. J. Higgs believed in him, he knew that a big future was planned for him, but he was unstirred, he was like somebody walking in their sleep. Now, listening to Nella, he felt something he had never felt before. He felt protective. There she stood, in front of him, tiny and not very noticeable, and very humble. He wanted to bare his muscles in her defence, to shout to the Corners and the Binns, and anyone who would listen, "Don't squash her, give her a chance, she's got more talent than any of you." At the end of the song he said in so interested a way that Nella was quite stunned:

"I don't see why you shouldn't sing. Your voice only wants developing. Would you like me to teach you?"

Her grey eyes grew rounder and rounder.

"Teach me! Why on earth should you bother?" His fingers ran up a scale.

"I don't know. I just want to."

The door of the hail swung open. The Corners and the Binns clattered in. Dulcie came first, and so she saw that Nella and Tom were talking. Tom had his face towards her. With that heightened sensitiveness which she had where he was concerned she was conscious that whatever he was saying had interested him, he was awake. Nobody would bother about Nella. Men never looked at Nella. It was more to cash in on his mood than jealousy that made Dulcie sweep forward.

"What are you two talking about?"

Tom would have told her, he would have cheerfully explained to all the family that Nella had talent and wanted training, but Nella intervened.

"He's been playing over a new version of your dance refrain to 'She Danced in Piccadilly.' He's been trying to get it the way you want it. Play it to her, Tom."

Nobody was more surprised than Tom when, without argument or fuss, he began to play the new version of Dulcie's dance. He looked at Nella to see if she were pleased with it, but she had shrunk back once more into her silent self, and seemed unaware that he wanted her approval.

Dulcie glowed.

"Oh, thank you, Tom. You're an angel. That's absolutely perfect."

* * *

Never was a trip started in better weather. It was not a bit like April, it was like mid-summer. The temperature went up to over seventy. The party succeeded in getting a carriage to themselves on the train. It had been difficult. Dulcie was wearing a rose pink coat over a light silk frock and no stockings. The sight of her slim legs and dazzling hair against the rose pink coat caused a flutter on the platform. Four young men made a concerted rush to follow her into the carriage. Alfie circumvented them. He leant out of the window.

"Sorry. We're full up in here."

He managed to sound so forbidding that, regretfully, the young men moved on, but Alfred continued not only to hang out of the window, but to block the view of Dulcie until the train started. He sat down at last, pretending to mop his forehead.

"Travelling with you, Miss, is like travelling a leopard. Bound to cause a crowd." He looked across at Alice. "If she was mine I'd travel her in a veil."

Dulcie had succeeded in sitting next to Tom. It was the result of planning. Before she got up that morning she had worked it out. "When we get on the platform I'll stick close beside him, and I'll let him get into the train first, then I can choose my own seat." She despised herself for thinking out these things, but that did not prevent a shiver of triumph when she had accomplished what she had planned. It was an over two hour journey to Comstock. So far she had come by very few chances to be next to Tom and make him conscious of her. If she travelled next to him for two hours surely he would become, like all the other men she knew, interested in her, and all that. She looked out of the window. Oh, goodness, what a lovely day! Suppose Tom did become human and ordinary; suppose he said could she come for a walk on the front or the beach to-night. She rather hoped he would not want to go to a restaurant. It would be pretty marvellous, in weather like this, out of doors by the sea. She wondered what it would be like if Tom made love to her. It was queer, but he was somebody she wanted to kiss. Staring out of the window she felt the colour rising in her cheeks. She hoped that she would be sensible. A girl only made herself cheap by giving things too easily. She had often heard that in the dressing-room. It had never come her way before. She had had no difficulty in remaining fastidious and aloof. Now she closed her eyes for a second, and let her imagination play. She gave a slight shudder.

Tom was talking to Muriel, who was on the other side of him. He turned to look at Dulcie in surprise.

"Goose run over your grave?"

Dulcie could not answer. She gave an assenting nod.

Tom intended to sit next to Nella. He found Nella very much in his mind. He knew that what he felt for her was what he would have felt for a sister if ever he had possessed one. During his time in the navy he had his experiences with women, and what he had felt then was so far removed from what he felt about Nella that he knew there was no love business in it. Tom was not self-analytical. He had taken extra trouble with his appearance that morning, he had shaved especially close. He was wearing a blue suit and he had discarded two ties before he chose the one he was wearing. In the navy he had been as fussy about the colour of his collar and the sit of the bow on his cap as any other seaman. When he had gone ashore he had expected his messmates to assist him, just as he assisted them, to turn out to the standard of sartorial elegance expected on the lower deck. That, however, was part of the navy and its tradition. Back on shore he had not thought of clothes much. He did not know that he had thought of clothes that morning, or at least he did not link his thinking about them with Nella. While, he was picking a tie he said to himself, "Poor little kid. Nobody notices her. Damn shame. Probably got more talent in her little finger than the whole lot of them put together." He had meant to put his arm through hers on the platform, and quite openly take her into the carriage with him. That was the way to treat a kid sister. She could do with a bit of petting. He never saw that brother of hers bothering much. But when he got to the station Nella had not been willing to be petted. She had drawn her arm in surprise away from his, looked up at him in fright and darted away, murmuring that she must see about the luggage. She had not come into the carriage through the same door as he had, she had gone in through another carriage and the corridor, and had planted herself between Betty and Dickie. Tom had to talk to Muriel, but he was still very conscious of Nella at the other end of the carriage. "Poor little kid! They'd squashed her so she was shy at the slightest kindness. Still, they'd all the summer before them, he'd show them."

Nella leant back and let Dickie and Betty chatter across her. Tom had scared her. In many ways Nella was still a child. She gave most of her interest to dancing; she spent any money that came her way on going to the ballet; her reading matter was mostly books on dancing; she had not so far attracted men, but she had, of course, met a good many and gone to dances, but none had shown more than a passing interest in her. She used her talent for being inconspicuous almost consciously. She liked being what she was, the quiet, the unnoticed. In a way it made her more herself.

She felt curtained off from the world, as by a fog. The very last thing she wanted was that Tom should pay attention to her; only too well she knew the results of that. Awful family jokes. "Who did I see holding Nella's arm this morning?" "Who's blushing?" Because Nella was undeveloped in many ways she was not unobservant. She could see that Dulcie was attracted by Tom. Living so close to Dulcie and travelling with her to and from the dancing school, she knew all about Dulcie's effect on men. She knew that they followed her around like needles after a magnet. She knew, too, how little Dulcie thought of this attention that was poured on her. She took it for granted. She was not the sort of girl who was silly about boys, she was just accustomed to worship, and that was that. Nella, standing in the corner at rehearsals watching Dulcie's manoeuvres, standing by the piano, leaning on Tom's shoulder, had been puzzled. Why should Dulcie, who never was silly about men, behave like that? Nella liked Dulcie, and there had been a time when she considered she was her best friend. One of the things she had liked best about Dulcie was the way she treated men. What was making her so queer now? Nella's idea of love was very secondhand, gleaned from films and from the very little that she had read. Could Dulcie have fallen in love with Tom? If Dulcie had fallen in love with Tom then, whatever happened, Tom mustn't make a fuss of herself. Of course, he had only caught hold of her arm on the station out of friendliness, but she did not want anything of that sort. Apart from just not wanting it, Dulcie might be annoyed. And annoying Dulcie was at all costs to be avoided. Dulcie was the star. Dulcie joining the concert party had made this lovely seaside trip possible. Because of Dulcie, Dad and Mum and herself and Dan were going to have a gorgeous summer all together.

Nella lay back in her seat, smiling a secret smile. Comstock was going to be heaven. The concert party was going to be fun. No silliness from Tom, or Dulcie, must be allowed to spoil things.

* * *

The camp was bathed in sunlight. The large blue swimming-pool glimmered, the yellow and blue chalets shone with fresh paint, nothing could look more inviting. The Corners, the Binns and Tom wasted very little time admiring their chalets and looking round. They made, as is the way of professionals, straight for the theatre. Alfred and John had done a good deal of advance publicity; they had sent down large photographs of Dulcie and posters, and Pinkie Barrow had done the rest. In an arc right across the front of the theatre was a sign "Here's Fun", and underneath, "Barrow's Campers' Concert Party". On the posters were their names in squares. Dulcie's a little larger than anyone else's. In the foyer were her photographs, large close-ups of her head, small ones of Dulcie in a bathing dress, evening dress, or various stage frocks. There was nothing for Dulcie to quarrel with; for the first time she was arriving at a theatre in which she was to star; she was properly billed, outside the sun was shining; and yet she felt thoroughly on edge. Seeing her name in large type for the first time and all the photographs made her nervous. Not for worlds would she have let the others know she was nervous. She threw up her chin, tossed back her hair and looked proud. "Of course I'm going to be success," she told herself. "Nothing in the world for me to worry about." But a raised chin and brave thoughts do not cure a sinking tummy.

John and Alfred decided on a run through of the show at six. The concert party was not to open until Monday night, but there might be minor adjustments to fit in with the size of the stage. There were four dressing-rooms. Two by the stage door, and two across the stage. John had suggested that Muriel and Dulcie should share, that another room should be for himself and Alfred, the third room for Tom and the two boys and the fourth the wardrobe in which Nella could dress. Muriel turned the idea down.

"Nonsense, it's the kid's first lead. Let her have a room to herself and feel important. Nella and I can share a room, all you men can dress together, and that'll give Alice the fourth room for the wardrobe."

John and Alfred accepted meekly.

"We may be the leading comedians and the manager, S'arnt," Alfred said, "but this is a family show, and if we want a pleasant summer we'll keep in with the women."

Once again Dulcie had nothing real to complain of. She had a nice little dressing-room to herself, just inside the stage door, but once more she was not pleased. The other room on the same side of the stage as her own was the wardrobe, across the stage were the rest of the company. It gave her a shut-off feeling, just herself and her mother that side of the stage. She explained her dissatisfaction to herself by, "All the fun will be the other side," but in her heart she knew that was not what was making her cross. She did not like being planted away from Tom. Of course, there would not be much time while the show was on to see anybody, but there would be an interval. Of course, he could come across the stage and talk to her, but would he? Crossly she slammed down a piece of chintz as a dressing-table cover, and the tray for her sticks of paint.

Pinkie Barrow turned up at the theatre at a quarter to six. He had been the sergeant pilot of a bomber, shot down over Germany, and, though much younger than Alfred and John, because of their mutual interest in stage shows, had got to know them fairly well in the short time he was in their prisoner-of-war camp. The *stalag* in which he had met them was an impossible place from which to escape, but that had not affected Pinkie. He had tried to escape from every camp to which he was moved, and no amount of punishment deterred him, so he was never in any camp for long. He was a gay young man who found everything in life amusing. If, underneath, he had his private worries and visions, he kept them strictly under lock and key. Any conversation in which Pinkie was embroiled quickly became ribald, he did not care for anything serious for long.

Alfred and John took him round his theatre to introduce him to his company. Dulcie's room had a window looking out on to the swimming-pool. She had not drawn the curtains as she was not going to dress. Pinkie had his breath quite taken away by the effect of her against the shimmering blue-water background.

"This is my daughter, Dulcie," John said.

Pinkie had easy, graceful manners. For once he was tongue-tied. Then he smiled his pleasant, slow smile.

"Sorry, but you winded me. I've seen your photographs, but I didn't know you were quite so pin-up in real life."

Behind his back Alfred screwed up his monkey face and gave John a wink. It was a wink which suggested, "Oh, boy, are we lucky! Dulcie doing her stuff." John turned a stern eye on Alfred, an eye which said, "I'll thank you to remember that Dulcie's my daughter and not something for sale in a slave market." Pinkie looked at his watch.

"We've got some nice lines in bars in this place, they open at six."

Dulcie always smiled at her managers. She smiled charmingly at Pinkie, but her heart missed a beat. Drinking with the management was not how she had intended to spend this evening. It was going to be a lovely night, so ridiculously warm for the time of year. If Tom did not suggest doing anything, she could stay behind after rehearsal and say something herself. Easy to ask him if he would like to come and look at the sea, or something of that sort. After all, there was nothing else he wanted to do, It was idiotic not to take advantage of weather like this. There were not going to be all that many chances of being alone. He was shy, of course, but it should not be difficult to break down his reserve.

"I'm afraid to-night's no good. We've got a rehearsal in half an hour, and that'll go on till about seven."

Alfred took a deep breath but John beat him to it.

"That's all right, Dulcie, we can manage without you."

Alfred nodded.

"We could take her numbers first if Mr. Barrow wouldn't mind sitting in the stalls for a bit."

Pinkie turned an amused face to Alfred.

"What's all this Mr. Barrow stuff? I was Pinkie last time I saw you."

"You're our manager now," John reminded him.

Pinkie, still looking amused, moved to the door.

"I dare say, but I'm still Pinkie, and you're S'arnt, and you're Corp." He looked at John. "And your daughter hasn't got to drink with me because I'm her manager. I'm just an ordinary young man with his eye on a bint." He looked over his shoulder at Dulcie. "What about it?"

Dulcie knew she was beaten. She had no possible excuse for refusing to drink with Pinkie. It was perfectly true that her numbers could be taken first, and the casual way in which Pinkie had refused to allow her father and Alfred to force her to drink with her manager had cut the ground from under her feet. If he hadn't said that it would have been easy for her to refuse, and then say to the family afterwards "I won't have you making use of me like that." Now her chance was gone.

"Right. As soon as I'm through. I'd love to."

For scenery John had designed painted boxes. They could be used in all sorts of ways. When the curtain went up on the concert party they were piled up in tiers, and on the top sat Dulcie, with the others grouped beneath her. It made a pretty opening. For this rehearsal Alice sat beside Pinkie in the stalls. Betty sat on his other side. Alice explained the colour scheme.

"The two men royal blue, Nella - that's the little dark girl, you know - and her brother, Dan, in scarlet, Mrs. Binns and my boy, Dickie, in green, and Tom Pollard at the piano and Dulcie in yellow."

Pinkie had an eye for colour. In his mind he redressed the different figures, and as he did it he saw an exchange of glances that he might have missed. He saw Tom look across the top of the grand piano at Nella. Because of the look that Tom gave her she ceased to need Alice's description, the little dark girl, and became a person to Pinkie. She did not look much in her black practice frock, but there must be something in her which that young man at the piano could see. He raised his eyes to Dulcie. She, too, was wearing a black practice dress, but oh, how different she looked! The black set off her fairness, her loveliness caught his breath. Alfred was giving a stage direction.

"Move a bit over, Dulcie, we want you dead centre, you're sitting a bit to one side."

Dulcie moved and, as she did so, she let her eyes rest for a second on Tom. Pinkie adored competition. He stiffened in his seat.

"What's all this? What's all this? Pinkie, my boy, you'll have to make a landing. Watch out for that flare-path."

Alfred said:

"We're going to take Dulcie's numbers first, Tom. She needn't do all of them, just the dancing ones to see how she goes for space."

The stage was cleared and Tom began to play "He Met Me at Waterloo". Dulcie felt all the frustrated annoyance of the day flood over her.

"I won't start with that. I'll start with 'She Danced in Piccadilly '."

Tom looked surprised.

"But that's to be in the second half."

Talk to him she would, even if it was only to quarrel with him.

"It doesn't matter where it comes. We're only having a run through now."

Alfred felt that their leading lady was not behaving at her best before the management. He came on to the stage.

"It doesn't matter what order she does them in, Tom; let her choose herself, it's only for space."

Tom began to play the opening chords of "She Danced in Piccadilly ".

"All right, it's all one to me."

Dulcie could have hit him. It was so palpably true. It was all one to him what she danced or where she was. He really was the most disobliging man. Alice whispered to Pinkie.

"This number comes in the second half. My husband has painted a fountain with Eros on the top. Dulcie sings the verses as the flower girl, but for the dance she throws aside her shawl and hat. I've got her a very pretty frock for this number."

Betty sighed.

"Scrumptious. It's like an autumn leaf."

Pinkie looked at her.

"Aren't you in the show?"

"Me! Goodness, no! I'm too fat, and I don't do anything except play the accordion a little bit."

Pinkie eyed her thoughtfully.

"I should have thought she'd do rather well to announce the numbers. Who's doing that?"

Alice's mind tore through the wardrobe.

"I've nothing to dress her in. I think Tom's sticking up the numbers on the top of the piano."

Betty was thrilled.

"Oh, Mum, I'd be much better than numbers on the top of a piano. Couldn't you, oh, couldn't you let me?"

"We've got a lot of that plastic material here, we're making our curtains of it," Pinkie suggested. "She might have a tunic of that."

Betty beamed at him.

"I do think you're a perfectly lovely man." Alice smiled.

"It's quite an idea."

They were startled to hear Dulcie's voice. She had stopped singing and her face was pink.

"If you want to talk, would you mind talking outside."

Everybody was appalled. What a display Dulcie was giving! Muriel made clicking sounds and Alfred shrank into the prompt corner. John felt horribly embarrassed. Shocking Dulcie was being, not so much to Pinkie, but talking to her mother like that. Dickie muttered, "Put a sock in it," and Dan said to Nella, "I bet Dulcie's going to spoil the whole summer." None of them understood. Dulcie was pleased with "She Danced in Piccadilly". Now the music was altered it suited her, and she knew her dance was charming. She had insisted on doing it first because she wanted Pinkie to be pleased. She thought he was sure to say something, and then she would be generous and explain

Tom's share in the business, how he had altered the music to suit her. Pinkie got to his feet and came to the edge of the stage.

"I'm terribly sorry. It was my fault. I was suggesting that your little sister should come on as announcer. With the changes of programme, you'll need somebody for that. It was dreadfully rude of me to talk during your number. Can you forgive me?"

Ridiculously Dulcie wanted to cry. What in the world was there to cry about? She stood there swallowing. Pinkie was touched, he held out a hand to her and looked into the prompt corner.

"She's tired. Can't I steal her for half an hour and bring her back?"

John had no idea what had got into Dulcie, but it was obvious she was in a state. He looked at Alfred, who nodded. He managed to give Dulcie a smile.

"Off you go. We'll have a run through of your numbers before the dress rehearsal to-morrow."

There were two bars in the camp. Pinkie led Dulcie to a table in a corner. He ordered a cocktail and gave her a cigarette.

"Are you still angry?"

"No." She found herself relaxing. She smiled. "I don't know what's the matter with me to-day. Everything's exactly as I want it and I'm not pleased about anything."

Pinkie lit both their cigarettes and put away his lighter.

"My nurse used to call that getting out of bed the wrong side, and my mother called it having a black dog on your shoulder. I call it browned off. I dare say it's the weather.

The Air Ministry say it is the hottest April since something or other. I always wonder who keeps all those weather charts, or do you think they just make it up? We run a magazine in our camp, and if we said that any special day was the hottest, wettest, coldest or finest day in Comstock for the last two thousand years, everybody would believe it." The drinks arrived. He put hers in front of her. He chattered on. "Very proud of myself for nabbing your show."

"You haven't seen it yet."

"I saw the old male version in our *stalag*. Proper riot. Lovely creature, a sergeant in R.E.'s, was the leading lady then. You've no idea what you've got to live up to. He had a red wig and the most fetching artificial bust." He raised his glass to her. "Here's fun in *Here's Fun*. Seriously, it's just the sort of show that I think our campers'll like. We're mostly a family affair, and your show's a family affair. Ought to be just the ticket. Very important to me that is. My old Dad has handed over the running of the shows to me this year, but he doesn't trust me farther than he can throw me. Always snooping around. I've got any amount of ideas up my cuff, but I can't get any of them going unless I have a free hand, and I won't get a free hand unless the old man sees that I can nab some good ideas. I'm trusting to this show to push that into his grey matter." He saw that Dulcie had calmed. He pushed the ash-tray a little nearer to her. "Tell me about your numbers."

Dulcie leant her elbows on the table.

"Some of it is Rose Reilly's stuff. I understudied her in London, and I have some other numbers out of F. J.'s shows, but, of course, Tom Pollard's songs are the interesting ones. They've been written specially for me."

"What sort of type is he?"

Dulcie, wishing she knew, spoke quite honestly.

"I don't know. He's not like anybody else. He's been in the navy."

"I've read up his publicity. Won a musical scholarship. Served with distinction in the navy. Attracted attention at a concert party on his ship and was sent to F. J. Higgs, who put him under contract. I can write that sort of thing myself. You don't know anything about a man by reading it. Take me, Pinkie Barrow, son of Leonard Barrow, educated at a good preparatory and small public school, joined the R.A.F. in 1940. Prisoner of war 1942, but what d'you know about me? Nothing at all. Might all be lies."

Dulcie finished her drink.

"Funny you saying that. I don't know anything about Tom. I don't know one thing more than there is in his publicity, except that he was brought up in an orphanage."

Pinkie beckoned to the waiter to bring two more drinks.

"Are you like me? Do you hate not knowing about people? I'm a proper old beaver, I like to burrow and burrow until I've worked my way along and found out everything there is." He waited for the waiter to bring the drinks. "Are you a bit of a beaver?"

Dulcie had turned her face slightly away from him and was looking down at her cigarette.

"I suppose I am rather. Though usually I'm not, because I think that men mostly tell you all about themselves without being asked."

"A vain and talkative sex. Tell me about you. Not what's on the publicity, I know that. The bits that aren't there. Hobby?"

"The theatre. Ever since I can remember I've meant to be a star. This is my first starring chance, if you can call it that. Of course, it isn't much, just the family."

"Don't forget, my girl, most of your audience change every week; thousands'll have seen you before the season's over. You might twinkle very nicely from here."

Dulcie's voice warmed.

"I want to be a proper star. Not somebody who slinks out of the theatre and goes home on a tube. I want to live like a star. Go about in a big car. My name in coloured lights all over the front of the theatre."

"And I should have it on a bus. I never think anyone's really got there until their name's on a bus."

"And on a bus," Dulcie agreed. "It's queer how much surer you are of doing the things you want to do some days than others, have you noticed that?"

Her hand was on the table. Pinkie patted it.

"We've all noticed it. Let's drink to your future. If you're a success here I go down big with my old man, so the toast is for both of us really. Here's to *Here's Fun*, and may you get everything you want."

Dulcie raised her glass.

"Here's fun." She paused. "And everything we want."

Pinkie gave her hand another pat.

"You shouldn't want two things at once though. Never get on that way. You stick to fame and your name on a bus."

* * *

Dulcie's departure left a feeling of awkwardness between the Binns and the Corners. Muriel thought, "What's the matter with the girl? I hope she isn't going to play up like this all the summer and spoil everything." Alfred's feeling was for John. "Poor old S'arnt! Difficult to know what to do with a girl like that. Too old to take a slipper to her, more's the pity." Dickie was ashamed. Everything was being such fun. Why on earth had old Dulcie behaved like this? Dan, fingering his billiard-balls, dropped one and mentally blamed Dulcie for it. Nobody could do anything right when people made scenes. Alice, in the stalls, was thinking of John. How unlucky! On their very first evening, too. There was so little understanding between Dulcie and her father. It was such a long way they both had to go, to go back to the happy father-and-daughter atmosphere of the pre-war years; it was maddening of Dulcie to have acted so stupidly. Betty kept her views to herself.

"I expect it's the sea air. I read in the paper, if you feel nervous and irritable on the first day of your holiday it's probably the air, and you ought to take some sort of salts, but I forget which."

John and Nella were thinking of Dulcie with sympathy, but both were fighting against accepting what their reason told them was true. "She can't be in love with Tom," thought Nella. "In any case, if she is, why should she behave like this? Men hate these girls who make fusses. I'm sure they do. It isn't like Dulcie to be like this, so there must be something. Of course, she's always thrown her weight about at home, but that was because she was in a job and nobody else was, but she never did at the dancing school, and I bet she didn't at the theatre. She can't be in love with Tom. If she was, Tom would be in love with her; men always are." John thought. "I believe I was right when I thought Dulcie might be keen on Tom. If she is, I wish she would trust me enough to talk to me. I'm sure she's barking up the wrong tree, poor little beast; that boy only cares for his music. I don't believe he knows that Dulcie or any other girl exists. If I'm right, I'm sorry. Poor little devil! How it hurts. How terribly being in love hurts."

Alfred suddenly became conscious of the general awkwardness. He pretended to sit on one of his boxes and fell off it. Muriel behaved as if this was terribly funny, and Dan and Nella smiled. Betty, whose great idea of humour was somebody falling off something, laughed louder than Muriel. Alfred said:

"Slipping a bit, aren't I? Come on, everybody. Let's get on with the rehearsal. We're at Comstock now. Put a snap into it."

Tom for once had not got his mind on his music. He found, for the first time since he had known them all, that he was aware of the Corners and the Binns as personalities. He had become conscious of Dulcie. Up to the minute Dulcie had said, "I won't start with that, I'll start with 'She Danced in Piccadilly'," she had been just another artist to him. F. J. Higgs had employed him to play at rehearsals, and in front of him had worked the chorus and the small parts, and the stars, and he had neither seen nor thought about any of them. His head buzzed with tunes, and he only waited for the artists to go and the piano to be free for himself. The Corners and the Binns had meant a little more to him; this time he was an artist, appearing on the stage, and so he felt more part of the company than he had when he was merely an accompanist at rehearsals. Dulcie had been, at first, "That fair piece". Then she became "That bad-tempered piece", and from there, because she annoyed him in wanting him to alter his music, "That fair bitch". He had been totally unconscious that she liked him. At F. J.'s rehearsals the small parts and the stars had often leant on the piano or against his shoulder when they were learning something. They even stretched across his shoulder and played a few notes on the piano. He found nothing noticeable in Dulcie's behaviour, but to-night everything was different. The show wasn't the Corners and the Binns, it was a show in which a little dark girl, who was to wear a red dress, was having a raw deal. The whole of *Here's Fun* took on new life from Nella. Each song he played and each little sketch the company ran through he re-cast, putting in dancing for Nella. He wanted to do something about her right away, speak to John and Alfred, but he was afraid. The little dark, dancing Nella, whom only he appreciated, had something about her which made him feel she would be angry if he interfered in her business without her consent. Of course, it didn't matter if she was annoyed, after all, she was only a kid, and all he wanted was to be a sort of brother to her. Still, caution prevailed. He would have a talk with her this evening. It was going to be a lovely evening. It would be nice on the beach. He needed his lungs filled with the sea again after months shut up in

London. Do little Nella good, too. A fine long walk, and a good talk about her future. It was queer how Dulcie had attracted his attention. She ceased to be that fair anything and, in one minute, became Dulcie. When she had raged up to the piano and said, "It doesn't matter where it comes, we're only having a run through now," he had glanced up at her and, in the new interest he was taking in them all, saw something he would certainly have missed even yesterday. There were tears in Dulcie's eyes. Nobody knew about those tears but Tom. She leant across the piano and he had seen them form in her eyes, and seen her swallow and angrily brush them away. It was because of those tears and not because Alfred had said it didn't matter about the order that he had broken into "She Danced in Piccadilly", and had said, "All right, all one to me." A queer thought had come to him as she leant across the piano. He had seen it happen before. Not to Dulcie's sort, but to tarts all over the earth. In saloons, when they had a day or two ashore, there would be girls. Everything had been going all right, plenty of drink and plenty of doings while the money lasted, and then suddenly it was over and they were sailing the next day, and the tart, just one probably, would care. It wasn't always about him, sometimes it was one of the other men. The tart had turned generous, didn't mind if the money was finished, paid for the drinks, and had tears in her eyes when they said good-bye. Dulcie looked that way. It was a special look that came on a girl's face when she cared too much. Dulcie caring! Could Dulcie, of all people, be caring for him? They had hardly spoken, most of the time she had been annoyed. Still, that was nothing, he'd been knocked out before now by a tart who had cried when he went away. Women were like that. Showed their love in funny ways. Spit at you, bit you, shout at you, and then be angry because you didn't know they were fond of you. He had never, since his training-ship days, been in one place long enough to know what you did next when some girl who was nothing to you decided to fall in love with you.

Alfred laid a hand on Tom's shoulder.

"Dulcie's 'He Met Me at Waterloo' comes next. Cut that and come to our nursery rhyme doings."

Tom played the opening bars but his mind was miles away. Cut that, he thought, better cut her altogether, if that's what she's feeling. Don't want any trouble there.

It was rather a muddled sort of rehearsal. It was not really possible to rehearse without Dulcie. There was no one to take her place in the full company numbers or the sketches. Everybody was glad when John and Alfred, after consultation, said, "That's enough. Dress rehearsal to-morrow."

Tom usually stayed on playing at the end of rehearsals. To-day he got up and came over to Nella where she was changing her shoes.

"I see supper is at seven. Would you come for a walk with me afterwards?"

Nella straightened up. Why had he asked her that? Whatever excuse was she going to make? No rehearsal till to-morrow and Aunt Alice had unpacked the stage dresses that afternoon. They had all unpacked. Childishly she said:

"Why do you want me to?"

That stumped Tom. Why did he want her to? He looked upon her as a kid sister, and people didn't want to go for walks with kid sisters. He decided it must be her talent, and his dislike of seeing it hidden.

"I think you're the most awfully good dancer. I told you so last night, and I think I could make you sing; I don't sing myself but I used to when I was a kid. I was brought up in an orphanage, you know, and there was a choir."

If he had not mentioned the orphanage Nella would have said no, but once he had mentioned the orphanage she could not make herself do it. It must be awful to be brought up in an orphanage. It must give you a terrible inferiority complex, you'd always feel you'd missed something that other boys had. It would be awful to say you wouldn't go for a walk with somebody brought up in an orphanage. There was a warm, friendly look in her grey eyes.

"Of course I will. I'd love to."

Pinkie brought Dulcie back to the theatre. She felt soothed by Pinkie He was the sort of easy, admiring man she was used to. He had put her world into perspective again. She was being a fool to be shy and stupid with Tom. He only needed a bit of encouragement, that was all any man needed. He was packing up his music when she came back on to the stage. She was helped by the two cocktails, which had lifted her tiredness and depression. Cheerfully and naturally she said:

"There's a dance here to-night after supper. Are you fond of dancing? Or we might go for a walk."

Nella had just folded the ribbon round her practise shoes. She gripped the shoes tightly. What was Tom going to say?

How dreadful if Dulcie was angry with her. Their very first night at Comstock, and she would never get away from her as they had to share a chalet.

Tom thought back to his waterfront saloon bar. Tell a girl who thought herself fond of you that you were going out with another girl and you'd get something thrown at you. He had no wish for a black eye before the first night. He looked apologetic.

"I can't to night, got a bit of business to do. Maybe some other night. After all, we shall be here the whole summer."

The camp was not a place in which it was easy to lose one another. In spite of the numbers of people walking about, there was always someone to see which way you went. From Nella's point of view there was Betty, the born reporter, who believed that everybody's actions were everybody's property, and that everybody liked to know what everybody else was doing. The camp had two large dining-rooms. The two families and Tom shared a table in a corner. They had no sooner sat down to supper than Betty said:

"It's the most super evening, do let's all go on the beach."

Alice and Muriel groaned.

"You children go on the beach by all means," said Muriel, "but I've had enough of rush and tear for one day. I shall be glad to get off the old dogs."

Alfred looked across at John.

"Lovely billiard tables here. What about it, S'arnt? We deserve some recreation."

Alice saw John's face light up and that easy relaxed look which both he and Alfred had when talking to each other.

Of course they would like to go off together and play a game of billiards. What men wouldn't? Only, in John's and Alfred's case, going off together had become too much of a habit. Her quiet voice broke in on the conversation.

"There's a dance every evening here in the ballroom. I read it in the programme of attractions. Muriel and I will sit and watch the dancing until you men collect us." She looked at John. "Then you can take us along to one of those bars for a night-cap before we go to bed."

John was amazed. Alice did not really like a drink. It was funny to hear her talking of sitting in a bar. Still, it wasn't a bad idea, make a nice round-off to the evening, and they ought to get to bed early, there was a busy day to-morrow.

"Right. Lucky that Corp and I sent the money along beforehand for club membership for all of us, or you wouldn't have been able to have a drink for twenty-four hours."

Betty, though tolerant, thought the ways of adults inexplicable. Fancy shutting yourself up in a room with a billiard-table when you could go into a ballroom. She turned to the rest of the party.

"Let's dance. You're all going to dance, aren't you?"

Dulcie, with her confidence in herself renewed by Pinkie's obvious admiration, was not going to let Tom think it mattered to her whether he danced or not.

"Of course I'm going to dance. You can wear a long dress here if you like, I shall change after supper."

Betty's eyes shone.

"What are you going to wear? And who are you going to dance with?"

Dulcie knew from experience that she would never want for a partner. There was also Pinkie in the background. However, she had no intention of being too explicit.

"Don't you be so curious."

Betty turned to Nella.

"Are you dancing?"

Nella shook her head.

"Not to-night."

Betty leant across to Tom.

"But you're going to, aren't you? It's free." Tom shook his head.

"I will one night."

Nella did not look at Tom, nor Tom at Nella, yet Dulcie felt uneasy. Then, mentally, she laughed at herself. Tom going out with Nella when he wouldn't dance with her! How could she be such a fool! She must snap out of it. This fixation about Tom was getting her down. Betty was cajoling Dickie and Dan.

"Come for just a tiny bit. I can't dance if you don't. You could take turns."

Dickie laughed.

"What an offer. Sitting out waiting to dance with the biggest lump in the room."

Betty knew her limitations.

"I don't expect it would be as bad as that really. By the time I've danced once with each of you you'll have both found something that you think snappy, and I'll be sitting out with Mum and Aunt Muriel. Life's like that, but I won't mind, at least I'll hear the band."

Pinkie caught Dulcie as she came out of the dining-room.

"Dancing?"

"Thought I'd look in at the dance for a little when I've changed."

"You going with anybody?" She shook her head. "Well, I'll call for you then. I can't stay long myself, more's the pity, I have to look in on all the entertainments during the evening to see everybody's having a good time, but it would be wizard if we could have a dance or two before the work of the evening starts."

Nella and Tom set out for their walk as soon as everybody had left for the ballroom. It was, of course, stupid to be so secret, and Nella knew it, but life was like that. It was stupid when you had to live at close quarters to make trouble for yourself. There was absolutely nothing in herself and Tom going for a walk. All there was to it was being manufactured out of the secrecy built round it. It was a lovely night. Incredibly warm for April. The sea made a gentle swishing accompaniment to their footsteps. There was a little breeze and it smelt of salt.

"Isn't it going to be simply gorgeous," said Nella, "our being here all the summer? I was never away much in the war. Betty was evacuated, of course, but I wasn't."

"I wonder you didn't go away. Can't have been very nice in London."

"It wasn't bad. Anyway, I was called up." Nella gave a faint laugh at the memory of herself. "I was a temporary civil servant. I was put to work in the Food Office. Gosh! How I hated it!"

Tom was horrified. Little, frail Nella forced to do work she did not like! He said gruffly:

"Lot of rot making women work."

"I don't see how we could have won the war if we hadn't. Of course, I don't mean that women won the war the way you did, but if you went away somebody had to fill in forms and things and make munitions. What did you do?"

"I was an ordinary seaman."

"Was it awful?"

"At the beginning. I was sick every day at one time, but I got over it."

"Must have been ghastly. Everybody's so on top of each other, nowhere to be alone, I should hate that."

Tom looked across the sea and his mind stretched back.

"As a matter of fact, you couldn't want anything nicer than the crow's nest, once you're used to the motion. Half the time there was nothing particular to do, and you were alone, of course. I'd never been used to being alone. I liked it."

Again Nella was torn with pity. Poor Tom, he hadn't had much of a time.

"Was it awful in your orphanage?"

Tom thought dispassionately back to his childhood.

"No. I don't remember thinking anything much. It was the same, you know, day after day, nothing ever seemed to happen. When I was eleven my teacher sent me in for a music examination and I got a scholarship. I still lived at the orphanage, but it was different. I went to school still, but I was always at my music lessons, when I wasn't they found a piano I could practise on. Then, when I was fourteen, I went to a college of music. That was fine."

Nella looked at him striding along with his head up and

his open shirt, his hands deep in his pockets. "That was fine." "Much the same, you know, day after day." "You were alone, of course." "I'd never been used to being alone and I liked it." How little had come to Tom. All the fun of ordinary things, the birthdays and the Christmasses and the little treats. He had nothing at all. It would be nice this summer if he could be made to feel part of them, look upon them as his family.

Tom said:

"I can't understand why you haven't more to do in this show. I'm no judge, but it seems to me that in dancing you're the tops."

Nella kicked a pebble on to the beach.

"Actually, I wasn't trained at the right place. I think I ought to have been sent to Sadler's Wells or somewhere like that, where you only have to dance. Nobody expects the girls at Sadler's Wells to sing. Still, I dare say I wouldn't have been good enough and they wouldn't have had me. Anyhow, now it's too late. Because of the war I didn't really have any training between seventeen and twenty, and that's put me back a lot. It was different for Dulcie, she didn't have to do any war work."

Tom was indignant.

"Why ever not? Why should you have been made to slave in an office if she wasn't?"

"F. J. Higgs got her exemption. She had to work awfully hard, you know. Shows on Sundays and all that, and she was quite a long time working for E.N.S.A."

Tom saw that even the Government had taken sides against Nella. It was a damned unjust world.

"What about these singing lessons? Will you let me try?"

Nella thought it was time to turn back. She pulled her coat round her.

"It's blowing up a bit. I think we'd better go home."

They turned their faces towards the camp. Tom said:

"You can make a little voice into a big one, you know. Your voice is awfully true. You're dead in the middle of the note. There was a kid in the choir at my orphanage who had only a whisper to start with and he became solo boy."

Nella had been going to refuse the singing lessons. It was going to be difficult to arrange. Dulcie was sure to find out and it might annoy her, but there went Tom again talking about his orphanage. She saw him as a little boy; he would have been very curly-haired then, thin probably, and, of course, terribly good-looking, only nobody would have noticed or cared.

"What did you wear at your orphanage?"

Tom was never surprised at side-tracked conversations. He was too tolerant and easy-going for it to worry him if people did not answer him directly.

"Jerseys in the winter and shirts in the summer. We were only allowed one shirt a week." He laughed at the memory. "I can smell it now, clean on Sunday morning. They were dark, didn't show the dirt."

Nella, as a small child, had owned a frightfully shabby, cheap doll. One arm had fallen off and its hair was apt to come out. Her mother used to say, "Do let me throw that old thing away." Because it was despised and rejected Nella took trouble with that doll, carrying it about and making a fuss of it long after she had ceased to care for dolls at all.

She had the same sort of feeling now for Tom. He must be petted and made much of. He must be made to feel terribly wanted. She did a thing which was foreign to her nature, she put her hand under his arm.

"It's awfully nice for us having you." She saw he was looking at her with a puzzled face. "I mean, I think perhaps we haven't all said how pleased we are having a pianist like you."

He liked the feel of her hand under his arm. He was not analytical and did not wonder why it pleased him to feel the hand of one he regarded as a kid sister under his arm. He did not want her to move it, but he did want to get the singing lessons fixed.

"I'm pleased to be with you all. I'd be even more pleased if you could come along to those singing lessons, only I suppose you might think it a waste of time. After all, I don't sing myself, you've got to take my word for it that I know something about it."

Nella could have cried at her blundering. So that was what he thought. He thought she was refusing to learn from him because he wasn't good enough. Fool that she was! Snubbing poor Tom, who had such a snubbing sort of life anyhow. She pressed his arm with her fingers.

"Of course I'd love to learn." Nella kept her head even when her sympathies were running away with her. "Only let it be a secret. I'm awfully silly, I hate family jokes about me, and there would be family jokes. Dad would call me Nightingale, and that sort of thing."

Tom nodded. No one could deny there would be jokes in the Binns family.

"Nobody need know. We could fix something. The camp's stiff with pianos."

"I'm sure we can fix something, only please, Tom, don't tell anybody. Promise?"

Tom promised. It was enough for him that the lessons were arranged. He began to hum, it was a pleased sort of hum and Nella had a warm feeling of happiness round her heart. It was, nicc to think that on their first evening at Comstock Tom was going to bed humming.

Their chalets were side by side. They stood in the shadow.

"Good night, Nella."

"Good night, Tom."

There was a little hesitation before they turned away. While they hesitated they both had the same idea. "I'd like to give him a kiss," thought Nella, "an ordinary good-night kiss, because I think of him as one of the family." "I'd like to give her a kiss," thought Tom. "The sort of kiss a brother might give a sister."

In the ballroom Dulcie was putting up a very fine performance. Pinkie had introduced her to the band and a few of the single young men, and in no time everybody in the crowded room knew who she was. She looked lovely in a simple black frock, nobody could help noticing her. Pinkie spent as little time as possible on his round of the amusements, then came back to her.

"What about a drink?"

She shook her head.

"I don't want a drink. We'll dance the next one if you like, and then I'm going to bed."

It was a waltz. He took her in his arms and they danced a few steps. He looked down at her.

"Tired?"

"No."

They danced half round the ballroom before he spoke again, when he squeezed her to him.

"It's difficult growing up, isn't it? But when you sort yourself out and know exactly what you want, you'll be, able to get it, and then everything'll be tickety-boo."

She raised her eyes to his.

"How do you know everything isn't tickety-boo already?"

"I've got eyes in my head and a story of my own which I'll tell you one day. You'll probably be glad you've got me ambling around before the summer's through. I'm an understanding type in my way. Don't forget."

The dance finished and Pinkie, without any further argument, saw her back to her chalet. He squeezed her hand.

"Good night and no dreams."

After he had gone she stood a moment looking at the hut next door. Tom would be asleep by now. Probably been asleep for hours, or had he? Again that faint feeling of uneasiness came over her. What had he done with his evening? What had Nella? Nothing, of course. Nella wasn't the sort that men looked at. She fumbled for her key to open the chalet door. Suppose Nella was out. Suppose Nella was out with Tom, what should she do? The chalet was in darkness. Betty and Nella slept in bunks over each other. From Betty came sleepily:

"Wasn't it gorgeous! Everybody was looking at you."

From Nella came no sound at all. Dulcie turned on the light and saw that she was curled up with her face to the wall. Dulcie pulled off her frock and hung it up. "Nella!" she thought. "My goodness, I am an ass!"

* * *

It was the first night. The little theatre was crowded. All day long the loud-speaker had reminded the campers that to-night was the first performance of *Here's Fun*. The first performance ever of Barrow's Campers' Concert Party. For the performances, which were free, the campers must ask for tickets, which would be allotted in order as the requests came in. In the dressing-rooms there was that tension and nervousness which belongs to all first nights. It took them in different ways. John became silent, Alfred noisy, Dickie, the quiet, voluble, Dan, the confident, pessimistic; only Tom, in the men's dressing-room, was outwardly quite unmoved. He had never appeared in a professional performance before and he needed instructions on his make-up. Alfred, glad of an excuse, shouted directions to him.

"Streak your whole face with number nine. Show him which is number nine, Dan." "Now, rub that smooth all over as if it was your own skin. See you don't get a mask, that means take the paint well down to your neck. Show him how not to get a mask, Dan." "Now you want blue for your eyes. Show him how to blue his eyes, Dan." "Now you powder well. Show him how to powder, Dan." "Now you do your eyebrows and your mouth. Show him what paint he uses for them, Dan."

Tom listened to Alfred's verbal directions and struggled to follow Dan's demonstration, but he had only half his mind on his make-up. This was very much a night for him in spite of his seeming calm. His songs were to be tried on the public. He'd not get a chance like this again of sitting on a stage and playing the accompaniment to his own songs making their first appearance. It would never be the same to sit in a box or the stalls listening to an orchestra playing your songs, your mind would be divided, you'd be wishing the conductor would take a quicker or slower tempo, and if the song did not get over, you'd be inclined to blame the orchestra. Sitting on the stage, playing your own music, there would be no division of the mind. You would feel if an air was catching on. Of course, there were always the artists to consider. They might put your stuff over badly. But from a position on the platform you could gauge how much there was of that. He was sure that two of his songs were good. "She Danced in Piccadilly " and "He Met Me at Waterloo". He had not got a clear view of Dulcie. At the dress rehearsal during "She Danced in Piccadilly" there had been a moment when he had thought to himself in surprise, "My word, that girl's good!" It was aggravating to remember that he thought that when she was dancing, and that it was the new version of the dance music which he was playing. Of course, he had changed it to please Nella, but he had to be honest and admit that Dulcie had asked for the alteration from the beginning. He wished now that he had altered the tempo of "He Met Me at Waterloo". She had asked him to alter that, too, though not as fervently as she had asked him to alter "She Danced in Piccadilly". Musically, the music was better as it was, but from a dancing point of view she might be right. Oh, hell! It was too late to do anything about it now. Queer how the thought of hearing the effect of your music could make you in such an uproar. Made him feel downright queer, and that was a fact.

Dan, struggling with his own make-up and Tom's, felt his spirits dropping lower and lower. He had always said that he was not going to appear in public before he was ready; he was not ready. It was true he could get his act right eight times out of ten, but before you appeared in public you ought to get it right ten times out of ten. It was all very well Dad saying look at his notices. What sort of audience had it been? People who had paid to see a show for charity, or shows in hospitals and camps, where everything was free. That sort of audience was uncritical. Easy enough for them to call you "The Boy Wonder Juggler". If he made an ass of himself to-night and bungled his tricks, he was going to refuse to appear another time and that was flat.

Dickie, sitting next to Dan, kept up a flow of conversation with snatches of singing.

"I say, Dad, do you think I want to be a bit paler against that green?" "I say, Uncle Alfred, I think you've told Tom to make himself up much too dark, he looks like an Indian." "I say, did you know that such a lot of people tried to get seats to-night that they were a queue that stretched all around the swimming-pool?" At intervals John said, "Shut up, old man, I can't hear myself think," but it made no odds to Dickie, who babbled on. He was wildly excited and overstrung. His heart was racing and he felt a little sick. To-night was the night of nights. His chance, he'd show them

Alfred and John thoroughly understood one another. They had so often made-up side by side, they knew that had they been alone Alfred would have whistled and made jokes and John would have been taciturn, but between them there would have been complete harmony and understanding. It was tiresome having the three boys in the room on this occasion, when they had not only got the responsibility of the show on their shoulders, but the responsibility of their families as well. Still, what had to be had to be, and nothing could disturb their good, solid foundation of friendship. There was a glow of quiet understanding in their corner of the room.

Muriel hummed as she made up. She always hummed on first nights. She was quite unconscious of what she was doing, it was a natural sedative to her and kept her from feeling too nervous. She found you got a bit more nervous as you grew older. When she had been a girl it didn't matter how she put a number over. She had always gone down well with the boys, they liked her red head and her curves.

People could say what they liked, but it wasn't every boy that wanted the skinny type. Now it was not so easy. Muriel was a realist, quite conscious that she had a certain amount of mental opposition to her appearance to get over before she could make an audience like her. Of course, her hair was very well done and maybe looked natural from the front, but you couldn't alter the fact that sideways there was a shocking bulge round her stomach, and her chin wasn't what it had been. Of course, the bright green helped, but a shape like hers took a bit getting over. It would be a shocking thing if the audience sniggered. An out-and-out laugh she could stand, but never a snigger. She hummed more loudly to drown her thoughts.

Nella was the least nervous of the party. She had so little to do she had not much to be nervous about. But with the acute sensitivity, which was part of her, she felt the nervous reactions of others. She saw Alfred and John, fathers as well as managers. The two boys getting their first chance. Dulcie, at last out of the chorus, with an opportunity to see what she could do on her own. Muriel, still singing beautifully, but a little self-conscious. A wildly excited Betty, to whom to-night and every night would be a party. Above all, she felt for Tom. Tom, who had spent such an unappreciated life, no admiring parents, no teasing but affectionate brother. "Oh, God!" she prayed, as she put on her make-up, "do let the audience stand up and shout for him." She frowned at her face in the glass. What a silly prayer! Audiences never stood up and shouted for the man who played the accompaniments. Still, his name was on the programme as having written the songs, but then, people never read things like that on programmes. She closed her eyes. "Let Uncle John or Dad make a speech at the end, please God, and let them lead Tom forward and say, 'This is the man who wrote the songs,' and then let the audience stand up and cheer."

In the wardrobe Alice was supervising Betty's dressing. She had made her shorts and a little shirt top in pink plastic. Nobody, even her mother, could consider that Betty looked well in pink plastic shorts. On the other hand, she would not have looked well in a pink plastic frock and, at short notice and without coupons, pink plastic was all that Alice could get. Betty thought she looked superb.

"Every inch an actress, aren't I, Mum?"

Alice tied a pink ribbon round Betty's head. Her straight hair was apt to flop over her face if it flowed loose, and she could not wear it in plaits on the stage. Alice looked at Betty's sparkling eyes and vivid colour and gave her a kiss.

"Every inch an actress, darling. For goodness' sake don't fall over or those shorts are going to split."

Dulcie wished she was not sitting grandly in a room by herself. She was feeling terribly sick. Two or three times while she was making-up she half rose to go over to the basin, convinced that she was going to be actually sick. So much hung on to-night. There was no excuse for not going over in a big way, she'd got the numbers. Now that the first night had arrived it was not Tom's numbers that she dreaded, but Rose Reilly's. She had said for so long that she could make a success of Rose's numbers if she only had the chance, well, here was the chance, and was she going to? Oh, goodness! If only she didn't feel so sick! How awful if she wasn't well enough to go on.

Alice opened the door.

"Ready for your frock, darling?"

Dulcie sat limply in her chair, looking at her mother.

"I feel most terribly sick."

Alice crossed the room and took Dulcie's yellow frock off its hanger.

"Just like your father, he's always felt terrible before the curtain goes up, but right as rain once he's on." She looked at Dulcie's legs. "Lucky you have those fine silk tights, your legs do look nice, dear. Step into the frock. Be careful you don't tear the little pants. That's right, I'll comb your hair after I've done you up." She fastened Dulcie down the back and stood away from her. She had made Dulcie's ballet skirts since she was a child and was a master hand at it. For this show she had a dress that was almost like an ordinary frock. There were long sleeves and a Peter Pan collar of yellow net. The close-fitting bodice and the brief skirt were of yellow satin. Under the skirt was the ballet skirt in every shade of yellow from the palest to deep orange. "Spin round, dear, so I see how it looks." She shook her head. "I suppose I shouldn't say it, as I made it, but you've never had a prettier frock than that."

Dulcie handed her mother the comb, she was feeling better. There was something very soothing about Mum, she made you feel that nothing could go very wrong when she was there.

"Give it a comb." She picked up a wreath of yellow and orange flowers. "Did you like the way I wore the flowers yesterday, or would you rather I had them a bit more over?"

The door opened and John looked in.

"Best of luck, Dulcie. Tom's going on now to play the overture."

Dulcie blew him a kiss.

"Good luck, Dad."

She fastened the flowers in place and stood back from the

glass to see how they looked. From the stage came Tom's music, a medley of the tunes in the show. Dulcie caught her breath.

"What is it, dear?" said Alice.

"I never wished Tom luck." Then, to cover the fact that she was worried by this omission, she added, "I meant to, you see, he's the only one that is not in the family."

Alice gave her a kiss.

"Good luck, darling. Not that you need it, you're bound to go down well and you look lovely." She opened the door. "Off you go, you'll have plenty of time to wish Tom luck before the curtain goes up, and you might give him a kiss from me."

* * *

On a first night the artists are too engrossed with their own performances, entrances and lines to be conscious how the show is going. It is only when there is tremendous applause or a scene or a number is supposed to be the high spot of the show that the artists snap out of their individual performances and think of the show as a whole. Only Dulcie knew how her performance was going. Rose Reilly's songs from F. J. Higgs' show were point numbers. There was one supposed to be in a bedroom, dance music was played supposedly over the air. The girl was having an imaginary conversation with her man not yet demobilized. Rose had worn a dressing-gown and the stage had been set as a bedroom. A dressing-gown was not pretty over Dulcie's yellow frock and she had no time to get out of it, so she sang it as she was, with only a small property dressing-table, which was brought on to show where she was meant to be. Her properties were the same as Rose had used, a big photograph of the young man, brushes and combs and toilet things. It had been Dulcie's duty to hear Rose sing that number, she knew every inflection she used. She knew the moment when Rose dropped her voice to the tiniest whisper and, though she had not gulped or anything like that, the audience had felt she was choked with tears. Dulcie could not help giving something of an imitation of Rose, she was too used to her work not to; but there were a few places where she used her own pauses and inflections. "Good night, George," went over beautifully, you could have heard a pin drop. At the end there was excellent applause. As Dulcie came off the stage her father and Alfred, who were waiting in the wings, murmured "Well done," and "That was fine," but Dulcie was not pleased. It was, of course, her first night, she would get the number better in time, but she had not got the audience as Rose had. When Rose sang that number there was a small pause between the end of it and the clapping. It was as if the audience could not snap out of the mood the song had put them into very quickly. When Rose sang half the theatre had tears in their eyes or a lump in its throat. Dulcie, back in her dressing-room powdering her face, felt again that stirring of discomfort that had disturbed her at rehearsals. Was she as good as she thought she was? She picked up her lipstick and remade up her mouth and frowned at her image in the mirror. "Nobody ever gets anywhere unless they believe in themselves. You're an idiot."

"She Danced in Piccadilly" came in the second half. It was a high spot of the programme, so the company stood in their dressing-room doors to hear how it went. John had painted a very good fountain with Eros back on the top. The steps were made with the boxes; on the bottom step sat Dulcie with a black shawl and a black straw hat and her basket of flowers, "Vi'lets, vi'lets, lady, vi'lets all fresh." Then she looked up and sang to Eros, a song to welcome him home after his many years of evacuation, telling him how, now he was back, they were expecting more love about the place, what the effect of that love was likely to be, including dancing in Piccadilly. At the end she flung aside her straw hat and her shawl and danced. She had a pin-pleated frock of brown chiffon over yellow. She kicked off her black overshoes and was back in her tights and ballet shoes. Sitting on the steps in her flower girl's shawl and looking up at Eros, Dulcie noticed that his bow was pointing straight at the piano. It flashed through her mind how nice it would be if that were the real Eros who could shoot a real arrow. Perhaps, because of the thought, she sang the song with exceptional charm. She had a tendency to over act, force and emphasize, but she sang to Eros quite simply. When she danced it was with true gaiety. She had been shot through the heart, love had come back into the world, she could dance in Piccadilly. At the end of the number there were a couple more lines showing that it was a daydream; Dulcie was back on the wooden steps, her shawl hugged round her, her hat slammed down on her fair head. Just as the lights were dimmed out her voice came plaintively, "Vi'lets, all fresh, lovely vi'lets, lovely vi'lets."

There was no doubt about the applause, it crashed out. There were whistles from the men. It was a number that appealed in itself. This one week's holiday was all that most of the audience could get, they were free for one week from food queues, housework and even, for many hours a day, the care of their children. It was a week of absolute rest, but everybody in the audience knew that outside the camp lay the hard, difficult world of 1946. How lovely to imagine, even for a moment, that when Eros came back to Piccadilly love and happiness would come back to the world. Dulcie, charming in the number and looking exquisite, could have afforded to have been far less delightful than she was. For its gay rhythm and escapist theme the audience had taken the song to their hearts.

The curtain came down at the end of the show amidst tremendous enthusiasm. They were all on the stage, Dulcie sitting on the piano, Nella and Dan, their arms round each other, a patch of scarlet up at the back, Muriel sitting on a box with Dickie beside her and, to set off the green of those two, in the centre of the stage were Alfred and John in blue, putting over the final chorus "Good night, campers". They had all had a hand in composing that song. The tune was easy and the words catchy. Alfred had painted the refrain on an enormous card, which was lowered from the sides for the audience to read, but they hardly needed it, in no time it was being roared by the entire audience. It became so popular that at last John had to call a halt.

"Just once more," he yelled at Alfred and nodded to one of the two stage hands. "Curtain after this verse."

The curtain came down and up, down and up; they took

curtains separately, starting with Betty. Betty had done nothing all evening except wander on and off with numbers hung round her neck, but it was so clear that she was enjoying herself that she soon became a favourite, and, before the evening was half over, each of her entrances was greeted with a whistle from the boys at the back. John and Alfred introduced the cast, they led each of them on.

"Betty."

The boys at the back were pleased to get her name, and amidst the applause they called for her. "Good old Betty!" Dickie came next. His dances had gone down well, his spots did not show behind his make-up and he looked nice in his green costume. He patter-danced on to the stage. Quite a lot of girls in the audience had learnt a bit of patter dancing, and they applauded heartily, saying to each other, "Good, isn't he?" Alfred held out his hand and Nella came on. Nella's scarlet frock had been made as differently from Dulcie's as possible. "No good having them alike in a harlequin effect," Alice had said. Hers, too, had a satin bodice, but it had short puffed sleeves. It fastened behind with a big scarlet satin bow. She, too, had tarlatan petticoats, though not a proper ballet dress such as Dulcie wore, for she had no dancing to do. She wore scarlet satin shoes. There was so little for Nella to do in the show, and none of the things she had to do suited her very well, that she had attracted far less attention even than Betty. As John called out "Nella" the audience clapped, and some of the older women said to each other that she looked a dear little thing, a nice, quiet type, but she got noticeably less applause than anybody else. It was bad luck on her that

Dan should come on next. Dan looked slim and very young in his scarlet costume, not a day more than fourteen. He had not made a fault in his juggling, and had built a niche in the campers' hearts. He got an ovation. Tom, at the piano, seethed. "Fools," he thought, "carried away by a bit of showmanship and looks. If only they knew it Nella's the jewel in the window, she's the one they ought to be after." Muriel gripped Alfred's hand tightly as she took her call. Both times that she had sung there had really been wonderful applause. "The Holy City" seemed to be a real success. Still, of course, it was a first night, and the campers were being kind. As a matter of fact, after six years with no holidays and not a glimpse of the sea, Muriel had opened to many of the older campers the doors of memory. Ever since they had toddled they had seen Muriel, or something like Muriel, in every seaside show, fat, highly-coloured, beaming, singing old ballads. The applause for her was a greeting to an old friend. It was none of your polite hand-clapping, but a proper, warm-hearted roar. It quite upset Muriel, who bit her lip, and her eyes filled with tears. She looked at Alfred. "Aren't they darlings?" Alfred and John went to the piano and fetched Tom. There was no question about his welcome. Every female of whatever age in the audience had been whispering about him ever since the curtain went up. "I say, isn't the pianist good-looking? They say they're staying in the camp. Wonder if we shall see him before our week's over. I'd like to get his autograph." "Isn't he tall? Just the type to wear yellow." "I wonder he isn't on the pictures, he's as good-looking as Stewart Grainger." Tom was completely indifferent to their applause. "Lot of fools who couldn't appreciate Nella. If he'd been in the audience, even with the little she had to do, he'd have spotted the talent in the kid."

Dulcie had been told to wait upstage. John and Alfred went to fetch her. She came out from behind the curtain looking, between her father's and Alfred's blue costumes, like a daffodil in a blue vase. She caught the breath with her beauty, her eyes shining, a faint flush showing through her make-up. She gave a ballerina's curtsey, her moonlight fair hair failing over her shoulders, her lemon and orange skirts billowing round her shoulders. The audience rose to her. Individually they might have preferred Alfred's and John's comedy, or the general numbers, or Muriel's singing, or Dan's juggling, but Dulcie was a star, she had all the attributes of a star, and the manner to put herself over. As she came on and curtsied again and again everybody felt what Dulcie knew, that they had been privileged to see a star in the making. Was she not a prodigy of F. J. Higgs? "I bet we hear more of her," they told each other, and, because she was a part of their holiday camp and, therefore, almost like a friend, they added, "I'm sure she'll do well. We must look out for her." Alfred and John held up their hands for silence. John was always the one to make a speech. In a slow, quiet voice he held the audience's attention. He did not think it necessary to get a laugh every time he came on the way Alfred did. He told the audience how he and Alfred had worked together in the prisoner-of-war concert party, and how they had met a certain sergeant pilot Barrow, and how all the company was made up of their sons and daughters. Then Alfred dived off the stage and fetched Alice, who was standing in the wings. Alice had no wish to come on, she had not powdered her nose nor tidied her hair, but she was not one to lose dignity, and it certainly put a paper hat on a nice evening when John said, "This is my wife, she's our wardrobe mistress. We couldn't have got the concert party going without her, in fact, she is the concert party." He squeezed her hand and she knew he meant it. Then Tom was fetched. John said just those things about Tom's music that Nella had prayed he would say. It was, John gathered, quite a surprise to the audience to hear what a lot of songs had been written by Tom. They all held programmes, but they had not read them properly. "Funny," they said to each other, "I never thought he wrote the music, I thought he was just playing it." Then the two stage-hands came on. There were flowers for all the ladies, even for Betty. For Dulcie there was a magnificent affair of carnations and orchids. John knew that the flowers were from Pinkie and he told the audience so and asked them, if they had enjoyed the show, if they wouldn't like to see the man who had provided it. Pinkie had not expected to come on the stage, but he arrived beaming but a little pinker about the face than usual. He said a few words about the concert party and the prisoner-of-war camp, and then, "I take it I needn't say any more about this show. I see you agree with me it's the tops. Going to be quite a slogan this summer *Here's Fun*." It was getting late, but the audience had not finished. It was a nice occasion, they were part of a reunion of men from a *stalag*, and it was a family concert party, the first night in the first season of holiday camps for seven years. Spontaneously they began to sing "For they are jolly good fellows". When that was finished the company returned thanks with "Good night, campers". The audience was still singing the chorus of that as they streamed out into the night.

* * *

The camp was called at seven-thirty through loud-speakers. Dulcie hated getting up early and had made an arrangement with Pinkie that she should have her breakfast brought to her on a tray when the ordinary dining-room breakfasts were finished. Betty became a junior camper; every week all children were signed on as junior campers, and they were kept busy from the time they got up to the time they went to bed. To Betty it was the most splendid existence in the world.

"It's absolutely marvellous, Mum," she told Alice.

"There's table tennis and physical training and skating and hikes and treasure hunts. I never sit down. Wouldn't you think that at the end of the summer I ought to be the most exquisite shape?"

Alice looked at Betty's radiant face, there was no sign of her losing weight. She was, in fact, palpably putting it on, and in the summer, when there was swimming added to the sports, she would probably put on more. Alice had always heard that swimming was developing, but she had no heart to discourage Betty. It was not only delightful to see her so happy, but it was a great comfort to have her off her hands. She would have been bound to want to help if she had been about, and really Alice found it easier to repair the wardrobe by herself.

Because Betty was a junior camper and out very early for physical exercises and Dulcie would not get up, Nella found it perfectly simple to have her singing lessons. Tom was an early riser and was through with his breakfast by eight-thirty and working at the piano in the theatre before nine. "I would have gone to the theatre every morning for dancing practice anyway," Nella thought. "It's not really deceiving anybody if Tom's there at the same time and teaches me to sing. I'd tell Dulcie if she asked me, but she never has, and it's much better not to tell her because, if she didn't like it, it would be easier to give in to her, and that would sort of snub Tom, and it would be most frightfully mean to snub somebody who's been snubbed so much already." Besides, how awful if the family knew Tom was trying to teach her to sing. How they would laugh!

Tom's and Nella's mornings followed a regular routine. Tom would sit at the piano, a sheet of music manuscript paper in front of him with a pencil on the top of it. Nella would come into the theatre, change her shoes and go to the back of the stage, where there was something she could use as a bar for practice. Very often Tom would be so engrossed in what he was composing he would quite forget that Nella was there. Then suddenly he would be conscious of her and would look at her over his shoulder. He would change what he was playing to a chord, and from there he would run up a scale.

"Come along, Nella. How are the vocal chords this morning?" Nella, out of breath from her dancing, would stand facing him across the grand piano, her heels together, toes in the first position, hands behind her back, a slight frown of concentration on her face. At first her voice was so soft it was all Tom could do to play sufficiently softly to hear her. By the time she had had a fortnight's lessons she was improving. At the far end of the theatre were busts of the King and Queen. In the middle of a lesson Tom would say, "Now turn round and sing for the Monarch. Go on, he can't hear. It's practically a shooting business if you make the Monarch strain his ears. Go on, louder."

Because he made her laugh, and smiling relaxed her larynx, more voice came from Nella. She had a tiny but really charming and true singing voice, and Tom's encouragement increased the volume. What he was competing with was not so much Nella's inability to sing as Nella's conviction that she could not sing and no one would want to hear her, anyway. But he could hear that she could sing. She would always need a microphone, but what of that? Plenty of stars needed microphones.

Since the day they had arrived Tom and Nella had not had another evening together. The weather had changed. It rained incessantly. The concert party was giving performances twice daily. All amusements were indoors. By the time the curtain came down in the evening, even had it cleared up, none of them had much energy to go out. Twice daily performances, with an ever-varying programme, is a big strain. Nella was thankful. The awkward situation when Dulcie wanted Tom to dance, and he was really going for a walk with her, must not happen again, at least Nella hoped it would not happen again, only Tom was not the sort of person you could order about.

Probably because he had been brought up in an orphanage, he was just a wee bit difficult sometimes. Nella had tried saying little things such as, "It's a lovely ballroom, they have dances on Sundays, you ought to dance with Dulcie one Sunday night," and "When it's fine you'll be able to go swimming. I'm not much good at swimming, but Dulcie is." Tom had either disregarded these hints or squashed them. Nella never quite knew what he was thinking when he looked at her and said, "It's a free world. People can dance with whom they like."

It was, as a matter of fact, difficult for Tom to get much chance to be alone with anybody inside the camp He was masculine idol number one. From the time he got up in the morning to the time he went into his chalet at night he was surrounded by fluttering girls. They called him Tom, they asked him for his autograph, they sent him small presents. Tom was rather like a puppy amidst chickens amongst them. He looked at them in a shy, puzzled way, and you had a feeling he was saying to himself, "I mustn't be rough, I might hurt these fluffy things."

It was even more difficult for Dulcie to be alone. Dulcie was the idol of the male population. She was glamour. She found it rather hard work being every man's idea of glamour, when you had to be under their eyes during practically all waking hours. Fortunately for Dulcie there were some shops in the camp, one of which pressed frocks, and with the aid of this and thanks to the fact that few of the campers had more than a week's holiday, she was able, more or less, to live up to what was expected of her. Every time she stepped out of her chalet to go across to the main buildings, it was as if an electric current ran through the population. Nobody knew how they knew, but all the men seemed to be about whenever she appeared. During the rains of May most girls tied bits of mackintosh over their hair and shoved on a mackintosh, to get to the main building. For Dulcie there was always somebody about with an umbrella, and somebody else saying, "Let me put my mack around you, it's bigger than yours," and somebody else saying, "Sit down and let me take off your gumboots, though, mind you, I like you in them, proper Puss-in-Boots." As well as admirers amongst the campers Pinkie, in his casual way, was more or less in constant attendance. He would find her before lunch and say, "What about a drink?" or he would fetch her after the matinée for tea. After the show there was usually a dance or some other amusement if she was not too tired. Pinkie would fetch her to it. Dulcie was trying to keep Pinkie at arm's length, but it was difficult. He took it for granted in his casual way that they were tremendous friends, yet Dulcie often had a feeling that she was amusing him and he was getting a quiet laugh at her expense. Saturdays were Dulcie's free-est days. The new campers only arrived that morning. If it was wet a few saw the afternoon show, and another lot saw it in the evening, but on the whole the campers had not got on to who she was. Every movement that she made was not watched and each step talked about. She was not left alone because, even without her stage background, she was the prettiest girl in the camp in any week. Saturdays should have been her days for Tom, but Saturdays were Pinkie's field days. He seemed to take a special delight in hovering round her. He would sing outside her door at breakfast time. One of Rose Reilly's songs had a refrain "So I 'ad a cup-a-tea". Pinkie was fond of this in the early morning. Dulcie, having her breakfast in bed, would be disturbed by a rattle on her door, followed by Pinkie's voice. When she did get up and come across to the main building he was always about on a Saturday. At last she tackled him about it.

"Everybody else is busy in the camp on Saturdays, why aren't you?"

He looked round at the groups of newly arrived but happy campers.

"The Barrow motto. Delegate. The full motto runs, "Pay your people to do the job and then don't interfere."

They were having a drink in the interval of dancing. Dulcie looked at him over her glass.

"I believe you do it on purpose."

He looked at her with wide-eyed innocence.

"Miss Corner! Surely I've made it clear that I'm your slave and follow you around day and night."

She took the cigarette he offered her but refused to play up to his teasing mood.

"I'm absolutely certain you do it on purpose. It's very difficult for a girl to have a private life in this place, and you know it."

"What sort of a private life does a girl want to have?" Dulcie scowled at her cigarette.

"I don't exactly want one at all." Suddenly she decided to take him into her confidence, or at least partly into her confidence. "It's Tom. We've been here weeks, but I never see him except on the stage." She saw that his eyes were twinkling. "The first time I met you you teased me, about wanting two things at once. I've thought a lot about that. It isn't that I want two things at once. Knowing Tom is important for my career. You see, he's under contract to F. J. Higgs, everybody thinks he's got a tremendous future. I want him to write songs for me when I'm a star."

Pinkie nodded:

"Name on a bus." He patted her hand. "That the only reason you'd like to know Tom better? Come on. Confide in Uncle Pinkie."

She pulled her hand away.

"You are inquisitive. I find him so odd. Every day we meet at meals, mostly we talk about the show, anyway, everybody's there. Every day, when it's wet, there's a matinée, goodness knows where he gets to afterwards, I never see him. Then we have another meal, more talk just about the show, then there's the evening performance, and then, I suppose, he goes to bed. He never dances, I hear him going out of the theatre, and I hear him call out 'Good night, everybody'. It's so odd, because other men aren't like that."

Pinkie was playing with his glass.

"I wonder why we all want the person that escapes us. I imagine that when we get old it's not the people who loved us that we remember, it's the ones we loved and never got any further with."

It was so unlike Pinkie to be serious that Dulcie was for once pulled from her own affairs.

"Are you interested in somebody who isn't interested in

you? You said you'd got a story of your own which you'd tell me one day."

In a moment he was laughing.

"Begone, dull care. Do you mean to say that you can't even get the fellow to take a cup of tea with you?"

She raised her shoulders and gave an expressive shrug.

"When do I ever have tea by myself?"

"This camp's admirable training for you. You said you wanted to be a proper star, that you weren't going to be the type that slunk out of the theatre and went home by tube, that you wanted to live like a star. I admit we can't do the big car stuff here, but you're living like a star all right. The glamour queen, every man's pin-up girl, the photographer's shop here says they can't begin to get enough stuff to print your photographs on. As fast as they get printed they're sold out."

"I know, but they all go away every week, and they don't mean anything to me, you know that."

"Does he?"

"I don't know. I don't know him, I keep telling you."

Pinkie considered her. He was perfectly certain that for some extraordinary reason she meant absolutely nothing to Tom. He doubted if Tom knew that she was interested in him. He adored a rival, but this abstract rival business was being tiresome, it was going altogether too far. Dulcie had been in the camp quite a time, and he had spent a large part of every day with her. Physically she attracted him enormously. Mentally she intrigued him. He wondered where she would get to, if her performance was good or easy and pretty and went over because of her looks.

Sometimes, he wondered whether, behind everything, there was real starring talent, something which might, if the gods were kind, break through. It was nonsense, in his opinion, Dulcie going on like this, neither getting to know Tom better nor getting him out of her mind. As it was, he was just a nebulous stumbling-block between Dulcie and a type like himself.

"I wouldn't let him slip me if I were you. Why don't you pin him down?"

"It seems queer to say so, but honestly, I never see him, except on the stage or at meals. I might on Saturdays, but you spoil that."

Pinkie beckoned to the waiter for more drinks.

"It goes against the grain to hand you to a rival; but I'll give you a tip. He practises in the theatre every morning, he goes there directly after breakfast, I'm always seeing him popping across."

Dulcie was surprised she had not thought of that for herself.

"I suppose he does." Then she made a face. "But I suppose everybody else is there, too. Still, I could try. Thank you for the tip."

Pinkie ordered the drinks.

"I bet you say thank you for nothing, and then perhaps you'll give up yapping after the fellow and pay a little more attention to the manoeuvrings of your Uncle Pinkie."

* * *

Dulcie swallowed her breakfast quickly. It was a fairly nice morning, she would go to the theatre. She would tell Tom she had come to practise. To give an air of truth to this, she would put on her blocked shoes. It would give her an excuse to hang about a bit. What should she ask him to do? It did not really matter much what as long as they were alone together. She stuck her head out of the window, she could hear her mother and Muriel calling to each other from their two chalets. In the distance she could see the back of her father and Alfred strolling off to have a look at the sea. Betty would be sure to be out with her junior campers; Nella was the catch. She was so crazy on her dancing she might turn up at the theatre, but probably she would go away if she saw she was there, talking to Tom. Talking to Tom! How stupid it was how she felt when she thought about him. Even imagining herself coming on to the stage and finding him at the piano sent a prickly feeling down her spine. She would ask him to come for a walk, or perhaps to take her out in a boat, he had been a sailor and would be sure to be good at boats. It did not look as though there would be a matinée to-day, it was fine, it would be grand to be alone in a boat, the only thing was she was sure to be sick. It would be difficult to enjoy being alone with Tom if she was being sick. Still, a boat was the best idea. She had seen lots of couples going out in boats, and once they were away from the beach they were by themselves, with nobody popping up and saying, "May I come, too?" A boat really was the only place she could be sure of getting anybody to herself. She wondered she had not thought of it before.

There was no stage door-keeper to the theatre. One of the stage-hands unlocked the stage door early in the morning and they all had keys to their own dressing-rooms. Dulcie went into her dressing-room to change her shoes. Then she sat on her theatre basket, one shoe half off, her eyes staring in the direction of the stage. She heard Tom's voice, not the voice she was accustomed to, rather casual, a little bored, but warm and friendly. "How are the vocal chords this morning? Come along and let's hear." There was a pause. "What will you sing?" Dulcie opened her door and peered on to the stage. She could not see who he was talking to through the crack. Who had he got hold of? Some camper? He smiled over his shoulder. "It's a nice morning, what about your favourite? Come and sit on the piano where I can see you." Nella came into view. She pulled herself up on the piano, she had on her short black dancing tunic, socks and ballet shoes, she was not a Nella that Dulcie had ever seen before. She was glowing and live-looking. She laughed at Tom and took a deep breath. He played a few chords.

"Sweetest little fellow,
Everybody knows,
Don't know what to call him
But he's mighty like a rose."

Nella sang the song to the end. As Tom played the last chords, he jumped up and took her by her shoulders and shook her.

"Wonderful. The Monarch almost heard every word. Now tell me I won't make a star of you." He gave her a kiss.

Dulcie closed her dressing-room door. She felt giddy. There were spots in front of her eyes and the room seemed to sway to and fro. She groped across to her dressing-table and sat with her head in her hands. Nella! Nella and Tom! Then another thought. Who says I won't make a star of you? Nella, the silent, learning, to sing. Nella, who could dance but had no personality, suddenly coming to life. Dulcie was no fool where the stage was concerned. The Nella who had just sung, sitting on the piano dimpling away at Tom, could be a success. Dulcie changed her shoes and let herself out of the theatre. Several men came forward to speak to her, but with a smile she got rid of them.

"Just a minute, I've been practising. I'm going to my chalet to change."

In the chalet she lay down on her bed. It seemed as if a different person had come back to the girl who had left quarter of an hour before. She clawed at the coverlet with her fingers. She had no idea it was possible to loathe anybody as, at that moment, she was hating Nella. "Sneaking out for singing lessons. Carrying on with Tom. I'll find some way to stop it," and then out loud, "I'd like to hurt her. Really hurt her. If she were to walk in now I would."

* * *

Dulcie, after the first storm of jealousy had swept over her, pulled herself together. She got off the bed, changed out of her dancing things and made up her face. She was just ready when she heard Pinkie outside. She leant out of the window.

"Good morning. What is it?"

She looked lovely, serene, charming, not a sign of the storm which had racked her.

"I've news. My old man's coming down to see the show to-night." A faraway look came into Dulcie's eyes. She was viewing her frocks in her mind and wondering if they needed tidying. Pinkie tapped her hand with a finger. "Don't look like that. My old man coming won't matter a damn to any of you, the campers like you and that's all there is to it. What does matter is that my old man should say, 'Bless me, there's more in that boy than I thought, shall have to give him a free hand next year.'

Dulcie was not listening, her mind had swerved to the programme.

"Have you told Dad and Uncle Alfred?"

"No. Haven't seen them. Do you know where they are?"

It seemed to Dulcie that it was another world in which she had leant out of her chalet window and watched the back of her father and Alfred strolling towards the sea, another world when she had heard her mother and Muriel talking. Yet her mother and Muriel were still in their chalets, still gossiping, and the men were not back from their walk. How short a time to grow up and to grow hard and bitter. It couldn't have taken half an hour. None of these thoughts appeared in her face. What was going on in her heart was her secret. She joined Pinkie outside the chalet.

"They went towards the sea."

"Good. So will we. Have you got proper shoes on?"

She nodded and then thought again about her clothes. She rapped on the window of her mother's chalet. Alice looked out.

"I say, Mum, Pinkie's father's coming down tonight to see the show."

Muriel's head shot out of her window.

"To-night! Have you told your Uncle Alfred?" Then she noticed Pinkie. "Good morning, Mr. Barrow."

Pinkie lit a cigarette.

"I was just telling Dulcie there is no need for any of you to get in a flap. You're the goods, delivered right on the target, but what I want is that my father should appreciate that it was I who found you, and that *Here's Fun* has been the high spot in every camper's holiday." He looked first at Alice and then at Muriel. "I can see I'm going to get no help from any of you. Mrs. Corner's already doing things in her mind with pins and needles and Mrs. Binns is choosing between 'Where My Caravan has Rested' and 'The Holy City'."

Muriel leant farther out of her window.

"What sort of songs does your father like?"

"My father lives, sleeps and dreams holidays for the masses. He'll judge what song he likes entirely by the applause of the campers. I'd pick on the ones that go over best. Dulcie and I are off to find your husbands."

It was nice walking down to the sea, the grass was beginning to sprout again after years of being crushed under army boots. There was a white chalky path down to the front, a nice, salt-tasting breeze blew up from the sea. Dulcie walked ahead, the wind blew her silver-fair hair back in a cloud; she had on a jersey over a light wool frock, the skirts of the frock blew out behind her.

"The best legs and the best shape the old man has ever had on his stages," thought Pinkie. Then his mind turned to Dulcie's performance. It was true what he had said to Muriel. His father judged everything in his camps by the pleasure it gave the campers. Nevertheless, he was a very shrewd judge of theatrical talent. Provided his campers were pleased, and, of course, they would be, the Binns and the Corners were all right. It was afterwards things might not be so easy, the old man was very much a law unto himself; one of his favourite sayings was that rough words broke no bones; never in his life had he flattered anybody, if he paid a compliment it was because it was less than the recipient's due. He was sure to come round and see the Corners and the Binns after the show, and equally sure to tell them what he thought. The rest could take it; he would warn them, and if his father was not tactful they would understand, but Dulcie was different. Dulcie was very much the star, and bitterly resented criticism. Pinkie was not in the least worried about Tom Pollard's songs; his father was sure to think they were all right, the trouble was going to come over Rose Reilly's numbers. The old man had seen Rose Reilly in all her shows, and thought her a genius. "And Dulcie, bless her heart, though there is not much else missing, is not Rose Reilly," he thought. He wondered whether it would be possible to suggest her using only Tom's songs cutting Rose Reilly's. He would have to wait, and see what the men had to say. Easy enough to take them more or less into his confidence.

John and Alfred were coming back from their walk. Alfred was as excited as a foxhound at a meet on hearing Pinkie's news. John was outwardly more calm. He glanced at the sky.

"Looks as if it were set fair for a change. Shouldn't think there'd be a matinée." He nodded to Alfred. "Come on, Corp, we'd better get along to the theatre." He turned to Pinkie. "Could you come in about half an hour, and see if you approve of the layout?"

The lay-out was not so easy. Every artist had their own favourites amongst their numbers, and they all wanted to perform them for Mr. Barrow. Of course, they knew that *Here's Fun* was going down well, but the coming of Mr. Barrow put them on their mettle. John went to Alice for support. He found her busy with the wardrobe.

"Of course, we haven't got a contract for the season. Our contract was always dependent on the way the show went over. We seem going over well, so Corp and I haven't worried Pinkie about our contract. Awkward if the old man doesn't fancy us."

Alice tried to look as if she thought he were being foolish, that there could not possibly be any cause for worry, but her heart missed a beat. She thought of the jokes she and John had in their chalet, of the discussions as they went to bed about Dulcie's dancing, Dickie's numbers and Betty. It was like old times, every week the war seemed to be slipping farther into the background. She shared, with all the other campers, the luxury of being catered for, the relief of no ration books, and not having to think about the next meal, and it was having its effect. She was so much less tired and strained, and so able to give more of her attention and personality to John. They enjoyed all the amenities of the camp. Betty catered for all day with her junior campers, Dickie often playing in matches, cricket or whatever it was, the staff against the campers, or, when he wasn't that way amused, there were plenty of other things for him to do. Dulcie seemed wonderfully happy. It was silly, of course, to get ideas, but Alice did sometimes wonder if Pinkie wasn't getting fond of her. Wouldn't that be nice! Pinkie was such a pleasant young man. Funny words men used. Awkward, indeed! If Mr. Barrow did not like the show it would be a tragedy. John and Alfred couldn't see themselves, they didn't know that every day they were becoming more their old selves, more the men she and Muriel had married.

Out loud she said:

"Old worry guts, aren't you? Of course he'll like the show. Now, pop along, I'm busy."

Pinkie tackled Alfred about Dulcie.

"Corp, the show to-night that you've fixed. It's fine, as I've just said to S'arnt, but there's just one thing. My old man is a Rose Reilly fan, and he's not always very tactful in what he says. Dulcie's grand, but no two artists put a number over the same, you know what I mean. I was wondering if you couldn't take out the Rose Reilly numbers to-night, and give Dulcie some of those extra songs of Tom's she does at matinées. Don't want her upset by my old man being tactless, and God knows he can be."

Alfred screwed up his monkey face and gave a slow, sad shake of his head.

"You needn't say any more, Pinkie. I understand you perfectly, but it can't be done, old boy. Dulcie might be very upset if your old man spoke his mind, but the rocket S'arnt and I would get if we tried to take out the Rose Reilly numbers . . ." He broke off and gave a whistle to express a large rocket rising into the air.

Pinkie gave a resigned moan.

"And I did want Dulcie and my old man to like each other."

Alfred dug him in the ribs.

"I don't doubt you did, but it's not going to happen at the expense of poor old S'arnt and I being blown sky high. Funny that about Rose Reilly's numbers. They go over all right, but she doesn't hit the nail on the head, does she, She knows it too, if you ask me. Those numbers are a red rag to a bull to her. It's having understudied them. Understudies generally get the idea they'd be as good and better than their principal if they only had the chance."

"She does them just like Rose Reilly, too, as far as I can remember. What's missing?"

"Heart, old boy. Very nice performance, every inflection good, but . . ." Alfred tapped his heart, "she doesn't feel it here."

Mr. Barrow arrived just before the evening show. Pinkie knew his father's habits, he had a box of cigars and a double whisky waiting for him, together with a plate of cheese sandwiches. Leonard Barrow never wasted words. He greeted his son with a nod, then took up one of the sandwiches and smelt it.

"Processed."

Pinkie waited until his father had drunk half his whisky and eaten three sandwiches before he spoke.

"I've got us seats in the middle of the dress circle. They've been going down very well."

His father turned an annoyed eye on his son.

"Every week I ask one in every hundred of my campers to write what their holiday had been like. They tell me."

Pinkie sighed. He had no doubt the campers did tell his father. He knew the most extraordinary letters reached the London office, but he also knew his father wouldn't tell him what the letters said. For all he knew four out of five campers had written to say the show stank, in which case it was out. There was no knowing what this visit portended.

"Hear that F. J.'s girl is a good looker."

Pinkie lit up. Well, that was something, anyway. Somebody had at least written to praise Dulcie's face.

"Clever, too. F. J. gave her permission to use Rose Reilly's songs." There was a queer, angry bark from Mr. Barrow. Pinkie hurried on. "I know. There's only one Rose. She feels that too, still, the campers like her. I'm afraid you will find there's something missing though. She doesn't get the heart into it Rose gets, but perhaps you'd say nothing about it to her, bit sensitive. Rose Reilly's understudy, you know." Leonard Barrow made another of his snorting noises. He swallowed the rest of his whisky and lit a cigar.

"Speak my mind. Always do." He looked at his watch. "Time we were going across. Come on."

Here's Fun had become a tradition in the Comstock camp. Holidaymakers who stayed for two weeks told incoming holidaymakers about it. It was part of the holiday to see the show once, if not twice. There was always a full House. The day had been fine, everyone was in a good mood. Pinkie and his father sat down in a theatre gay with laughter and chatter.

Alfred was peering through a hole in the curtain.

"They're in. Strike up, Tom, old man."

Tom began his medley of songs out of the show. Although most of the campers had only arrived on Saturday, and this was Monday, they had already picked up a lot of the tunes. They were played by the orchestras, and were whistled by the staff. Long before the curtain rose they were humming and whistling. Mr. Barrow smiled round and relaxed. This was the atmosphere he liked. Friendly, homey, cheerful. This was the service he tried to give. Pinkie looked at his father out of the corner of his eye and relaxed. "Thank God, the old man's coming unbuttoned."

The curtain went up. It was a gay scene with the mixed colours of the dresses, and Dulcie, posed on the top box, with her lemon-orange ballet skirts spread round her, really looked lovely. The audience often clapped the rise of the curtain. They did to-night. It was too much to hope that his father would join in the clapping, but Pinkie noticed that he pursed up his mouth in a way that only happened when he was pleased. The company were on top of their form, and that they were on the top of their form communicated itself to the audience. Pinkie settled down to enjoy himself.

"Eight." Pinkie glanced idly at his programme. He saw "Good night, George" and, in brackets, "By special permission of F. J. Higgs." Simultaneously his father looked at his programme and snorted. "Gosh," thought Pinkie, "Alfred might have managed to hold up the number. No need to put the old man's back up before the show's half begun."

The lights dimmed, the little dressing-table was pushed on. Dulcie was leaning on it looking in the glass. To-night, because of the specially arranged programme, she had made time to change out of her yellow frock. She was wearing a dressing-gown as Rose Reilly had done in the London production. It was a plain, tailored dressing-gown, and Dulcie looked childish in it. The gramophone off stage which was supposed to represent a wireless set softly played a waltz tune. She turned the big photograph of the young man on the dressing-table towards her, and picked up her comb and mirror. There was something in the way she did it, something purposeful, that touched the audience's heart. There was dead silence in the theatre. Then Tom began the accompaniment.

All day Dulcie had lived in a haze. Outwardly she was herself, inwardly she ached. Tom was not a dead fish of a man, he was as capable of being fond of a girl as anyone else, there was no mistaking the way he had looked at Nella. Nella and she had always been friends. Why had she sneaked off with Tom behind her back? What was all this about singing? Why did Tom want Nella to be a success? More extraordinary still, he looked as if he might make something of her. She always had danced, if now she were able to sing . . . "Not in this show, she won't," thought Dulcie. "I've got a little power here, and I'm not having two people trying to star. Besides," she told herself honestly, "Nella dances better than I do, only she can't put herself over." Can't put herself over? She thought of that queer, husky, childish voice. The Nella she had heard that morning was not the Nella who could not put herself over. Something had happened. It had been a busy day, and Dulcie had no chance to dissect herself. Why should she care so much about Tom? Never once had he shown the slightest sign of caring about her. It might, of course, have been injured pride, but she knew it was not that. It did hurt her pride, of course, that Nella should succeed where she had failed, she who had never before known failure, but it was more than that. She wanted Tom, and she was not getting him. She would have been shocked if she had known how much she wanted Tom physically. For the first time in her life she was swamped by a violent physical need. She had been slow in developing, and had been cold, now she burnt and ached, and slept badly. Because she had not understood her own feelings the deeper had been her sufferings, and now a new suffering was added. Frustration. She was never to be satisfied. His interest was in Nella. To everybody there comes a choice. Shall unhappiness soften or embitter? Dulcie did not appreciate that what she had to fight was choosing the hard road of embitterment.

It had been her choice that her first number should be "Good night, George." She had never cared for singing it in her yellow frock, which had nothing to do with the song and made her feel silly. As she sat down in her dressing-gown a queer feeling came over her. She was not herself. She was somebody different. She was the girl who knew the man in the photograph. All artifice fell away from her. She did not bother about what inflections Rose had used or had not used, she sang the song straight, the photograph blurred before her eyes, the George to whom she was supposed to be singing vanished, and in his place was Tom. In her song George was not yet demobilized. She could only imagine dancing with him, talking with him. Tom was on the stage with her, but she could only imagine dancing with him, talking with him. There was the line, "I want your arms round me." It nearly broke her. At the end, just as the lights were dimming for the black-out, she had to kiss the photograph before singing a final "Good night, George." Dulcie kissed the photograph and said, "Good night, George," but her mind said "Good night, Tom." It was bitter to kiss a bit of cardboard when you wanted the living, breathing man. Her voice could hardly be heard, it broke on the whispered, "Good night, George."

There was quite a pause before there was any applause, then it came with a crack. Pinkie was sitting bolt upright in his seat, looking as though he had received a shock. Betty came on and announced number ten. Leonard Barrow snorted as he looked at his programme.

"Doesn't get the heart into it! Stupid fool, Pinkie. You always were."

On the stage the lights had gone up on Alfred and John in a patter number. For once Tom failed them. He started their accompaniment late. When Dulcie had finished singing his hands had dropped off the piano and his mouth had fallen open. He was still half stunned when John and Alfred had come on. "I'll be fried and frazzled," he thought.

"That was beautiful, perfectly beautiful, and I'd have sworn she couldn't do it."

* * *

Leonard Barrow looked upon the visitors to his holiday camps as his family. He would no more have dreamt of visiting a camp and not speaking to them than he would have dreamt, when his children were small, of coming into his house without visiting his nursery. The curtain was no sooner down at the end of the show than he was on the stage. He held up his hand for silence.

"Evening. You don't know me, but I'm Mr. Barrow." There was a roar of applause. Nobody had quite visualized him in the flesh, he had been like the Holy Ghost to them, invisible but highly influential. He went on to tell them a little of the history of the concert party. He took them into his confidence, leaning forward and lowering his voice, as if Pinkie could not hear. "I thought my son a bit of a fool. You know how it is. We're all apt to underrate our children, but he found this concert party for me, so it doesn't look as though he's quite such a fool as I thought. What d'you think?" There was another roar of applause. Pinkie was a familiar figure round the camp, every camper knew that he was old Barrow's son, and they also knew that he had been a sergeant pilot who was a prisoner of war in Germany. Leonard Barrow crooked a finger. "Come on, young man, come and say thank you." He then took a more serious note. "Every one of us likes to feel we have discovered somethin'. It's all very well to read about other people's discoveries, but the fun is to do the job yourself. Sittin' in the dress circle to-night I reckoned that you campers have discovered somethin'. Quite true my boy here put the discovery in front of you, but you, with your appreciation and your applause, have done the digging, if you understand me, and brought the nugget to light. It won't surprise me if, when you're back home and this holiday is only a memory, one Sunday you'll open your papers and say, 'Look, that's our girl, that's Barrow's Holiday Camp girl. I knew she'd be a star'." He held out his hand to Dulcie. "Come here, young woman, I'm old enough to be your father, so I think I might give you a kiss."

"Gosh! " thought Pinkie. "The old sauce-box."

There was tremendous applause. Dulcie, with her beauty, and her light charm, had pleased them all, but the audience to-night had been moved. They had no idea they were the first audience that Dulcie had moved, they just thought she was always that good. As they clapped they said to each other, "Bet he's right." "Hope we do read she's a star. Be fine, wouldn't it?"

Old Barrow asked the company and Alice over to the office for a drink. It was a small room and with the Binns, the Corners, the Barrows and Tom in it, was quite full. Dulcie, without manoeuvring, found herself next to Tom. They sat side by side on the sofa. Leonard Barrow was on her other side. She was very conscious of Tom's thigh against hers, but for quite a while she had no chance to speak to him. Old Barrow had not brought the company along to talk to each other, he had got them there to congratulate them. But there came a moment when he wanted to talk business. He got up and went over to John and Alfred.

Tom wanted to say something to Dulcie. It had been at the back of his mind ever since they reached the camp that he ought to, do something about "He Met Me at Waterloo". Of course, the change in "She Danced in Piccadilly" had come about through Nella but, he had to be fair, Dulcie had always asked for it. She had always asked for alterations to the other numbers, too. He was conscious that he had been a bit difficult about the whole thing. She had annoyed him. She had put on airs, and he did not think there was anything in her work to give her the right. She flaunted herself as leading lady over poor little Nella. If it were not for Dulcie, Nella would at least have had a chance by now. Nothing to do with him, of course, Nella was only a kid, and no more to him than if she was his sister, but he hated to see anybody given a raw deal. And now, to-night, his ideas had changed. God knows what Dulcie had been playing at all these weeks. Why, in the name of heaven, when you could put over a number like that, give an artificial performance that any hack could manage. Maybe that was what they called the artistic temperament. Still, whatever they called it, she had what it took, and he had to admit it. He turned to her.

"I should like to alter the tempos of those dances the way you want. Particularly 'He Met Me at Waterloo'." Dulcie was so surprised that she was silenced. She turned her eyes to his. She looked so puzzled that he added, "You did want me to alter them, didn't you?"

She was thinking. What had caused this? Why was Tom

suddenly being nice? It couldn't possibly be because old Barrow had made a fuss of her. Tom's future was secure anyway, he went back to F. J. in the autumn whatever happened. He was playing up to her for some reason. Now what? She answered cautiously.

"That's very nice of you. It would be easier if they went a bit slower."

He nodded.

"Could we rehearse them some time to-morrow?"

Her face was perfectly calm, but her mind was like an adding machine. Put this to this and what did it add up to? She said sweetly:

"It'll have to be early then. How about directly after breakfast?"

Nella was sitting on the other side of Tom. Dulcie thought she moved nervously. At the back of Tom's eyes she caught a fleeting anxiety, but he answered quite easily.

"Right. To-morrow morning, directly after breakfast." Then he added with a smile, "I didn't know you got up that early."

"Sometimes, when I have a reason."

Her voice was like honey, but inside she was seething. "I know you didn't know I got up that early, and I bet you didn't want to know." So it was deliberate. Tom and Nella's meetings were planned when she was out of the way. Goodness knows why Tom was making up to her now, it was all part of some scheme, she might be sure of that. Well, two could play at that game. She would go to rehearse with him all right, but with her eyes open. She moved her body as far away from his as she could. How maddening it was when you wanted to hate a person, to be so incredibly excited by touching him.

The Binns and the Corners had gone to bed. Leonard Barrow poured himself and Pinkie out a last drink. He carried his glass to the window and looked out.

"Queer to think that only last January this place was a sea of mud, troops stamping all over the place. We're coming along fine. Shall be using you a bit more, son." Pinkie knew his father too well to make any comment. This was what he was waiting for, but he must show no sign of excitement. "Quite an idea this family stuff, make very good publicity for next season. I'd like you to fix this lot at the big camp next year, and you might look around for other talent. This could be our try-out spot. Leave it to you." Pinkie swallowed. Gosh! But this was being a good evening! His father turned back from the window. "You're an ass though. Telling me that kid, Dulcie, hadn't any heart. She's not Rose Reilly, you don't get a genius like Rose twice in a generation, but, my word, she's a nugget all right. What a looker!"

Pinkie cleared his throat.

"You - think she'll be a star? Pity really. We could have done with her."

The old man laughed.

"I bet you could, but she won't stop in our shows. What's more, I shall see she doesn't. Not at all a bad thing if we made a first-class star. Probably get known as the Barrow girl, like I told them this evening. I've got ideas about her. I'll drop in a word in the right ears."

Pinkie fiddled with his collar.

"Don't you think another season would do her good? I mean, if I had her at the big camp next year . . ."

The old man swallowed his drink. He jabbed a finger into Pinkie's waistcoat.

"None of that, none of that. Can't combine business with pleasure. That girl is going to twinkle a long way out of your reach, my boy. Can't stop her."

Pinkie watched his father walk off into the night, then he turned to put out the lights and locked the office.

"Blast," he said to himself. "Damn and blast."

* * *

Dulcie was on the stage early the next morning. Tom was alone. As always, when it was a question of his music, he was thinking of nothing else.

"Listen, how would this do?"

He played the dancing refrain. It was a point number with a sad little undercurrent of tune. Up till now the dancing refrain was played in a major key and he swung it. Now he had kept to the background refrain but had built it up. At the end of the song a wedding was mentioned, and at the end of the dance, although he kept the sad little rhythm, he had inserted a background of church bells. Dulcie was so charmed that for a moment she forgot she was angry with him.

"That's heavenly. When on earth did you write it?"

"In bed last night. Dan and Dickie were asleep. I got some paper, wrote it by the light of my torch. Come on, see how it goes."

There was no question how it went. It was the tempo that Dulcie had always wanted. It gave her a chance for the pirouettes and attitudes at which she was good, it gave her an opportunity to finish each step neatly. At the end she came to him glowing.

"Perfect. Have you altered the others?"

He was playing a little tune.

"No. Hadn't time, but I will. They aren't quite so important as that one. 'Waterloo' and 'She Danced in Piccadilly' are the numbers that go best. I'd like F. J. to hear them."

"So would I. He said he would come down. I wonder when he will."

"I heard from him the other day."

She was jealous.

"Did you? What did he say?"

"Asked how things were going, and said would I let him know when I was ready for him to hear anything."

"Have you told him you want him to hear those two?"

"No. I'm not ready yet."

Dulcie flushed. Who did he think he was!

"I'll be ready next week if you let him know."

Tom seemed to have forgotten her, fiddling with his little tune.

"I shan't be though."

She was going to make an angry answer when she was struck by what he was playing.

"What's that?"

He sang the answer without thinking.

"You ought to see the coast there
When the poppies are in bloom."

She leant forward, her eyes glowing.

"Go on, sing the rest of it, it's heavenly. Let's put it in next week."

He crashed down on a chord and took his hands off the piano. His face was sullen. He looked, she thought, like a small boy caught stealing sweets.

"No." Then, feeling some explanation was necessary, "No, I don't want it in the show yet."

"Why not?"

"It isn't ready."

"Nonsense, it is ready. It's perfectly charming." His face was sulky.

"I tell you it's not going in the show yet. I ought to know, I wrote the damn thing."

She was so angry that she lost her head, and before she could hold the words back she blurted out:

"You mean, it's not for me?"

Tom looked at her. This was awkward. Her face had the look on it that used to be on the faces of girls in the dockside joints he had known in the war, the look they got when they were going to hit somebody over the head with a bottle. All girls were dangerous when they were angry. Dulcie was probably doubly dangerous since she was a good artist. He smiled at her.

"Don't be cross."

Dulcie was quite beyond discretion.

"It's for Nella. I know what you've been up to. Sneaking

in here giving her lessons."

Tom did not know he could be so angry, especially not with a girl.

"And why shouldn't the kid have a chance? Why should she always be pushed into the background? She's a beautiful dancer, and you know it."

Dulcie did know it. Why, indeed, should Nella always be pushed into the background? For no reason at all except that nobody had bothered to pull her into the foreground. Nobody had torn aside the reticence that hid the real Nella until now. She fixed on the one point about which she could argue.

"You make her sound as if she were about twelve years old. Her birthday and mine are exactly a month apart, and actually she's a month older than I am."

"But you've had all the chances."

Dulcie knew she was being idiotic. She knew she was taking up an entirely untenable position. She could not say, "I won't have you writing songs for her because I won't have you two getting together." But she was past reasoning. Tom, flushed and angry, was even more attractive than Tom elusive and controlled. But the effect was different. She lost her longing to touch him and run her fingers through his hair, instead she wanted to run her nails down his face, to see his skin torn and his blood trickling down his chin. She beat on the top of the piano with her fists.

"I'm not having any other girl starred in this show."

Alfred's voice broke in. He made it as loud as possible. He was standing at the back of the pit with Leonard Barrow and Pinkie.

"What's all this, you two? What's happening here?"

Tom answered.

"It's about a song I've written. It's not ready yet. Dulcie wants to sing it."

Alfred wrinkled his monkey face.

"Let him finish it, old girl. Don't want to taste the pudding before it's cooked."

The entrance of Alfred and the Barrows had the effect of a pail of cold water on hysterics. Dulcie shuddered and in a moment was herself. It was very unfortunate that they had to come in at that minute. She must smooth things over somehow. At all costs she must keep Tom from blurting out the real cause of the quarrel. She came down to the front of the stage.

"Good morning, Mr. Barrow. Good morning, Pinkie. We're having an early rehearsal. I'm afraid you kept me up a bit late last night and I'm bad-tempered this morning." She did not need to look at Pinkie, she could trust him for tact, not by a blink of an eyelash would he show his surprise at finding her out of bed at this hour. She used all her charm on old Barrow. "Tom has written a different version of the dancing part of 'He Met Me at Waterloo'. It's simply lovely. Would you like to hear it?"

Leonard Barrow was entirely unmoved by Dulcie's tantrums, he had known plenty of leading ladies in his time, many of them with far less talent than Dulcie, and they all made scenes. He did not know the full arrangement by which Tom was with the company, he looked upon him as an employee. Old Barrow had many employees, and they all jumped to obey him when he issued a command.

"I'll hear this new song, even if it isn't finished. What's it called?"

Tom wished that Nella was there. Nella, for all she was such a child, would know how to handle this situation. She knew he had been working on this song for her, she had laughed at him and told him it was much too good and he would never be allowed to waste it on her. But she had been sweet and encouraging, and she certainly would understand that he was not going to be forced into giving the song to Dulcie. But what would she do now? He cleared his throat. His voice was grumpy.

"Poppies for England."

Leonard Barrow was a bit of a gardener. His camps, before the war, had been a mass of flowers. During the war years, when he had been making plans to reopen them in peace time, he had seen them in his mind's eye. One was near a river. It had kingcups along its banks in the spring. There was one in the north-west. It lay close to a mountain, and he never thought of it without seeing the purple patches of heather. When he remembered Comstock he saw poppies. Field after field flaming scarlet against the greyish salt-bitten grass. He moved towards the stage.

"You've got somethin' there. 'Poppies for England'. I'll hear it."

Unwillingly Tom began to play. The delicate, wistful little tune that he had first conceived as being sung by an airman returning from a bombing raid, and later had changed into a song for Nella, drifted out into the theatre. It held Alfred and the two Barrows spellbound. It was the kind of song that caught at the ear, that sent audiences out into the night humming, and kept them humming for days. At the end Alfred gave a low whistle.

"You've certainly hit it this time, Tom."

Old Barrow smiled at Dulcie.

"What about the words? Let's hear them."

Dulcie hurried to say that she did not know them, or to say anything that would get Mr. Barrow away from that song, but Tom was before her. It was not a question any longer of what Nella did, or did not, want. They had heard the song, it was his best. Quite likely the best he would ever write. They were not going to let the matter drop. Nella might be angry, but he had to speak up.

"I've not written this song for Dulcie."

Alfred said:

"Who for then?"

"Nella."

Alfred's eyes were on Dulcie's face, in his ears all the nice things that old Barrow had said about her last night. He felt the only thing to do was to turn the matter into a laugh.

"Nella! That's good! My wife always says it's easier to hear a bat squeak than Nella sing."

Old Barrow considered Tom's song a matter of important business that needed to be settled.

"Who is Nella?"

Alfred quite accepted that Nella might have escaped his attention.

"My daughter. I dare say you wouldn't have noticed her much. Little dark girl in red."

It was more than Tom could bear.

Wouldn't have noticed her indeed! Little dark girl in red! That was the kind of way they always thought of her. Shoving the poor little kid around, never giving her a chance. He'd like to put his fist in all their silly faces. Instead he stood up and shouted.

"That girl's never had a chance. She's a beautiful dancer and it's nonsense about her voice. It's perfectly clear and true and it only needs bringing out." He scowled at old Barrow. "Yours would need bringing out if you were snubbed every time you spoke above a whisper."

Alfred thought this really was going too far.

"Quietly, old boy. Nobody's snubbing Nella that I know of."

Tom was not to be silenced.

"You are snubbing her. You're treating this whole conversation as a joke. None of you believe me. You won't sit down in those seats and have the girl in and see if I'm not right."

Alfred made a face to silence Tom.

"Another time, old man. Mr. Barrow's busy."

Old Barrow needed no help from Alfred or anybody else in the managing of his affairs. He tapped Pinkie on the shoulder.

"Run along and fetch Miss Nella. See for myself what she can do."

Nella was sitting by the swimming-pool with Dan. They were having a deep discussion on Dan's future. It never struck either of them that Nella might have a future to discuss.

"You see," Dan told her, "this is just the sort of experience

I ought to have. Full house every night, different audience all the time, but easy. It's a mistake in my line to start with too difficult an audience, like you get on the halls. My patter isn't up to much yet, and you need patter to hold them. Doesn't matter how clever you are on the halls, if you can't hold them you're done, and you've got the bird before you can look round."

The loud-speaker set up round the swimming-pond began to crackle. A voice boomed, "Calling Nella Binns, calling Nella Binns. Will you come to the theatre at once please, Nella." Nella and Dan gaped at each other. What on earth could anyone be calling her for? She turned quite pale.

"Gosh! You don't think Dulcie's fallen down and broken her leg or anything?"

Dan caught her arm.

"Come on. Don't make that thing yowl for you again. Anyway, I wouldn't fuss, if Dulcie had broken her leg they wouldn't put you on, even if you are the understudy. You couldn't get the stuff over." They were nearly at the stage door before he spoke again. "More likely something's happened to the wardrobe and Aunt Alice wants you."

Nella's heart had been racing, now she slowed down and smiled.

"Aren't I a fool, fussing! Of course that's it."

Confident that the crisis was wardrobe, the two sauntered into the stage door. They passed Dulcie's dressing-room and looked in at the wardrobe.

"Funny," said Nella, " Aunt Alice isn't here."

"Probably in our room or yours," said Dan. "Come on." Still quite calm, they strolled on to the stage. In a second

Nella sensed that something was wrong. She saw Dulcie first. Dulcie had never looked at her like that before. Nella's heart looped the loop. Dulcie glaring at her, her father and Mr. Barrow in the stalls, there could be only one answer to this. Tom had said something stupid. Dan looked round in amazement. "What's up? They called for Nella over the loud-speaker."

Alfred had never been more nervous. Whichever way things turned out, it was bound to be awkward. If Nella gave the poor sort of performance she was likely to give, it would take the hell of a good joke to make old Barrow laugh. He was not the sort of man who liked his mornings wasted. If Nella did well, which was fortunately unlikely, there was going to be a hell of a mess-up. Tom would want her to sing this new song of his, Dulcie would tear the place up, and he didn't blame her, it wasn't the way to treat a leading lady, and it was going to make things awkward between him and John. S'arnt was a reasonable type, but he was going to think it a bit queer if Tom wrote music for Nella behind everybody's back. He tapped a seat beside him.

"Come down here, Dan, old man. Tom's written a new number and he wants Nella to sing it. Mr. Barrow's going to hear it."

That was too much for Dan. He looked first at Tom and then at Nella, and he burst into a roar of laughter.

"That's a wow of an idea." He looked at Mr. Barrow. "She'll have to come and sit beside you, sir, if you're going to hear her voice."

Tom could have hit Dan. Miserable little pipsqueak,

talking like that about his sister. He'd show them.

"You can criticize Nella when you've heard her. If you ask me, there's been a damn sight too much criticism in your family. If you want to know, she's got more talent than the whole lot of you put together."

Nella saw that drastic action must be taken.

"Don't be silly, Tom. You know that's not true." She looked at Dulcie. "I can't sing his new song. I've kept telling him so."

Dulcie looked, at her with hostile eyes.

"We shall know that in a minute or two." She made a gesture. "The stage is all yours. I shall go and enjoy the concert from the stalls."

Nella forgot old Barrow and her father, Dan and Dulcie. She did not hear Pinkie come back through the front of the house. She gave all her mind to Tom.

"I can't sing it. You know it's true, I hardly know the words. And nobody will hear me."

Tom thought, "She's going to stall on me. It's because she doesn't want a family row. It's quite true she doesn't know the song very well, but she knows enough of it to put it over." She had got to sing it. Not only for her own sake now, but for his. He had known as he played the refrain that he had written a winner. He had watched old Barrow move from the back of the theatre towards the stage, he had known he had got him when the old man said, "You've got something there." He had seen, as the little tune finished, that he was holding not only old Barrow, but Pinkie and Alfred, as if he had mesmerized them. It was in an awed, respectful tone that Alfred had said, "You've certainly hit it this time, Tom." If he had hit it, and he believed he had, it must go into the show. He believed it was the sort of song that F. J. Higgs was hoping he might write. It was the sort of song that F. J. Higgs would come down from London to hear. His face was hurt; he looked like a snubbed small boy, he spoke in a low voice so that they should not catch what he was saying in the stalls.

"I've got everybody interested. It's my big chance, but if you won't sing it, all right then. I'll tear it up."

Nella was torn. What on earth was she to do? She could not possibly let poor Tom tear up his lovely song. It was his best. It might make his name. It was so important that Tom should make a name. People who had no chance in life and were brought up in orphanages ought to be famous when they grew up. It was a sort of compensation. She leant on the piano.

"Tom, be reasonable. Let Dulcie sing it." Tom set his mouth.

"You or nobody. If you don't care to help me you needn't."

That settled it. It was unlike Tom to speak like that to her. He was always so gentle. He must be very worried about the song. It was unfortunate, it was going to be difficult to smooth things over with Dulcie, but Tom wanted Mr. Barrow to hear his song, and Mr. Barrow should hear it. She was not dressed for dancing, she had on a teddy bear coat and a jersey and skirt. She was wearing sandals. They wouldn't be so bad, but they wouldn't be right. She pulled off her coat and laid it on the top of the piano. She gave Tom a smile.

"All right. I'll do my best."

Tom had never mentioned how the song was to be sung. He had made her sing it as she sang "Mighty Like a Rose," sitting on the piano. She swung herself up there now, she was terribly nervous, it was awful having to sing to that critical audience, and there was no microphone. Even though they were all in the front row, could she make them hear?

Tom ran his fingers up and down the keys. He played the opening bars. Then he whispered, "Let the Monarch hear." The words made Nella feel at home. This was a singing lesson. She and Tom were alone. She looked out over the stalls to the bust of the King.

The delicate, sad little tune fell like a tiny pebble into a pond, ripple after ripple of melody whispered into the stalls; it wound itself into everybody's heart. Nella, sitting casually on the piano, singing earnestly to the King, had exactly the right quality for presenting that song. Her clear, true, tiny voice had the sexlessness of a choir-boy. She put in no emotion, no feeling, she just sang. At the end of the second refrain she thankfully slipped off the piano. The dance came now, this was easy, this was what she knew. Long ago she had planned her dance. The first steps took her into the fields, the grass blew to one side, and in a flash the world was scarlet with poppies, she caught her breath and took a pose expressing ecstasy, then began to pick the flowers, arm-loads of them. At the end, her arms full of poppies, she danced back through the fields, and so off the stage.

Old Barrow lay back in his stall. He made no comment

for a moment or two, his mind was busy with a number of things. Why had this daughter of Binns been given nothing to do? Must be something here he didn't understand. What? She was not Dulcie, of course. The sort of talent that this girl, Nella, had was of a very rare kind. She was a collector's piece. You never knew where you were with collector's pieces. Might crash up into the top sales or be worth nothing. She would be nothing like as popular as Dulcie with the camp audience, still, if young Tom Pollard would not let anyone else sing the song, then this little girl had better put it over. She would need the microphone, of course, but that wouldn't matter. The camp was certainly going to hear that song. He looked at Nella, who was by now standing awkwardly on one leg, wondering what she ought to do next. Queer little thing, but she certainly had something He knew nothing about dancing, but she had been a pleasure to watch, she got you when she moved. He could see the situation was tricky. Young Dulcie would have to be handled. Still, leading ladies always had to be handled, and that was Pinkie's business. The boy wanted his chance to show what he could do, well, let him show it now. He got up.

"Very nice." He looked round to see if Pinkie was back. "Get that song into the show as soon as you can, it's a knockout." He turned to Dulcie. "Sorry the young man's determined about who sings it. Still, you've got all the other good numbers." He turned to go. "Have a nice day, everybody."

"S'truth!" thought Pinkie. "What a hope!"

* * *

John had not of recent weeks been giving much thought to Dulcie. She seemed happy, and they had all the summer before them. In the back of his mind was the plan to get on the old easy terms with her, but it could wait. Alice was the cause. He felt almost as if he were meeting her for the first time. In the years that he had been separated from her he had forgotten such a lot of things about her. The quiet way she spoke, but the firmness behind what she said. He loved her smooth head; of course, there were a few grey hairs, but they seemed part of her charm. He liked them. He was so glad of Alice's smooth, unchanged hair, he would not have cared for all that dyeing and touching up that Alfred had to put up with from Muriel. He had forgotten the way Alice's nose freckled. When they had that hot weather in April she had come out in a mass of freckles. He liked the way she dabbed lotions on her nose, believing freckles could be cured. Dear Alice, she had such a simple faith in the goodness of everything, even lotions for freckles. Living at the Comstock camp Alice had more time than she had possessed for years. There were no rations to get, no housework to do, no cooking, no entertainments to plan for the children; all day long, for those who wanted it, there was something going on. Everything was catered for, there was even a church service on Sunday. "It's a pity, in a way," Alice said, "that we haven't got a toddler. I'd like to take advantage of the whole thing while I'm here. Just imagine what it's like to these young people with a baby of two or three. The week they spend here is like enough the only week the wife's known when she hasn't had her baby under her feet every hour of the day. I like to see these young mothers going along with their keys to the nurse on duty in the evening. I like to see the young husbands and wives having a good time dancing, knowing there's a nurse keeping an eye on their baby and if it cries they'll be called on the loud-speaker. I like seeing 'Mothers' Free Hour' written down on the day's programme. A mother needs a free hour or two, especially just now, when she's got her husband home for good, and not just on leave. She wants time to get to know him." John put his arm through Alice's. He did not say, "And so are we getting to know each other." It was foreign to him to make remarks like that, but Alice knew what he was thinking. If John had not been so engrossed in Alice he would have perhaps sensed a little more of what was going on. Certainly if Alice had not been so wrapped up in John she would have spotted that Dulcie was not quite herself. Since that first rehearsal when she had acted so queerly there had been no incident to draw their attention to her.

The first news of what had gone on in the theatre came from Dan. Alice and John were wandering up to one of the cafés to get a cup of coffee when they ran into him. John said:

"Come to have a cup of coffee?"

Alice, to make conversation, asked where he had been.

"At the theatre. There's been a bit of a rumpus." John moved on sucking calmly at his pipe.

"What's happening?"

Dan fell into step beside them.

"Matter of fact, it's rather queer. I never knew Nella could sing."

"Nella!" Alice was amused. "Your mother always says she's got a voice like a bat squeaking."

"That's what I thought, but she does. She'll have to use the microphone, but it's all right. We never thought Nella could do anything, but she can. Mr. Barrow said it was very nice, and the song was to go into the show as soon as possible, and it was a knockout."

Dan had his audience now. John and Alice spoke together.

"What song?"

Before Dan could answer Alfred came rushing across from the theatre. He gave Dan a push.

"Clear out, son; I've been looking for you everywhere, S'arnt. We're in a hell of a mess."

Alice said quietly:

"Come and have a cup of coffee and let's hear about it."

They chose a table out of hearing of the campers, and Alfred poured out his story. At the end John asked:

"Is Nella good?"

Alfred fidgeted with his cup.

"She's not Dulcie, but she's got something. I'm knocked all endways really. My Nella! Talk about finding a cuckoo in your nest!"

Alice stirred her coffee.

"Where's Dulcie?"

Alfred fidgeted with his cup.

"With Pinkie, I expect." He looked apologetically at them both. "I wouldn't have had this happen for the world. I didn't know anything about it. I didn't know Tom had written the song, and you could have knocked me down with a wisp of hay when he said he wanted Nella to sing it. I thought he was being funny. Been giving her singing lessons. I could take the hide off Nella. Why couldn't she have told us?"

John held out his cigarette-case.

"Have a cigarette, Corp, and keep calm. I'm sorry this has happened, but there's nothing for us to worry about. There was nothing to say Dulcie was to sing everything that Tom wrote. There's no reason why Nella shouldn't have a number."

Alice had to break in there.

"I don't think we can say quite that. It was understood that Dulcie was leaving F. J. Higgs to star for us, and it was understood that Tom was to try and write some good numbers for her."

John looked at Alfred.

"Is it good?"

"It's the tops. In another class to the rest of his stuff."

John went on placidly smoking.

"Well, it's out of our hands. If Mr. Barrow says it's to go into the show, it's to go into the show, and if he says Nella's to sing it, she's to sing it."

Alfred shook his head.

"He didn't exactly say that. He said, 'Very nice,' and then he told Pinkie the song was to go into the show, and that it was a knock-out. But you've got the picture all wrong, old man, if you think that you can sit back and say that's what Mr. Barrow said, and that's what's going to happen, you've not seen young Dulcie. I tell you straight it wouldn't surprise me if we opened to-night and found that girl missing. She's just in the mood to walk out on us."

Pinkie was with Dulcie in her dressing-room, or rather he was pressed up against her dressing-room door while she raged up and down. Every now and then she paused in front of him, shaking him by the lapel of his coat or forcing her point over with her finger on his chest.

"It's the meanness I won't stand - sneaking along behind my back - can't sing! It's quite true she can't. I never heard such a miserable noise - you can barely hear her - nobody would hear her without the microphone - what gets me is that she's been planning it from the beginning - I always did wonder why she wanted to wear a crimson dress, and now I know - she meant to sit on top of the piano and sing about poppies - I don't blame Tom so much, he's the sort of man that a girl who wanted to be unscrupulous could twist round her finger - well, I'm not going to stand for it - if Mr. Barrow wants Nella he can have Nella - I shall go back to town this afternoon - I left the West End to come to this lousy camp, and when I get here I'm insulted - I'd like to see any other leading lady put up with what I've put up with - I say that I like a song, and I want to sing it, and what happens? - the pianist, a mere nobody, is allowed to say no, you can't, and everybody backs him."

Pinkie had to interrupt there though he knew it was dangerous.

"He did write the number, darling."

"It was an understood thing that every number he wrote I was to sing. Anyway, it doesn't matter now, I'm going to pack."

"I think you're taking a rather exaggerated view of all

this, aren't you?"

That Pinkie failed to understand was the last straw. Dulcie was at that moment standing by the dressing-table. She seized her sticks of lipstick and broke them in half, and threw the bits on the floor; she ground her rouge into the carpet, she picked up a shoe and smashed the mirror. Pinkie wanted to laugh.

"Go on. Smash the place up if it does you any good, but grease paint is hard to come by, I believe, and that was a nice mirror. If you could spare the electric light fittings I'd be glad. We had those put in especially for you, and they're nicely matched. If you're going I must get this room fixed for Nella. I suppose she'll move in here. Funny how the world goes, isn't it?"

Dulcie swung round to him.

"Do you mean to say that if I go to London you think Nella will have all my numbers? That would be funny."

"Oh, I don't know. I'm not so sure of her in 'Meet Me at Waterloo' but she ought to be a wow in 'She Danced in Piccadilly'." Dulcie swooped over to him. He caught her by her shoulders. "Don't hit me, sister, I'm only a frail little man."

"Do you really mean to say that you seriously think that Nella could go on for me and be as good as me?"

"Grammar! Grammar! I never said that. I just said, if you walked out on us she would have to go on. Who else?"

"You said she'd be a wow in 'She Danced in Piccadilly'."

"She'd be all right in the dancing part. Quite a dancer, young Nella, but she wouldn't be you." He felt the atmosphere was calmer. He put his arm round her. "Come on, it's a lovely morning, let's go out in my car somewhere. My father's going off in half an hour, and I shall be free then. Let me take you out to lunch. You'll feel a lot better if you get away from this place. See things more in perspective. You don't really want to go to London to-day, you know. Perhaps you'll want to leave us, but if I were you I'd think things over. What do you think my old man said last night?"

"What?"

"That he thought you were going to be a first-class star."

"He didn't. You're saying that to calm me down."

"No, it's a fact. I'll tell you exactly what he said. He said, 'That girl is going to twinkle a long way out of your reach, my boy, and you can't stop her'."

Dulcie's eyes were shining.

"Did he? Did he truly?"

"He did and the old man's no mean judge, and, what's more, he means to see it happens. That's to say, if you stay with us. When the old man decides to do a thing he always does it, and he's decided to make you a star."

Dulcie hunched her shoulders and scowled.

"But that was last night. I expect to-day he's thinking of making Nella a star."

Pinkie took his arm off her shoulders. He knelt on the floor and picked up the bits of grease paint. He laid them on her dressing-table.

"You can be a fool, duckie. What the old man liked was the song. Anybody would like it, it's a winner. But he's not kidded. He saw that we couldn't have the song unless Nella sang it so he gave in, and that was all there was to that."

Dulcie's eyes narrowed.

"I'll never understand how Tom could behave like that. It's the meanness I mind - it's . . ."

Pinkie was picking up the pieces of mirror and putting them in the waste-paper basket. He held up a finger.

"Don't get all worked up again. You'll be sorry you smashed this up. As it is, you'll have to make shift for a mirror this evening." He got up from the floor. "The first time I met you I gave you a word of advice. I said you shouldn't want two things at once, you stick to fame and your name on a bus. It's my bet you're nearer those last two than you think. It's tough about Tom, believe me, I know just how it feels, but if you're not his type, then you're not. Only an idiot would ruin her career for him, and you're not that."

Dulcie came over to the dressing-table. She tidied her broken paints. She thought, "He's perfectly right. Only an idiot would spoil her career for Tom; but I wonder if Mr. Barrow really is going to try and make me a star, or if Pinkie's just saying that to smooth me down. It's all very well for Pinkie to say don't mind about two things at once, but I do. I can't help it. I want Tom to like me. I hate Nella." Her head was bent and Pinkie could not see her expression or the half-smile round her mouth. It would be idiotic to leave and give Nella the chance Tom wanted for her. Just playing into their hands. Besides, if she stayed, she might get a chance to get even with Nella. All sorts of chances cropped up in the theatre, you never knew. Besides, Tom couldn't really care for her. And if he did - people changed.

"All right. I'll stop."

"And you'll come out to lunch with me?"

She weighed that. Should she stay and let them know that she was angry? Or would it be more clever to slip off and leave them wanting to talk to her and wondering what sort of mood she was in. Probably that was the best thing to do. Let them spend the whole day wondering if she was going to play to-night or not.

"Where's your car?"

"Across the road."

"All right. I'll come with you if we go at once. I don't want the others to see me going."

Pinkie's eyes twinkled. He saw exactly how her mind was working and adored her for it.

"Right, my poppet. I'll just stick my head round the office door to say good-bye to my old man and then we're off."

* * *

"Poppies for England" did not go into the show immediately. It was Nella who caused the delay. She was torn between pleasing Tom and upsetting the happiness of the company. It was an entirely new idea to her that she might be a success. She had for so long accepted that she had not got the personality to put over a number that she could not believe that she really was the right person to sing Tom's song.

She thought, "Tom's only wanting me to sing it because he's sorry for me, and Mr. Barrow only said I could sing it because Tom said nobody else could sing it. Dulcie would do it much better than I could do it. It's very nice of Tom, but it's silly of him."

Nella was backed in this idea by her family. They, too, had so long accepted that they'd only one brilliant child, and that was Dan, that they could not visualize Nella as a success. They were glad that Tom had written so charming a number, and that Mr. Barrow was pleased, but they could not see it was worth all the fuss that was going on. Nella might be able to put it over, but Dulcie would put it over better, and meanwhile the strain was appalling. Dulcie would not speak to Nella at all. Fortunately, in the chalet there was Betty, who was quite unmoved by quarrels and chattered first to Dulcie and then to Nella, otherwise not a word would have been spoken. It made meals very awkward. The two girls were at the extreme ends of the table, but there was a tendency for there to be two camps. There was an effort made to placate Dulcie by taking a tremendous interest in anything she said, but this was counteracted by Tom, who was determined that Nella should not be neglected. After over three weeks of this John said he must put an end to the miserable situation. He came to Dulcie. It was after the show and she was taking off her make-up.

"Could you have a word with Nella about this song? Everybody's been at her, but she says she won't sing it, that you'd be better in it. It's awkward because Mr. Barrow said put it in as soon as possible, and Tom won't let anybody else sing it."

"Don't see why I should. I want to sing it myself, I've said so, it's Tom who's being unreasonable."

"I know. But somebody's got to be big, and I thought it might be you. You've been a surprise to me in lots of ways. The girl I left when I went away had it in her to be very generous. I haven't seen much of that side of you since I came back, but the girl I left when I went away wasn't the artist that we've heard lately. The way you've been putting over Rose Reilly's songs is amazing. Some nights you bring a lump into my throat, you did to-night. Especially in that song at the dressing-table."

Dulcie went on cleaning her face. Funny, she thought, and I don't even work at that number. I just think of Tom and there it is, but then, Dad doesn't know that. Still, she was pleased by what he had said. On the other hand, she was not going to Nella for anybody. She was not going to be soft-soaped by Dad or anybody else into telling Nella she didn't care who sang that song. She did care; it was going to be the best song in the show, and if managers came down to see the show they were sure to notice it. A good song could often run away with a show, no matter who sang it.

"If I'm all that good, why doesn't Tom, want me to sing it?"

John took a risk.

"Tom's not in a fit state to judge who should sing a song. He's fallen for Nella. I don't think either of them know it, but that's what's happened."

Dulcie played about with her make-up. Her father's words seemed to hang in the air. The words had been said now. The words she was frightened to hear. "Tom's fallen for Nella." Oh, God! Was that true? What happened when he and Nella were alone? Did they kiss each other? Did

Nella run her fingers through his hair? She shuddered and then began to cry. It was the last thing she wanted to do. If she had to cry, she had no wish to do it in front of her father. These weeks since the row had been an appalling strain. She was never alone, never got a chance to relax. She would lie awake, looking across the chalet in the direction of Nella's bunk, turning over schemes for getting even with her, racked with jealousy. When she went to sleep she slept badly, often waking up tired and heavy-eyed. She needed a good cry and now, relentlessly, sobs were torn out of her. John looked pityingly at her heaving shoulders. He would have liked to have touched her, but he was afraid. He knew so little of this grown-up daughter. She would probably resent his sympathy. He said diffidently:

"Poor old lady."

Through her sobs Dulcie began to speak.

"I can't think why I like him - he's an off-hand, rude devil, but I do like him - I keep saying I won't think about him any more and then I do - I don't even care about being a success - I only want Tom . . ."

John nodded as if to himself. He had been right then. Back in those days at rehearsals in London. If he had not been so busy getting to know Alice again he would have seen the way the wind was blowing. Poor little devil! He was sufficiently carried away to put his hand on her head and stroke her hair.

"Poor old lady." There was nothing very much one could say. "You've got to put him out of your mind, you know he's not for you. You won't agree with me, of course, but it's a good thing. He's not the type to make a husband for you. You want somebody who'll put you first, manage your affairs; Tom will always put his music before everybody. I wish I hadn't had to say that, but it never does any good not to face the truth. I really think you'll feel better yourself if you put an end to this squabble. Nella's got to sing that song, a word from you could straighten things out."

Dulcie raised her head and choked back her sobs.

"I'd rather die than go to Nella. But you can go to her if you like. You can tell her that I've given in. I don't want to sing the lousy song. But I tell you, when she sings it I'll pray every night she's a failure."

John was too thankful to have gained his point to say more, nor could he think what to say. He gave her hair a final stroke.

"I'll tell her. What are you going do to-night?"

She looked at her face.

"I was dancing with Pinkie, but I look such a mess I shall go straight to bed. I'll sneak out of the front of the theatre and miss all the crowd who are hanging around waiting. Would you explain to Pinkie?"

John went to look for Nella. It was good Dulcie had given in about the song. It was awkward they had been so long putting it into the show, but he felt miserable. How hard it is, he thought, that none of us can help each other when it comes to the big things of life. We can say we're sorry and that's about all. Poor little Dulcie, struggling along. I hate to think of her unhappy, but there's nothing anyone can do, she must find her own way back to happiness.

* * *

"Poppies for England" had its try-out towards the end of June. It had been a wet week. Although the camp offered every sort of indoor amusement, it was hard when it rained on a holiday. There had been a matinée every day and the theatre had been packed. John and Alfred tried to help by varying the concert party programme as much as possible, so by Thursday they had run through their repertoire.

"Quite a lot of the poor blighters will have seen the show before," Alfred said, "we want a bit of variety for them. Mind you, if they must have a wet holiday, they've been much better off here than they would be in most places. At least it's only a step to all the amusements, but one can't help feeling sorry for them."

John looked out across the dripping camp.

"You've said it, Corp. What most people need these days is a bit of sun on their bones. They're dead tired and it would brighten them up, all the indoor amusements in the world can't compensate them for no sunshine. What I'm afraid of is that we get a bit browned-off ourselves with all this rain and twice daily shows. I think to-night's the night to put on this poppy number."

Alfred looked at John out of the corner of his eye.

John caught the look and they both laughed. Alfred said:

"Thank God we can laugh. If you had told me when that song was written that it was going to make us famous from one end of the world to the other, I should still have said, 'You know where you can put it.' Talk about trouble! Perhaps it will clear the air when it's in the show."

John shook his head.

"Doubt it. We're not pleasing anybody. I forced Nella to agree. Never knew a kid so determined to remain in the back row as your daughter. I persuaded Dulcie to let me go to Nella, but I can't say that those two girls are all love and kisses."

Alfred kicked angrily at the leg of his chair. "Such a fuss about a song."

The words spilled into the air. John and Alfred listened to them. Then they looked at each other, and laughed again. John said:

"Come off it, Corp. It's got very little to do with the song, and you know it."

Alfred was still laughing.

"It's the funniest set-up I ever knew. If there's anything between Tom and Nella, things have changed a lot since I went courting. All Nella wants to do is to sit and darn Tom's socks, and all Tom wants to do is to force Nella to be ambitious. I don't believe they even hold hands."

John was lighting a cigarette. He looked at Alfred over the flame of his lighter.

"And here's Dulcie, who only has to raise her little finger and she can have all the boys trailing after her, crazy about him. Aren't women contrary?"

Alice and Muriel were less frank in discussing their daughters. Alice, although she fought against it, could not help taking sides with Dulcie. To her there seemed something underhand and sly about the way Nella had got hold of Tom, persuaded him to write a song for her. There seemed something funny about the way those two had got together without anyone knowing anything about it. Alice would have considered Tom the last person to make a suitable son-in-law. He was not at all her idea of the man Dulcie should marry. But when it came to seeing Muriel's daughter walk off with him under Dulcie's nose, all her mother-love rose to defend her chick. Tom might not be the man she would choose, but if Dulcie wanted him, Dulcie ought to have him. Both women were far too intelligent to let the affair blow up into a quarrel, but there was a coldness between them. Muriel talked to Alfred about it by the hour.

"Such swank they put on about Dulcie. You'd think that Nella had stolen something from Dulcie the way they go on."

Alfred did his best to pour oil.

"Well, Dulcie did leave a job in the West End to come out with us on the understanding she was to be the lead, and it is a bit thick to have the best song Tom's written snatched from under her nose."

The two wives did their best to get the husbands to take sides.

"I can't think how you and John can go on as though nothing had happened," Muriel grumbled. "You ought to tell them to take a slipper to Dulcie. Do her a lot of good."

Alice did not risk her newly found happiness with John by too open criticisms of the Binns family, but she did say:

"I wish you'd make Alfred see that it's not Nella having the number anyone minds, it's the underhand way it's been gone about."

There was even an effort made by the two mothers to

separate their children.

"Now, Dan," Muriel said, "I don't want you about with Dickie all day. He's all right, but they've got funny notions, that family."

Alice said to Dickie:

"I'm sure you don't let Dan say anything silly about Dulcie, but it's difficult not to discuss it when you two boys are about together all day. Couldn't you make friends with some of the other young men in the camp?"

Dan and Dickie repeated these conversations to each other, and laughed themselves sick. Over just one point they were agreed. It was quite understandable that both Dulcie and Nella wanted Tom. They shared a chalet with him, and thought him a grand type.

It was agreed by John and Alfred that the news that to-night was the night for the appearance of the controversial song should be told individually to each member of their respective families. They expected trouble, but actually, everybody was a little relieved.

"I'll get round to the wardrobe," Muriel said, "and put some extra tarlatan to Nella's frock. I've had it waiting. Can't ask Alice to do it."

Alice said

"If she is going to do it, to-night is as good a night as any other."

John went to Dulcie's chalet. When there were two performances a day she did not get up until about twelve. He sat on the end of her bed. She was wearing a coral pink nightdress, and he thought he had never seen her look prettier.

"I'm putting Nella on to-night."

Dulcie looked at him with cold, expressionless eyes. "I don't care."

He had hoped for something more than that. Since her tears he had thought they were a little closer to each other, but he saw that for the moment she was as far from him as ever. He offered her a cigarette, and changed the subject.

Alfred went to the theatre where Tom and Nella were practising.

" 'Poppies for England' goes in to-night. I'll be with the electrician at twelve. To try out the lighting effects and the microphone."

Tom and Nella said nothing for a moment. They watched Alfred's retreating back, and heard him shut the stage door. Nella was the first to speak. Her voice was a whisper.

"To-night. Tom, I can't."

Tom took his hands off the piano, and caught hold of hers. They seemed very small and had turned cold with fright.

"You can, and you've got to. I had a letter this morning. F. J. Higgs is coming down to see the show soon, he's coming specially to hear this number."

Nella's eyes were round with horror.

"Tom, I couldn't, not with him there. Let Dulcie do it."

He gripped her hands more firmly. Oh, gosh, he thought, what they've done to her between them! Will she ever get over thinking she's no good?

"Listen. You've got to snap out of this, you're going to be fine. You've got more talent than Dulcie's ever heard of."

That made Nella laugh.

"Don't be silly." Then her face sobered. She withdrew one hand from his, and stroked his sleeve to soften her words. "Seriously, when you get Mr. Higgs to come would you let Dulcie sing it? It's only going to make the most awful row, and we don't want another. Besides, it would give the song more chance."

The queer, sulky, little boy look, which she knew so well, came over his face.

"If you won't sing it there's no point in his coming. That's the song I want him to hear."

She was moved as usual. Poor Tom, thinking she did not want to sing it. He always thought things like that, but it was no wonder, brought up as he had been with no one to love him. If only he would be reasonable, and see that it was not that she did not want to sing it, but she knew she would not be good, and even if she was good it really was not worth the row that had been going on. Still, she could not let him look like that.

"Don't be silly. I'll sing it if you won't let Dulcie." She climbed on to the piano. "Come on. We'd better rehearse it."

As Tom played the opening bars she thought how stupid this is. This isn't what I want at all. I don't want to sing. I don't even want to dance. If only Tom would notice how nicely his things are washed and mended, instead of worrying about my voice, it really would be much better for everybody.

"Poppies for England" was put on towards the end of the second half of the programme. It was put in in the place of one of Muriel's songs.

"Can't see why I've got to be cut out of the programme," Muriel said. "By rights this should take the place of 'She Danced in Piccadilly'."

Alfred screwed up his face in comical horror.

"For a reasonably sensible woman you can talk more rot than any person I know. Cut Dulcie's song indeed. Simpler really to drop an atom bomb on the theatre."

For the number Alfred had painted a backcloth. The fields outside the camp with the poppies in full bloom. He and the electrician had arranged some very pretty lighting, a mixture of sunlight with patches of crimson. Before all special numbers there was a blackout. When the blackout lifted before "Poppies for England" Nella was sitting on the top of the piano, her crimson skirts billowing round. She sat childishly, her knees slightly apart, her hands clasped between them. She leant a little towards the audience, her dark hair falling forward, her grey eyes wide with fright. Tom was in the shadow. He was side view to Nella, and she could not turn to look at him, but she could see him perfectly clearly in her mind. His dark head raised, and his fingers running up and down the keyboard. Poor Tom, she thought, what an awful mistake making me sing this song. I must try not to let him down.

It was only the refrain which was actually sung. As far as the verses were concerned it was a point number. The first bars of the sad little tune were falling into the theatre, and over them Tom whispered: "Keep your eyes on the Monarch."

Nella looked towards the bust of the King.

The audience sat so still that the rustle of a programme

was disturbing. Nella's voice came softly through the microphone. When she broke into the refrain the choir-boy quality of her singing brought half a smile and half a lump into the throat. She sang just as she had for Mr. Barrow, no emotion, no feeling, but her phrasing was perfect. It was more as if a wind instrument were accompanying the piano than a girl singing. At the end of the second refrain she slipped off the piano and started to dance. Then the true Nella appeared. Not the Nella of the dancing school, but the buried Nella. Tom enjoyed her dancing, Tom did not mind her having no personality, so she danced for him. Few of the audience knew anything about ballet, they did not appreciate that what caught their breath was the liquid way one movement faded into the other. They did not appreciate her technical proficiency, they just loved her, and that was that. At the end, followed by a crimson spot, she danced off holding in her arms an imaginary sheaf of poppies. There was an appreciable silence before the applause. There were not the whistles and shouts which came for Dulcie. It was more a warm rush of feeling which turned into applause. Nella was a very undeveloped artist, she had, apart from her dancing ability, a queer, childish quality; half the audience would have liked to have hugged her. But away and beyond the applause for Nella was the applause for the song. That was something. Nella took her calls, and then Alfred came on.

He had prepared for the situation. He held up his hand for silence. He told them they were seeing the first performance of Tom's new song, and he made Tom stand up. This brought out the whistles as well as the applause usually reserved for Dulcie. Alfred again silenced the audience.

"You like the song? I thought you would, so why shouldn't you learn it? Come on, Tom, strike up."

He clicked his fingers to one of the two stage hands and one of the large song boards which he loved was lowered with the words of the refrain. It seemed that the audience could not get enough of that song. They sang it and sang it, and John, smiling in the wings, replanned his programme, and had to cut out his own and Alfred's last number. He whispered to Dickie:

"Pop along round to everybody and tell them we'll go straight into the finale from here, or we'll run over our time."

It was a very pleased audience who streamed out into the night. Their pleasure was added to by finding that the rain had stopped. Stars were twinkling, and a watery moon was struggling through the clouds. As if in thank-offering for a fine night, the campers spontaneously started to sing. It was as if a conductor lifted his baton. "You ought to see the coast there. When the poppies are in bloom."

In the theatre there was jubilation. Tom was congratulated, and Nella was congratulated. Alice buried the hatchet and kissed Nella.

"You were splendid, darling."

John patted her on the shoulder.

"Talk about hiding your light under a bushel."

Pinkie nodded and waved to her.

"Fine. Congratulations."

But his eye was towards Dulcie's closed door. What was

she thinking about in there? He would have to go and see her. What would it be tactful to say?

Dulcie was standing re-reading a letter which had come by the evening post. She folded it, and put it down the front of her frock. She looked at herself in the glass. Her face was nicely made up. She gave herself a smile. She and her reflection knew what they were up to. She straightened her shoulders, flung open her dressing-room door, and, every inch a leading lady, walked on to the stage. She went across to Nella and gave her a kiss. Her voice was perhaps a fraction artificial, but only a fraction.

"Darling, you were marvellous."

Pinkie eyed her in admiration and amusement. A beautiful performance, he thought. Now I wonder what the hell she's up to.

* * *

Nella and Tom were sitting on the sand. The change in the weather the night before had not been just a break; it was a glorious sunny morning, the sea blue and sparkling. Nella played with the sand. She let it run through her fingers. Tom looked at her, and felt warm with affection. She was so small, childish and defenceless, sitting like that, playing with sand like a kid. But she had something on her mind, and, though he could not imagine why, he felt he was to blame. Because he wanted so much to understand his voice was gruff, almost angry.

"I thought you'd be on the top of the world, today, everybody's talking about your success. They're treating you quite differently. Look at the way they all talked to you at lunch."

Nella frowned in a worried way. Tom could not see this because her hair fell forward and hid her mouth.

"I think you've got a wrong idea of what's important - at least important to me. I never want to be noticed. You're wrong if you think I minded not having anything else to do in the show. Even now I'd much rather Dulcie sang the song."

"Well, she won't. She was nice about it last night, wasn't she?"

Again the faint smile crossed Nella's mouth.

"Very." She looked up at him laughing. "We're now in that stage of being awfully polite, if you know what I mean. We've only one dressing-table in our chalet, and she says, 'You use it first, Nella,' and I say, 'No, of course not, you, Dulcie.' She used to give me a shove and say, 'Get outside, I want to do my face.' I liked it better that way."

"Your family are no end pleased."

Nella laughed again.

"The only sensible one is Dan. He said to me this morning, 'What a silly ass you are. Why didn't you say you could do all that before?' I tell you who has been nice though, Aunt Alice and Uncle John. I think it's nice of them, particularly of Aunt Alice. She hates anybody to have anything that Dulcie wants."

Tom dug a hole in the sand, forcing his finger in with angry jabs.

"I suppose you won't be a bit interested when I tell you I'm writing another song for you."

Nella looked at him in wide-eyed horror.

"For goodness sake, do you like rows?"

He snapped back.

"I want you to be a success. You want that too. You're pretending when you say you don't. You've been so frightened and bullied you're scared what everybody's saying."

Nella was sorry she had hurt him. She laid her hand on his.

"Don't be angry with me, Tom. I think 'Poppies for England' is a simply lovely song, and you've had an enormous success with it, but don't try and rush me, I got away with it all right last night, but you know as well as I do that it's a funny sort of getting away with it that I do. I just sit up there and sing into the microphone, and they like it, but I don't know a bit how I do it. That's a frightening sort of feeling, getting somewhere without knowing why."

"That's rubbish. It's just people telling you you can't do something that's made you at last believe you can't. After you've done the song a night or two it'll be absolutely fixed and you won't have to worry at all."

Nella sighed.

"I suppose not, but you can't make me enthusiastic, Tom, whatever you say. I still wish Dulcie could sing it. I feel most peculiar here," she laid her hand on her solar plexus, "because I've got to do it again to-night. Up to yesterday I never felt anything at all, I just went to the theatre as if I were going to clean my teeth."

Tom looked at her thoughtfully. Was this a good moment

to tell her that he had heard from F. J.? His coming down was almost fixed. Probably not. It was not like him to be tactful, but he could feel that he had to be a little cautious with Nella. He never could be sure that he had her. It would be only too easy for her to stick in her toes and refuse to sing. He said softly:

"I never knew a girl who fought so hard against being a success."

Nella got up. She stretched and gazed at the sky.

"Oh, what a lovely, lovely day." She looked at Tom over her shoulder. "I'm not sure that the sort of success you want for me is the sort of success I want for myself."

"What do you mean? What other success could there be?"

She had her head turned from him. She spoke in a detached way.

"The sort Aunt Alice has. She's making Uncle John happy, a heavenly mother to Dulcie, Dickie and Betty, but no outside success like my mother has. She's quite happy just sewing at the wardrobe and never being seen by anybody."

Tom tried to fathom her thoughts. Mrs. Corner was nice; from the day he had arrived at Comstock she had treated him like one of the family. It was she who fetched him for meals when he forgot the time playing the piano. He had never thought about her before, he had just taken it for granted that there were Mrs. Corners in the world, who were put there to be nice to other people. But he could not put Nella into that category. Nella was a dancer and an artist. He burned to see her triumphing, he longed for F. J. to come down and, in front of everybody, say, "This is the most talented member of the company." He liked to imagine the gaping faces of the Corners and the Binns and Dulcie's fury. Little Nella, the despised, being put in the place of honour. If only Nella were different. Not that he wanted her different in herself, he thought she was quite perfect as she was, but it was a pity she had no ambition. It was very hard to push a person on who had not got that.

"She's all right. I like her awfully. Of course, I never knew my mother, but if I'd known her, I'd have liked her to have been like Mrs. Corner." He was going on to say that Nella was different, that she was born for great things, but Nella interrupted him. She leant down to him and took him by the shoulders and shook him.

"Oh, Tom, I am a beast, don't listen to me. Don't say that about having no mother, it makes me feel miserable. 'Poppies for England' is the most lovely song, and if it pleases you at all, I'll work and work to get it as perfect as I can. I'll even sing another of your songs if you want me to, only please don't write one."

Tom was gazing at Nella in a bemused way. He felt queer. There was something electric about her hands, there was something electric about her hair which fell forward and brushed against his cheek. He tingled all over. Then he flamed with shame. What an awful thing to want to take Nella in his arms and kiss her. Whatever would she think if he behaved like that? She looked upon him as a brother, and quite right, too. He was dismayed at the surge of passion which swept over him. How appalling if Nella should guess how he felt. He jumped up quickly, his voice rough.

"Come on, we ought to be getting back. I should think it was time for tea."

Nella glanced at her watch. Only half-past three. Their meal before the show was two hours away. She smiled understandingly. Dear Tom, he never thought of anything but his music. He couldn't bear being away long from a piano. Meekly she followed him up the beach.

* * *

Alice had not accepted Nella's success as easily as Nella had supposed. After the first performance of "Poppies for England", when she and John were safely in their chalet and the door was shut, she said:

"She can't be heard without a microphone."

John was sitting on his bed taking off his shoes. He thought, "I know how she feels about Dulcie, but it won't do anybody any good if she's narky over it."

"She'll be useful. I'm going to have a talk with Alfred. See if we can give her another number. Bound to have wet days, and we could do with some extra stuff for the matineées."

Alice undressed a while in silence.

"If only I could get it out of my head that there was something underhand about it all. It seems so funny she and Tom planning all this behind everybody's backs."

"You don't mean everybody's backs. You mean Dulcie's back. I don't think it was underhand, Nella's not like that. The way I see it is that she didn't want to be laughed at. You know what they are in that family. Alfred would do anything to get a laugh, and up to the time Mr. Barrow heard Nella sing there would have been a hell of a laugh if she had said Tom was giving her singing lessons. I don't think Nella's got any ideas about herself now. I still think she thinks putting her on to sing is half a joke."

Alice was at the dressing-table brushing her hair.

"I don't see why she should, she's very good."

John came over to her and put his arm round her.

"That's more my old Alice."

She looked up at him, her face against his arm.

"Do you think there's anything between those two?"

He tightened his grip on her.

"About the same as there was between us two when we first met."

Alice let her mind run back through the years.

"Couple of comics we were. What I wanted to do was to look after you. I remember a frayed collar you once wore. I'd have given everything I had to get hold of it and turn it."

John gave her a kiss.

"Some time you might have a look in Nella's work-basket. I'll be very surprised if you don't find a couple of Tom's socks waiting to be darned."

* * *

Pinkie and Dulcie were out in his car. It was a Sunday. The weather had stayed fine and the temperature was now in the eighties. Dulcie was wearing a leaf-green frock, her bare legs were the colour of sunburn stockings; against her feet her sandals looked extraordinarily white. Pinkie gazed at her with appreciation. On the whole, he thought, she's the most completely good-looking girl I've ever known. The car was open and her hair blew behind her, her eyes were on the poppies flashing by.

"Penny for your thoughts."

She turned on him a wide-eyed, innocent look.

"It wasn't worth a penny. I was thinking how lovely the poppies were."

"Like hell you were," thought Pinkie. "That wide-eyed, innocent look doesn't mean that your mind's on poppies." He grinned at her.

"I should just love to know what you're up to."

"What do you mean? Up to?"

"Come off it, Naïve. For over a week now you've been all sweetness and love, with now and again a pretty burst of enthusiasm when you say loudly, 'Doesn't Nella put over that song charmingly?'."

"She is charming, don't you think so?"

"Charming, but I'd take a snappy bet that you don't think her as charming as all that. I remember a day when I grubbed round your dressing-room on my hands and knees picking up broken grease paints and bits of mirror."

"That was my artistic temperament."

"Might have been. I know that's the polite word for it in the theatre. I should have called it temper." He added, apparently inconsequently, "Rather slow getting off the mark, those two, aren't they?"

She flashed round at him.

"What two?"

"Tom and Nella."

The colour went out of her day. There he went, he was saying the same thing as her father had said. It was nonsense, there was nothing between Nella and Tom. Nothing except that she was a mouse of a little thing saying, "Yes, Tom; no, Tom, three bags full." He was a shocking egoist. He thought his music perfect. He did not believe anybody knew anything about it except himself. He liked people who said "yes ".

"You are a soppy fool, Pinkie, always trying to pair people off. There's nothing between them, and you know it."

"I don't know anything of the sort, and I can't help being pleased, I've a hankering after you myself." He broke off there, whistling to hide how furiously he was thinking. Dare he tackle this question of Tom? Dare he show Dulcie what was in her mind? For all her sophisticated manner, she was very innocent in a lot of ways. Would she be horrified if he explained to her exactly what her feeling for Tom was? He said, "The number of times I've told you you shouldn't want two things at once. You want to stick to stardom and your name on a bus. If you don't mind my saying so, it ill befits a lady of your talent to go yapping after an unknown song writer."

"I'm not yapping after him."

Pinkie sighed.

"I hate to be coarse, but the simile that slips into the mind is a cat on the tiles."

She felt the blood pouring into her cheeks. How horrible! How did Pinkie guess at the thoughts she had about Tom? It was hateful that he could guess. She had hoped they were hidden from everybody. Of course, there was that day when she had been silly and cried to her father, but he would never have gone to Pinkie and told him what she had said. Her tone was truculent.

"I think you're very vulgar, and don't fuss about me, I'm quite all right, thank you. I know where I'm going."

"That's fine then. Everything's tickety-boo. We're all as happy as happy."

The word tickety-boo lined up in her memory. It brought back her first night in Comstock. She had danced with Pinkie, it was a waltz, he had said, "When you sort yourself out and know exactly what you want, you'll be able to get it, and then everything'll be tickety-boo." She had asked him how he knew that everything wasn't tickety-boo already. That was the queer thing that often puzzled her about Pinkie. He was usually so silly and laughed at everything, but he did know things without being told. He had not known her half a day at that time and yet he had felt that she wasn't happy about something. Just now he was being intuitive in the same way. Everybody else thought she was being nice about Nella, but she hadn't fooled Pinkie. What made him so sensitive? There was something else he had said. This was a good chance to keep him to his promise.

"You said you'd got a story of your own that you'd tell me one day. Tell it me now?"

Pinkie thought, "There we go. I did promise her, too. Might be a good day to dig up the dirt. There's bits of my story that tag on to hers if she's got the sense to pick up the bits."

"I've been married."
Dulcie was lighting a cigarette. She was so surprised that she dropped her lighter. Her voice came muffled from the floor of the car.

"Good gracious! You don't look a bit like a married man."

He looked down at her fair head.

"Have you found that thing? Married or single, I don't want to be a headline in to-morrow's paper, 'Car mystery. Two charred bodies found on east coast'." She came up flushed, holding the lighter. "We're divorced."

In the theatre there were plenty of broken marriages, but Dulcie had never thought of one in connection with Pinkie. She was surprised to find that she minded. She did not like to think of Pinkie being married, and still less did she like Pinkie being divorced. You couldn't be divorced without somebody else coming into the story. She had begun to think of Pinkie as her personal property, not somebody that she wanted particularly, but somebody who was always there if she did want him. It was annoying to find that he belonged to not one, but two, other people. However, it would be a mistake to let Pinkie know how she felt. She said with polite brightness:

"Go on."

"I met her at a dance. She worked near where I was stationed. She drove an ambulance. She had red hair and that skin and those blue eyes that you get sometimes with red hair, and her name was Annabel. I was an innocent little boy learning to fly and she was everybody's pin-up girl. We sergeants hadn't a look in. Squadron leaders, commodores and even, it was rumoured, Air Vice-Marshals fell for her. She used to come to dances at the station. We queued up for a chance to dance with her. To me she was a hell of a lot more than a pin-up girl, she got under my skin. I wanted her so badly I couldn't sleep; I nearly lost a Wellington because of her; my mind wasn't on the job, you know. The funny thing about her was that for all her red hair she wasn't the flaming, passionate type. What she liked was to talk about books, high-brow stuff, too. God knows what she saw in me."

"How did you get to know her?"

"Her ambulance broke down one day. I was tootling past on my cycle, fell off the dam' thing I was so excited to find I had got a chance to crash in at last. I mended the ambulance, and she talked to me about Bernard Shaw. Spent all the next three weeks mugging up Bernard Shaw. I met her every day. Hell of a job keeping up with her. One day we'd have a nice cosy on *St. Joan*, and I thought I'd got that taped, and the next day *St. Joan* was out and we were deep in *Man and Superman*. Shocking it was. Our padre ran the library, he got hopes of me, seeing the stuff I read, and asked me to read the lessons. Then one day, when she was looking particularly marvellous, I couldn't hold it back any longer, and I told her that I loved her. She turned those blue lamps of hers on to me and said that she thought marriage ought to have a mental kinship, didn't I? I didn't know what she was talking about, but I didn't care what kind of a kinship it was as long as I got her. Anyway, we were married."

"Were you happy?"

"Was I hell! She wouldn't give up her job so we only met

when I had leave. I was doing bombing raids at that time. All the way out to the target, and all the way back I thought about her, I pictured our next leave; not to put too fine a point on it bed had a place in my thoughts. She told me she had thought a lot about our leave, too. Her mind wasn't on bed, it was still on Bernard Shaw. Funny, she always got her way. I got to bed all right, but she spent half the night talking about *Blanco Posnet*. Ever read *Blanco Posnet*?"

"What happened next?"

"I was taken prisoner, and when I got back she had gone off with somebody else."

Dulcie's spirits flew skywards. So he had divorced her, she had never thought of that.

"What a shame! I know lots of girls who left their husbands like that, I do think it was mean when they were prisoners of war."

Pinkie shook his head.

"Couldn't have been more pleased. She wrote and told me she had found her soul mate, he was in the navy. Sometimes I think of the poor mugger. I suppose he's about at the *Blanco Posnet* stage now."

Dulcie was puzzling over the story. There didn't seem very much in it to make Pinkie human and understanding.

"It was funny you didn't know that she was a different sort of person to you before you married her."

"Not funny at all. If I'd faced the facts I shouldn't have yearned after her. I'd have known that I couldn't make what is known as an improper suggestion to her, she wasn't that sort, but I might have come round to realizing that an improper suggestion was all I wanted. Very confusing, love, you know. Very easy to mistake something else for it."

Dulcie again felt the blood rising to her cheeks. There he went again. Perhaps he didn't mean it this time, but he sounded as though he meant it. He was trying to say she was not in love with Tom, but just attracted to him physically. Was that true? Were all the thoughts she had about Tom just that? Was the fury which came over her when she thought about Nella jealousy? Was there a way to get all these things out of her mind? Could Pinkie help her? Was she going to weaken in what she planned to do?

It was unlucky that, at that moment, Pinkie, uncertain what was meant by her silence, and slightly embarrassed at having laid his story bare, changed the subject. However frivolously he had talked of Annabel a little of the hurt she had left behind had probably sneaked out. Had he failed to be funny? Horror of horrors, was Dulcie being sorry for him?

"My inside is rattling like an old plum stone in an empty jam jar; look at the map, ducky, and see how far it is to the Royal Hotel."

Dulcie was still struggling with the map when the hotel came into sight. For the rest of the day Pinkie was funny; there was no further chance for serious conversation.

* * *

"Poppies for England" became one of the high spots of the show. It was not so much Nella, though she was a great success, but the song itself. The weather was lovely, the poppies were flaming all along the cliff side, the queer, sweetish smell of them mixed with the salt of the sea would be in the campers' nostrils when this holiday was only a memory. Back in their homes, factories and offices, it would be fine to bring the smell back. "Poppies for England" would do that for them. It was not only in the theatre that they sang until the roof lifted. They made the orchestras play it. They sang it in groups as they walked about the camp.

Unwillingly, because of her song, Nella found herself something of a personality. The campers pointed her out to each other as she passed by. "Look, there goes the girl who sings our song." "Funny little thing, isn't she? She gets you, somehow." "You can't say she's an actress exactly, seems to come natural." "Very different from that Dulcie. Now she's an artist to her finger-tips." Few of the audiences could have defined what they meant. When they were in the theatre and Dulcie was on the stage she put things over, tears or a laugh, and people said, "Isn't she clever? Doesn't she do it well?" With Nella, sitting on the piano and swinging her legs and chirruping away into the microphone, it seemed so casual and unforced that they might almost have done as well themselves. Of course she danced beautifully. Even that was dismissed. Nella danced for her own pleasure and because Tom liked it, and again it seemed too easy. When Dulcie danced with her yellow frock and her moonlight fair hair you felt you really were seeing something, there was a showmanship about her.

Night after night Alfred would stand at his dressing-room door listening to his daughter, his head on one side, his face screwed up in perplexity. When "Poppies for England" had been in the bill for a week he could stand it no longer. After the show he burst out to John.

"You could knock me down with your little finger, S'arnt, but young Nella's got something. She gets you. Funny thing is I don't think she knows how she does it or cares either, if it comes to that."

They came into the dressing-room. Tom and the two boys were chattering. John spoke softly.

"I was going to speak to you about her. I think it's time we gave her another number."

Alfred looked doubtful.

"Can't hear her beyond the front row without the microphone, and I doubt if she could do it twice."

John smiled.

"You're stalling. You think we'll be in for another rumpus." His face grew grave. "But we're here to serve the public, get another run of bad weather and we need all the variety we can raise."

Alfred saw John's point, but he still had to argue. "Don't put in an extra number for Nella unless you've squared Dulcie."

"I won't. Matter of fact, all that seems to have blown over."

Alfred was taking off his make-up. He slashed some grease over his face.

"You never know with women. It's not Dulcie especially I mean," he added hastily, "but just women. A couple of them can be hating each other's guts, and if you listen to them talk the only word you catch is darling."

John looked across the room to see that the other three were not attending. The air had been cleared between himself and Alfred when they had placed the row about "Poppies for England" in its proper place, not a row about a song, but a row about a man.

"I'll have a word with Dulcie before we see what else we can give Nella to do, but it's my belief Tom hasn't got another song up his sleeve at the moment."

Alfred's face was buried in his towel. He emerged to give a broad wink.

"Praise God from whom all blessings flow, S'arnt, hope that's true."

Dulcie thought it was Pinkie tapping at her door. When she saw it was her father she gave him a sweet smile. John hated to be greeted with that artificial bright look. He wanted to rumple her hair and tell her not to put on an act for her father, but he had come on business, and this was no minute to rub Dulcie up the wrong way.

"Your Uncle Alfred and I were thinking we might give Nella another number. This weather won't last for ever, and we could do with an extra number at matinées."

Dulcie had taken off her theatre make-up, and was putting on her street make-up. She had promised Pinkie to dance with him after the show. John watched her face in the glass. For a fraction of a second he saw a cautious, calculating look in her eyes, then it passed, and in its place was the pleasant, serene leading lady who had greeted him when he came in.

"Why not?"

John felt a fool. With those two words she had made him

feel that he and Alfred had manufactured trouble where none existed. Why not indeed? Did he come to Dulcie and talk to her about it when Dickie had a new dance routine? Dan some extra juggling? Muriel an extra song, or when he and Alfred were trying out a new comedy number? He did not, and that Dulcie found it puzzling and surprising that he should bother her about a new number for Nella was implicit in those two words. John could have kicked himself for feeling awkward and embarrassed. How ludicrous to feel awkward and embarrassed with your own daughter! He could not think what to say next, he could not even think how to get out of the room comfortably. He had come in portentously knocking on the door, and here was Dulcie dismissing what he had come about as if it did not concern her. Dulcie added to his aggravation, she said sweetly:

" Did you come to see me about anything special, Dad?"

He could have slapped her. He would have liked to have taken her by the shoulders and shaken her well and said, "You know ruddy well I came to see you about something special. It's only a few weeks ago that you cried your eyes out about Tom giving Nella a song, and you know it, you little devil." He was spared answering by a knock. Dulcie called out, "Come in." She looked at Pinkie over her shoulder.

"I shan't be long. Dad's held me up." She turned to her father. "What else was it, Dad? You can't only have knocked on the door and come in all managerial to tell me Nella's going to sing a number at matinées. Why should I care?"

Pinkie lit a cigarette, and leant against the door. He passed his case to John. "Better take one," he thought, "you'll need, it to soothe the nerves if she's in this mood." He said:

"What's Nella going to sing?"

John took the cigarette and shrugged his shoulders.

"Don't know. Some simple little thing. She's not suitable for putting over a difficult number. Haven't had a word with her yet, as a matter of fact."

"More something to dance to she needs, isn't it?" Pinkie suggested.

Dulcie got up and took her evening dress off a hanger. She looked at it thoughtfully, as if deciding whether to wear it or not. Then she turned to her father.

"I tell you what she sings. I heard her practising it once. 'Mighty Like a Rose'."

John was surprised.

"Does she? I should have thought that more up her mother's street. Shouldn't have thought young Nella could have tackled it. She can't very well dance to it. Pity really she shouldn't dance, it's her long suit."

Dulcie slipped off her wrapper, and pulled her evening dress over her head. She came over to Pinkie and turned her left side to him.

"Do me up. I should have a word with Tom, Dad, if I were you. When I heard her I thought, 'That's pretty good, actually'."

John moved towards the door.

"Thanks for your help. I'll have a word with Tom now."

Dulcie was not going to let him go as easily as that. "You

still haven't told me what you came about." John could not resist it. He made a face at her, and shut the door. Dulcie giggled.

"I adore Dad when he's like that. Did you see him make a face at me? He knows I know he came in to see what kind of a row I was going to make about Nella singing another song. I pretended that I couldn't possibly be interested in whether Nella sang or not."

"Will you stand still when I'm doing you up, or I'll put a hook into your skin. I'm not at all sure you wouldn't deserve it. How nice people like your mother and father gave birth to a minx like you puzzles me. There, that's the last hook."

Dulcie was wearing a flame-coloured frock. It had a wide gold belt to match her gold shoes. She took the belt off a hook and clipped it on. Her eyes were dancing, she hummed softly, "Sweetest little fellow, everybody knows." Pinkie picked her coat up from off a chair and put it round her shoulders.

"Come on, you, come and dance." He took her arm and led her out into the night. "Is there any chance that you are going to tell me why you so hopefully suggested that Nella should sing that song? Can't she sing it? Or did you select it because there's no dance possible?"

Dulcie looked up at the stars.

"What a beautiful night. As a matter of fact, if you want to know, she sings it most awfully well, better than 'Poppies for England'." She started to hum again. " 'Don't know what to call him, but he's mighty like a rose.' You've such a despising sort of nature, Pinkie. I suppose you couldn't think that just for once I was just being nice and helpful."

Pinkie laughed.

"Like hell I could. Come on."

* * *

"That's fine, Nella. At least it will be when you've got the microphone. You haven't anything else with a dance refrain?"

Tom thought Nella's rendering of "Mighty Like a Rose" superb. He had expected ecstasies from Alfred and John. This casual sauntering along with mild praise and the suggestion that perhaps she'd rather dance, made him mad. They went out of their way to crush the talent in the kid. What was she going to feel to-night when she started to sing "Poppies for England" and remembered her father's words. "Haven't you anything else with a dance refrain?" The sort of satirical thing her family were always saying. Just like that crack about the microphone. Nella had been thankful to hear that "Mighty Like a Rose" had been suggested. If she had to do an extra number at matinees, then here was one she knew and would not have to learn. She had seen that her father and John were quite pleased. She smiled at them happily.

"I haven't really, and I'd rather . . ."

Tom interrupted her. He got up and marched to the edge of the stage.

"What's wrong with the way she sings 'Mighty Like a Rose'?"

Alfred did not want a repetition of the scene that Tom had produced for Mr. Barrow on Nella's behalf. He said soothingly:

"Nothing, old man, only dancing is Nella's cup of tea."

Tom glowered.

"Who said so? Doesn't she tear the house down night after night with 'Poppies for England'?"

John came forward.

"Of course she does, and puts over 'Mighty Like a Rose' splendidly. We just thought it a pity she shouldn't dance, that's all. Still, if she's happy with 'Mighty Like a Rose', so are we. Come on, Corp. What about some coffee?"

Outside the theatre Alfred gave a comic imitation of a man removing bucketfuls of sweat from his forehead. He screwed up his monkey face at John.

"You know, S'arnt, we're in the wrong business. It'd be a damn sight easier and a whole lot safer if we travelled with a wild animal act."

On the stage Nella looked reproachfully at Tom. Why was he so silly? What made him blunder about fighting battles for her that she never wanted fought?

"Why are you being so angry, Tom? Dad and Uncle John were quite right; dancing is what I do."

Tom was back at the piano, hunched over the keys. Poor little innocent! Can't even see when the whole lot are trying to crush the spirit out of her.

"You sing that song fine. You'll bring the house down. It'll be in the evening bill before you know where you are, you see if it isn't. That's why they don't want you to do it. They want the evening bill kept for their precious selves."

Nella slipped off the piano and sprawled across it, so that her face was somewhere on a level with Tom's.

"Tom dear, that's not true. Nobody's trying to keep me out of anything, and please, Tom, promise me you won't try and get it put into the evening bill, I'd simply loathe it. Already I feel sick every night about 'Poppies for England'."

Tom played a crashing, angry chord.

"All right, if you don't care, I can't make you. If you like to believe all of them instead of me, then that's your look-out. I suppose they all know more about singing than I do."

Nella's heart contracted with compassion. Goodness, what an inferiority complex Tom had. No wonder he was difficult.

"I do think it's marvellous what you've done, Tom. I never would have sung at all except for you, and I do see that people like me singing 'Poppies for England', and of course you know more about singing than anyone else, because you're a musician. The only thing you're wrong about is thinking that I want to have a lot to do in the show. Truly I don't."

Tom spoke gently. He had to play softly while he spoke, because his inclination was to get up and take that serious, earnest little face, with its great eyes staring at him, in his hands and kiss her and kiss her until she had forgotten what they were arguing about; but Nella was not that sort of girl. She would be horrified if he did a thing like that.

"What you don't seem to know is that you're an artist. I know you say you don't want to sing, but that's because everybody has crushed the spirit out of you."

She could not leave things there, she must, somehow, get

this fancy picture of her out of his head. She started to speak, but before she had said a word Betty rushed on to the stage.

"I met Dad and Uncle Alfred and they said you were here. The post's come. There's a post-card for you, Nella, from Grandmother. She sent me one, too. There's a typed one for you, Tom. Oh, gosh! It's hot. I'm going for a hike. All along the beach, there's a prize for who gets the most different shells."

Nella glanced at her post-card.

"I never knew anybody so marvellously happy as Betty."

Tom made an absent grunt. He was reading his letter. He raised his eyes from it and looked at Nella consideringly. Then he laid it down and broke into "Mighty Like a Rose".

"Come on, you must get working."

Nella climbed on to the piano. She was not facing the theatre, but three-quarters towards Tom. She started to sing.

" 'Sweetest little fellow, everybody knows. Don't . . .' " She broke off, staring at the letter which Tom had put down. "Tom, that comes from F. J. Higgs' office. Has he written to say when he's coming down?"

Tom was staring at the keyboard.

"Don't be inquisitive and get on with your practice."

"But, Tom, if he's coming it's not inquisitive, it's everybody's business."

He shrugged his shoulders.

"My private letters aren't everybody's business."

Once more she leant towards him.

"Tom, dear Tom, don't be so prickly. You take everything

that anybody says as if it were something to row about. I'm not inquisitive, but if F. J. Higgs is coming, everybody'll want to know. Dad and Uncle John will want to make up a special programme, and Aunt Alice will want to do something to the dresses . . ."

His fingers rang savagely up a scale.

"And you'll want Dulcie to sing 'Poppies for England'."

"I won't. If you know that F. J. Higgs is coming, and will go round and tell everybody about it, I'll sing 'Poppies for England' without one more word, though I'll hate every minute and probably have a bilious attack for days before."

A look flashed across Tom's face, a look which said, "I bet you would, too." It was followed by a protective smile. Nothing was going to drag news out of him that would worry poor little Nella. He would be crazy to let out something which might spoil her performance. He couldn't lie to her, there was something about Nella's honest grey eyes which made lying difficult.

"Has it never struck you, you silly little thing, that F. J. Higgs pays me my salary." He extracted a cheque from the envelope and laid it on top of the letter.

Nella was all contrition.

"Oh, Tom, I am sorry. It was terribly impertinent of me to interfere with your letters, but I do so want everybody to like you, and you can't pretend that some of the family don't think our singing lessons a bit secret." She saw the sulky look on his face, the small-boy look that she could never resist. She hurried on. "You and I know how it happened, but I don't think they do quite. Please don't be angry with me, Tom."

He felt a cad. To hide it he spoke gruffly.

" Are we going to rehearse this song, or aren't we?"

* * *

Dulcie and Pinkie were having a before-lunch cocktail. They were sitting out of doors. Dulcie stretched her legs in front of her. She looked towards the theatre and laughed.

"Listen to Tom. Those two in there practising! Nella knows that song perfectly, but they've been at it all the morning. Sooner her than me on a day like this."

A porter came out to them.

"You're wanted on the telephone, Miss Corner. It's a London call."

Dulcie gave Pinkie her drink to hold and went to the telephone.

"Hullo, Who? Mr. Higgs' office; yes, I'll hold on. Is that you, Miss Grey? Saturday week? You are an angel. Nobody's let me know. What? He does? Well, if he knows he hasn't told me. He can only have got the letter this morning? Oh! Yes, I dare say he'll tell us later in the day. Thanks for the tip, anyway, good-bye."

She put down the receiver and sauntered smilingly back towards Pinkie. As she sat down Nella and Tom came out of the stage door. She pointed to them.

"Ask them over for a drink. I don't believe you've stood them a drink since we've been here."

Pinkie got up to fetch them.

"Nella only drinks lemonade and Tom doesn't seem to drink at all. Still, far be it from me to interfere with your sweetness and light programme."

Nella, painfully conscious that she had spent the morning rehearsing another song, came over to Dulcie shyly. Dulcie greeted her with a radiant smile.

"Darling, I hear you're going to sing 'Mighty Like a Rose'. We heard the accompaniment from here; of course, we couldn't hear you as there wasn't a microphone. But I'm sure you'll be divine." She looked at Tom. "Oughtn't it to go into the evening bill?"

Torn gazed at her sulkily. Now what was she up to?

Pinkie broke an awkward silence.

"Lemonade, I know, for you, Nella. What'll you have, Tom?" He saw the way Dulcie was looking at Tom and added: "Better make it a Guinness, gives you strength."

Tom scarcely heard the question about his drink. He accepted that it would be a Guinness with the briefest nod. His mind was working furiously. It would be better if Nella sang a second song. It might be that F. J. would think it was the song and not the singer if she only sang the once. Already he had decided that "Poppies for England" would have to be moved to the beginning of the programme. News of who was in front seemed to reach actors and actresses by some kind of tom-tom system. Nella must sing it when she was not nervous. He sat beside Dulcie.

"It would be a good idea if she had something in both parts. I rather think 'Poppies for England' would be better in the first half."

Dulcie finished her drink thoughtfully. The first half! That was what he was playing at. Wanted his little star to shine early on so that she wouldn't be nervous. A picture of an evening came into her mind. It was all she could do not to giggle. She turned sweet, limpid eyes on Tom.

"Why not? I'll go and speak to Dad about it right away. Take my glass, Pinkie."

Tom gaped at Dulcie's retreating back. Nella looked after her almost with awe. She turned to Pinkie.

"I do think Dulcie's generous."

Pinkie took her lemonade and Tom's Guinness from the waiter. "Poor babes in the wood," he thought. Out loud he said:

"Dulcie is a girl whom I should describe in every way as a dear little thing."

* * *

Pinkie was in his office. Saturday was a busy day for him, campers departing, campers arriving. On this Saturday his mind was not entirely on his work. Things were going on and, moreover, things which he knew nothing about. Apart from his job as the man in charge of entertainments, Pinkie had a natural curiosity which made him dislike things going on which he knew nothing about. What was Dulcie up to? These last days she had been avoiding him and, when she did meet him; she talked very fast about a great many things which meant nothing at all. Now why? Why had Tom come to him and asked to have one seat reserved for Saturday night? He had asked for a good seat and had not said who it was for. Any of the artists could ask for seats. Why not? But somehow it was queer the way Tom had done it. Funny, thought Pinkie. I like the fellow, but when he came in about that seat he looked furtive. Like a type in a film who's trying to bury a body in a garage. Above all the other points to distract Pinkie's mind was Dulcie as a person. He had always sworn he was never going to get serious about anybody after his trouble with Annabel, yet here he was thinking of Dulcie morning, noon and, above all, at night. Queer how he could be in such a state about Dulcie, for he wasn't fooled about her. If ever a double-crossing little so-and-so walked, it was Dulcie. "Queer thing," he mused, "I like her for it. Fancy me falling for somebody that I know is a double-crossing little so-and-so!"

He had been working for half an hour when the telephone bell rang. His father's voice barked at him over the line.

"Want two good seats for to-night."

Pinkie was surprised.

"To-night? Thought you were in the north."

"Speaking from London. Don't waste time and money askin' silly questions about where I am. Now, listen, and don't talk."

Pinkie listened. As he listened his eyes grew rounder and rounder. At the end he said:

"But can't I tell Dulcie?"

"You get more of a fool every day. You can't. I want him to see her just as she is every night, no special performance with frills on it. She's not to be told. That's an order."

Pinkie thought of Dulcie's queer behaviour the last few days.

"Are you sure she doesn't know already?"

One of his father's best snorts came over the phone. It hurt the drum of Pinkie's ear.

"Damn it, boy, I've been angling for this for weeks. Come back from the north on a mere chance. He only got back from America yesterday, and I only knew last night. How do you think she knows?"

Pinkie rubbed his ear, which was still tingling.

"What time are you coming?"

"Just before the show. Have drinks and stuff waitin'." With a click the receiver was down.

Pinkie went back to his desk. Angrily he dragged forward some papers he had to sign. All this secrecy, we ought to be Scotland Yard. The door opened and the secretary came in.

"You wanted to see me. I'm afraid I'm a bit late, but there seems something queer with the printing press."

Pinkie pointed to a chair.

"If you ask me there's something queer with the whole works this morning. Do you ever get hunches about a day? I've got a feeling this is going to be a very rum Saturday. Now, look, what I was going to tell you was that I wanted a seat kept for a friend of Tom Pollard's. Now I've had a telephone call from my father. He wants two seats kept for him. Better put them together. Those three in the centre of the circle, but nobody is to know my father's coming. That clear?"

* * *

It had been a lovely day, the *Here's Fun* company were in good spirits. There was a lot of talk and laughter as they made up. Only Tom and Dulcie were not their usual selves.

Tom was acutely nervous. F. J. Higgs had said he might be a minute or two late. Thanks to Dulcie "Poppies for England" now came half way through the first half of the programme, and "Mighty Like a Rose" half way through the second half. Suppose F. J.'s car broke down. Suppose he missed hearing "Poppies for England." Of course it could be done privately for him afterwards, but that was a different thing to seeing its reactions on an audience. Very different for Nella. He wanted F. J. to see the light come up on her crimson frock, and the effect of her queer, serious little face on the audience. He wanted him to hear the hush that came over the theatre, and the crack of the applause as she danced off at the end. There was something there for F. J. to see, he was convinced, something rare and unusual. In another moment came the opposite wave of feeling. Of course he was right about Nella, but was he right about the song? Was it as sure-fire as everybody thought? What a hell of a thing if he had brought F. J. down to hear that song and told him that he ought to have an eye on the girl who sang it, and all the old man said was that it stank, or something like that. What on earth would he say to Nella if he had boosted the poor little kid up into thinking that when F. J. came he would like the song, and the whole thing fell flat?

Dulcie was in a hard, brittle mood. As she made-up she hummed. There was no one to mind her humming, and yet she hummed as though in defiance of voices which cried, "No, no. You can't do that, Dulcie. You can't."

Alice brought in her frock.

"There, dear, I've done it up as you asked. I can't find

anything wrong with it. I've freshened up the tarlatan, but it didn't really need it."

Dulcie swung round.

"I said it was to be renewed."

Alice hesitated.

"Not all new. There's some new tulle at the top, the tarlatan was perfectly fresh."

Dulcie got up, and went to the dress. She picked it up and examined it. She could find nothing wrong with it. This made her the more annoyed.

"Nobody ever does anything I want in this theatre. I didn't say would you add a bit of tulle. I said the whole thing was to be renewed."

Alice wished that Dulcie was still of an age when she could give her salts in the morning. Must be out of sorts. There was nothing wrong with the frock.

Dulcie turned the frock upside down, the lemon and orange tu-tu fell backwards. It looked like some giant yellow daisy. It was exquisitely pressed, and in perfect order.

"You've been in the wardrobe all the week, what on earth were you doing?"

Alice took up Dulcie's comb and brush.

"Let me do your hair. It's getting fairer than ever with this sun." To herself she thought, "For all she's so sweet to her I'd better not tell her I've been busy with Nella's dress." It was Tom who had drawn her attention to Nella's frock. It had come in for a stitch, and was hanging beside Dulcie's in the dressing-room. Tom had run his hands under Dulcie's frills and had said, "I wish Nella's stuck out like that." Alice had been feeling bad about Nella and Tom ever since her talk with John. Maybe they were in the early stages of falling in love. That funny, incoherent stage. In Tom, standing there admiring Dulcie's dress, she had seen the young John. Of course she had never worn a ballet frock or anything like it, but if John had seen something pretty on one of his sisters he would have been likely enough to have said, "I wish Alice had a frock like that." The equivalent really to Tom's, "I wish Nella's stuck out like that." She had smiled at Tom. "So it can. I'll make the frock over." Tom had lingered. "Will it take very long?" She had laughed inwardly at that. He was impatient, of course, to see Nella in it. She wouldn't look different, but Tom would think she did. She had said, "I can have it ready next week if I work at it." Tom had looked strangely embarrassed, and then touchingly anxious. "Would it be ready by Saturday?" She had laughed. "Saturday, without fail." It was the next day that Dulcie had demanded an entirely new tu-tu. She could not have it. Alice had not got the material; she would have to send away for it. She had not told Dulcie outright she couldn't have it. No good meeting trouble half way, besides, with a few new frills it would be as good as new. Now, combing Dulcie's hair, she was faced with her slight dishonesty. Pity Nella was wearing her new ballet underskirt tonight. Dulcie had eyes like a hawk, and was certain to spot the difference. She finished combing Dulcie's hair and then said gently:

"Put the frock on before you scold your old Mum. If you can see anything wrong with it then I'll send away for the stuff next week."

Dulcie stepped into her frock. Alice fastened it down the back. As she did up the hooks she noticed a tautness about the girl, it was as if, she thought, she had stiffened up to dive, or something of the sort. "Queer, I wonder what's wrong." Then her mind turned to Pinkie. Of course John would call her an old match-maker, but could there be anything in that? Dulcie had been looking tired and jumpy these last few days, come to think of it. Making up your mind over a man made you tired and jumpy. That would be it. She gave Dulcie a kiss.

"Now look in the glass, pet. Anything wrong with that?"

Dulcie looked at her slim, radiant image. There was a lump in her throat, she wanted to cry, she wanted to be a child again, and sit on her mother's knee, and confess. In those days when you confessed a thing the world became serene again. She twitched at her skirt, and turned half on to the mirror, then her eyes hardened. Fastened into Alice's frock was a needle, and from it hung a long, crimson thread. Dulcie gave the thread a little pull.

"Been busy with Nella's frock, have you? No wonder you hadn't time for mine."

Alice looked guiltily at the thread.

"You know that isn't true. I've done all I could to your frock. There isn't any more stuff in the place, I'll have to send away for it."

Dulcie laughed, a queer, sharp, hard laugh.

"I don't mind. Let Nella have a brand new dress for all I care. I think it's rather a good idea." She giggled and added to herself, "She'll need her looks."

"There," said Alice, thankful for the diversion, "there's

Tom striking up." She went to the door. "You're being very silly, darling. You look lovely, and you know it."

In the dress circle Pinkie mopped his forehead. Here was a pretty set-up. Tom bringing F. J. Higgs down on the quiet. What on earth was Dulcie going to say? If only he could get round and tell her. How like the old man to say, "Sit there and don't move, I may want you." Might have known there were funny goings-on. Or did he know? He was a sharp old soul, he well might. Tom's overture was coming to an end, the curtains rose on the company. Dulcie, sitting on her boxes raised above the others, looked superb. Old Barrow turned to his guest, who was smoking a cigar.

"There she is. Lovely, isn't she?" He got a snort equal to any that he could give himself."

"Letmeseesomethin', letmeseesomethin'. Beauts are two a penny. What I want is the whole works."

On Mr. Barrow's other side F. J. Higgs settled back in his seat. He looked at all the company with approval, then he leant over to Pinkie.

"I suppose the girl in red is Miss Nella Binns."

Pinkie nodded. To himself he said, "So that's it! Oh, boy, oh, boy! The best place for you, Pinkie, when the curtain comes down is locked in your office with a guard on the door."

Unlike all other theatres the Barrow's camp audiences were most difficult on Saturday nights. The campers had only arrived that day. They did not know the company by sight, they had not begun to feel possessive about them as they would by next week, when they would say, "Our concert party." This Saturday they were an easy audience.

Lovely weather had greeted them. From arriving hot, dusty townspeople by mid-afternoon they were relaxed holiday-makers, splashing in and out of the bathing pool or sitting in chairs watching the bathers, the men in open shirts and flannel trousers, their wives in summer frocks or slacks, and the girls in sun suits. By the evening, full of Comstock air, they had almost forgotten the clanging, queuing, rushing world outside the camp. They were given over to a holiday mood, those who had tickets for the evening show were the lucky ones, a concert party was the right way to round off the first day by the sea.

Alfred and John, coming off after their first comedy number, raised their thumbs to each other. "The tops, aren't they, S'arnt?" "You've said it, Corp." Betty with her numbers was being whistled for by the boys at the back after her third entrance; Dickie's first patter dance went over with a bang; Muriel got an ovation for "My Little Grey Home in the West." She came off beaming, and ran into Dulcie.

"Lovely they are to-night, dear. Never knew them better." Dulcie gave a vague smile, but did not seem to have heard. Funny, thought Muriel, looks kind of strung up somehow. Wonder what about.

When Dulcie had talked her father into putting "Mighty Like a Rose" into the second half of the programme, she had arranged a switch of her own numbers. She wanted "Good night, George" in the second half and "She Danced in Piccadilly" to come immediately after "Poppies for England" in the first half. Neither John nor Alfred liked this lay-out.

"Putting our best stuff rather close together," Alfred said to John. "We don't want 'Poppies for England' on too early before the audience has settled down."

Dulcie's reasons seemed clear enough to John, as he supposed they were to Alfred. She wanted "She Danced in Piccadilly" to come after "Poppies for England" so that she could take the shine out of Nella. Tiresome of her though he thought it was, theatrically it was reasonable enough. She was the star, and any star wanted the lay-out so arranged that all their best numbers came at the most advantageous spots on the programme. All the same, he wished she had not asked for the switch over. She had been generous about Nella, generous as the old Dulcie that he had known before 1940. It was a pity to spoil things.

"Better put our 'Private Jones, Private Brown' number between 'Poppies' and 'Piccadilly'," he suggested. "It's our best sure-fire laugh, and will just give us time to change back into our concert party costumes before the finale to the first half." The new lay-out had been tried earlier in the week. It worked all right, though Dulcie did not get the applause for "She Danced in Piccadilly" which she had got in her old place on the programme. Before, it had been the best charming dancing number, and took all the thunder. Now the audience's hands were sore from clapping "Poppies for England." After two nights of the changed programme John said to Alfred, "Suits us all right. 'Private Jones, Private Brown' never went better. Just the place for that sort of comedy number, but I should think Dulcie would want the lay-out changed again before the week's out."

Alfred murmured, "Shouldn't wonder." He had not looked directly at John, there was no need to. They both knew what was implied. It was a surprise to them that they reached Saturday night with Dulcie apparently quite contented with the new lay-out as it was.

Betty came on with number four on a card, Dulcie's first solo. It was an old song of Rose Reilly's, "Fancy That!" A point number with a great many laughs. It was not an easy number for Dulcie. She got it over by her blue-eyed innocence. It seemed doubtful as the double-edged lines fell from her lips if the little darling could really know what she was singing about. Rose Reilly was an actress who could convulse the house by a half-lift of one eyebrow. It was an acknowledged fact that nobody could put over a Rose Reilly number as she did.

Dulcie came down stage centre. She folded her hands in front of her like a small girl about to recite. A gold spot fell on her, she looked amazingly lovely, and an expectant and hopeful hush fell over the theatre. In the theatre Leonard Barrow leant across F. J. Higgs to speak to Pinkie.

"Why's she doin' this? Thought she sang 'Good night, George' here."

Pinkie whispered.

"The programme is often changed. 'Good night, George' is coming in the second half."

F. J. Higgs said to no one in particular.

"Couldn't touch 'Good night, George'."

Leonard Barrow snorted.

"Not Rose, of course, you found a genius when you found Rose, but you wait." He turned to his other guest. "Was

I right? Is she a looker?"

He was greeted by a snort even louder than his own.

"Looks are three a penny. I want the works."

Whatever Leonard Barrow's party might think, the audience adored Dulcie. Audiences vary from night to night, some are easy laughers, some prefer the romantic moments, some are slow and some are quick. This Saturday night audience was a quick-minded audience. A funny point number was just their cup of tea. They thought Dulcie, standing there as exquisite and innocent as a buttercup, putting over rather doubtful lines, irresistibly funny. She left the stage amidst a roar of applause. Betty bounced on announcing number five, which was Dan. Then the whole company were on in their nursery rhyme number. Seven was a sketch with Dulcie as a mannequin, eight a funny song from John and Alfred. Then Betty came on with number nine and the lights dimmed. Slowly they came up on Nella. The stage was flooded with its patches of crimson light, Tom played the opening chords, softly the refrain of "Poppies for England" slipped into the theatre. The audience, who had been rocking and mopping their eyes at John and Alfred, sat back. There was a charmed silence. Nella looked earnestly in the direction of the bust of the King, and half sang, half spoke her opening lines:

"He said, if it's flowers you are wearing -
Will you please wear a poppy for me."

F. J. Higgs stiffened. He was an old hand in the theatre, not easily carried away, but there was something here. He knew it from the opening bars.

Leonard Barrow looked round in a pleased way at the rapt faces of the audience. He had said they would like this song and they were liking it. He was always pleased to find he was right.

Pinkie relaxed. No doubt there would be the hell of a rumpus afterwards, these big-wigs in front with, as far as he knew, Dulcie knowing nothing about it. Still, nobody, not even Dulcie, could say the show could have gone better than it was going. He had never heard her put over "Fancy That!" so well, it needed a bite which she had not usually got. She had it to-night all right.

There was something wrong. Tom was still playing, but Nella had stopped singing, or rather she had stopped being heard. She was still opening and shutting her mouth, but not a sound reached anybody beyond the front two rows. The audience grew restive, someone said, "Sing up, dear." Somebody else laughed. Other voices said, "The mike's gone wrong, what a shame!"

There is something unutterably ludicrous about an opening and shutting mouth through which no sound comes. It was like watching a film when the sound track is out of action. Nobody meant to be unkind, but the audience could not help itself. It giggled, the giggles became laughs, the laughs roars. Behind the scenes there was confusion. John and Alfred were half changed into their uniforms for the next number, they sent Dickie and Dan round to join the stage hands and see what had gone wrong with the mike. On the stage Tom, of course, knew in a second what was wrong. The lead of the microphone was plugged in outside the wardrobe. He looked across to see if someone had tripped over it. In a split second he saw, from the corner of his eye, the flick of a yellow skirt. His eyes blazed, then he turned his attention to Nella.

"Cut the song, we'll go into the dance." He took his hands off the piano and began the dance refrain. "Cut the song, we'll go into the dance."

Nella was past hearing Tom, the piano or anything else. This was the sort of thing that happened in a bad dream. She had always said she couldn't sing, well, now everybody knew it. Oh, listen to the audience! They were giggling at her, they were laughing at her, they were roaring at her. Oh, poor Tom! His lovely song. It never crossed her mind to stop trying to sing. Tom had said he wanted her to sing the song, doggedly she went on.

John and Alfred, pulling on their trousers and buttoning their khaki tunics, were in the wings.

"The mike's gone, Tom. Cut to the dance."

Tom had his hands off the piano. There was such a noise in the theatre it did not matter how loudly he spoke.

"I can't stop her."

Muriel came as near the piano as possible without coming on to the stage.

"Dance, Nella dear, dance, the mike's wrong."

By now the audience could see Tom's despairing face, and the anxious face and bits of gesticulating Muriel, and the laughter rose to a crescendo. Tom could bear no more, he got up, picked Nella off the piano and literally pushed her off the stage.

John and Alfred were too old hands in the theatre game

to be put off by a microphone going wrong or a house out of hand. They did not need a microphone, nor did Dulcie, and it could be mended in the interval, but they made capital out of the accident. Alfred opening and shutting his mouth when he came on, and John saying to the audience, "Doesn't Private Jones sing nice?" They were not helped by Tom who, though back at the piano, was off his form. He was not following the comedians in his usual faultless way, he was looking off-stage towards the microphone with eyes that burned and smouldered, his mouth a grim line.

In no time John and Alfred had the audience in hand. It was a pity about "Poppies for England", but there were other nights. They went off amidst plenty of applause, perfectly happy. Dulcie was next. "She Danced in Piccadilly" was always a riot.

Betty came on with number eleven, the lights dimmed, the stage hands pushed on the figure of Eros, Dulcie sat down on the steps, her basket at her feet, her shawl hugged round her, the lights came up slowly, "Vi'lets, lovely vi'lets." She started to sing.

John and Alfred were in their dressing-room changing. Dickie, Dan, Muriel, Betty and the stage hands were gathered round the microphone lead. Nobody was attending to what was happening on the stage. Nobody noticed that Tom was playing the song in another key and to a new tempo. Dulcie struggled. She tried to change the key. She tried to change the tempo. Then, in despair, she spoke the lines. Tom was ready for that, he had powerful hands, he crashed out the tune, drowning her voice. She gave up. She flung aside her shawl, pulled off her hat and, discarding the second verse of her song, began to dance. She had to improvise, but she looked lovely in her brown and yellow frock and could have managed something, but Tom was waiting for her. If she pirouetted, he swung the tune, if she posed he played fast, if she broke into a few fast steps he played slow chords. She was beaten. She looked, she knew, unrehearsed and awkward, her charm and beauty could not help her now. There was almost no applause and she left the stage.

Alfred and John burst out of their dressing-room. "What happened? Is the number over?"

Dulcie was in such a tearing rage she could hardly speak.

"It is, and you can do your finale without me. Send Tom to my dressing-room the moment the curtain's down."

By superhuman effort the rest of the company got the finale over. The audience were restive, the fine, gay mood of the evening had been dispelled, nobody could help the mike going wrong, that had been an accident, but the queer, muddled number they had just seen had meant nothing. In theatrical parlance, Dulcie had let the audience drop. It was hard work for everybody to get them back. As the curtain came down Alfred mopped his forehead. Then he turned to Tom.

"Whatever went wrong with 'Piccadilly'?"

Muriel tugged at his arm.

"The microphone was cut, it was deliberate, the stage hands say."

Alfred gave her a nudge with his elbow. If the microphone was deliberately cut during Nella's song, only one person would have done it. What was to be done or said would have to be gone into, but the less said at the moment the better. If Muriel started saying the microphone had been cut, the next step would be her saying that Dulcie had cut it, and, though that was probably true, they did not want Alice and Muriel at each other's throats, which they certainly would be. He turned to Tom.

"We'll get the microphone mended. You go to Dulcie, she wants to see you in her dressing-room."

Tom got up from his piano seat. He had nobody's feelings to consider, he did not care who flew at whose throat. He was in a blinding rage. It was sickening enough that Dulcie had ruined "Poppies for England" with F. J. Higgs in front, but it was nothing to the fact that she had ruined Nella's song, and got Nella laughed off the stage.

"And I want to see Dulcie. She'll be lucky if she's fit to come on in the second half when I'm finished with her, the dirty little bitch."

Dulcie, a flame of scarlet showing on her cheeks through her make-up, was standing by her dressing-table. She started to speak as Tom came into her room.

"Shut the door."

He shut it and came towards her.

She said:

"This is the last time you'll play in this theatre. I'm telling my father and Uncle Alfred after the show, either you go or I do. And I know who they'll choose."

Tom clenched his fists. He had never in his life hit a woman, but he had to control himself not to hit Dulcie. His voice was almost a whisper.

"All right, but you can hear a thing or two. You deliberately ruined Nella's song. What that poor little kid's ever done to you, I don't know. You've done your best to crush her from the beginning. You're jealous, that's what it is. You know in your silly, miserable little soul that she's got more talent in her little finger than you have in your whole body. You're scared of her, that's what it is, but however scared you were, I never thought you were capable of a mean, dirty trick like that."

Dulcie's voice rose to a scream.

"Mean, dirty trick! What about what you did to 'She Danced in Piccadilly', ruining my song with F. J. Higgs in front."

Tom let out a great breath.

"Ah! So that was it. You knew he was in front. That's what all this altering of the programme meant. I thought it was funny. You meant to have her number laughed off the stage, you meant to scoop all the applause for 'She Danced in Piccadilly'. Well, things didn't work out that way, the audience understood about her, they knew the mike had gone wrong, but you looked like some unrehearsed amateur."

Dulcie gave a kind of howl and flung herself at him, beating him with her fists.

"I know I did, and it was your fault, you beast, you beast."

He gripped her by the elbows.

"Stand still, you little hell-cat, and hear what I've got to say. I'm going to do the same all through the second half. I'm going to make a laughing-stock of every one of your numbers. You wait till you see what I can do with 'Good night, George '."

Dulcie ceased to struggle.

"You wouldn't. Tom, you can't."

He gripped her tighter than ever.

"I can, and I will, you watch."

She stared at him, her eyes terror-struck.

"Tom, you can't. This may ruin my whole future."

"You should have thought of that before you ruined Nella's numbers."

"Nella. Always Nella."

"And why not Nella?" Suddenly words came from him that he hardly knew he felt. "I love Nella."

She seemed to slip in his hands. Suddenly she was crying.

"I know you do, that's what I can't bear. I wanted you to love me. I've always wanted it since the first time I saw you."

He gave her a shake.

"Love! You don't know the meaning of the word. You've never loved anyone in your life except Dulcie Corner. You've got to have everybody following you around, you've got one of the nicest men God ever put breath into trailing after you, but that isn't enough, you want everybody. The only reason you want me is because I'm not interested in you."

Dulcie gaped at him, tears dripping off her nose.

"Do you know, I think that's true. At least, it's partly true. I don't know what I feel about you. When you came in I hated you, now I don't feel anything. Nothing at all."

"You'll hate me again all right before the curtain's come down."

In a flash she had taken her mind from her personal affairs, and was back in the theatre. She choked back her sobs.

"Tom, you can't ruin all my numbers. There's the audience to think about."

"I'm not thinking about anything but what you've done to Nella." She pulled away from him.

"Let me go. I've thought of something." She went to her dressing-table and tidied her face. When she turned again to Tom there was a calmness and a strength about her that he had never seen before. "All right, I did cut the microphone. I did ruin Nella's song, and you ruined mine. I'm going to father. I'm going to tell him what I did, and I'm going to ask him to let me go out to the audience and tell them that the muddle with the microphone was my fault, and that they mustn't miss 'Poppies for England,' so it's going to open the second half. Will that satisfy you?"

He gazed at her.

"You wouldn't do that."

"I will, and we'll give as good a second half, to make up for the bad first half, as we can give." She faced him. "Friends?"

He saw she was sincere, that there was no intention in her mind to cheat. He held her by the shoulders and gave her a shake.

"You're the most awful little cad, but if you'll do that I'll play your numbers straight. Friends." He kissed her. "Go on, get on with it."

* * *

From the moment when the microphone had broken down in Nella's number Pinkie had said, "Here we go. This is it. That's Dulcie doing her stuff." Out of the corner of his eye he looked at F. J. Higgs. F. J. Higgs had come a long way to hear "Poppies for England." In an exceedingly busy life it meant rearranging quite a number of things to fit in this appointment. Miss Grey, his secretary, had been planning this trip to Comstock for weeks. He had heard the telephone ringing, and Miss Grey's precise voice, "No, not that week-end. Mr. Higgs has an important engagement in the country." "No, Mr. Higgs won't be in London that Saturday. He has an important fixture on the coast." "Don't you dare let anyone talk you out of Saturday's engagement at Comstock," Miss Grey had said to him. "I've had enough trouble fixing it, and I don't want to start all over again." "I've not a great deal of stuff that it's worth while your coming to hear," Tom Pollard had written, "but there are two songs, 'She Danced in Piccadilly' and 'He Met Her at Waterloo,' which are Dulcie Corner's numbers, but the best I've done so far is called 'Poppies for England.' I would be glad if you could find time to come and hear that. It's put over by a girl called Nella Binns, I want you to hear her, she's a great find, I think."

Well, here was "Poppies for England," and here was Nella Binns, and here was a trip all mucked up by a blasted microphone. Years in the theatre had made F. J. Higgs philosophical. The curtains came down at the wrong places on first nights, leading ladies sprained their ankles or had babies, young discoveries, who had just begun to make good, were lured into the films. He was inured to disappointment. He would have to hear Tom Pollard's song after the show. Pity. He could tell so much better how a song went if he could hear it with an audience. As far as the girl was concerned he couldn't see it mattered much. Funny little thing with her brown hair and her earnest face. Probably could have put the song over quite nicely if he could have heard it, but she didn't seem to have much personality, certainly no technique. Queer a daughter of Alfred Binns knowing so little about the stage that she could sit there opening and shutting her mouth, when she must have known that not a sound could be heard, and the audience were rocking with laughter. He turned to Leonard Barrow.

"Bad luck, the microphone going."

Leonard Barrow was annoyed. In his camps things shouldn't break down. He growled.

"Pity. Best song in the show."

It was not till Dulcie had started "She Danced in Piccadilly" that the party in the dress circle knew that something was really wrong. Pinkie was the first to get on to it. He knew "She Danced in Piccadilly" so well he could have sung it himself. He did, in fact, sing it to himself in his bath every morning. From the first wrong note that Tom struck he sat up briskly like a terrier after a rat. With eyes goggling he watched Dulcie's brave, but hopeless, effort to compete with the piano. He watched her give up the struggle and lose her charm, and, instead, throw blasting glances at Tom. With a mixture of pity and thankfulness he saw her exit before an almost silent audience.

F. J. Higgs tugged at his ear, his eyes twinkling. He said

quietly:

"As pretty an exhibition of tempers on the stage as I've ever seen. Didn't know young Pollard had it in him." Then he scowled. "Shocking behaviour." He turned to Pinkie as if it was his fault. "Actors are in the theatre to serve the audience, private quarrels should be kept for the dressing-room."

Leonard Barrow was furious. With the utmost difficulty he had got his guest to the theatre. He had sworn that time and trouble taken to see Dulcie would be rewarded. Now look what had happened! Although she had been charming in the beginning of the programme she had not registered. The guest had murmured "Letmeseesomethin', letmeseesomethin'." He should have seen something in "She Danced in Piccadilly." Dulcie was charming in it. Now, for no reason at all, look what she had done. Messed it up, looked a shocking failure. He clenched his hands and scowled. What was he going to say to his guest when the curtain came down? Bound to blame him. Probably think he was a besotted old idiot who was interested in the girl. He would never believe now that there really was talent.

The guest had slumped in his seat, bowed with boredom, from the time the curtain went up. He hated concert parties, he loathed cross-talk comedians, he thought Muriel Binns a museum piece, he thought the whole entertainment something out of Noah's Ark. He was busy, important and immensely influential. As it happened Leonard Barrow was busy, important and immensely influential, but he was also very canny. When he had said, "Come to Comstock, it's going to be worth while, I've got something there for you," he believed him. His heart had fallen like a stone when the something for him had proved to be yet another fair, doll-like beauty. God! How he hated fair, doll-like beauties ogling at him, and trying to attract his attention. He watched Dulcie's entrances and exits with eyes glazed with ennui. "Oh, Lord!" he prayed, "give me strength to endure this evening, give me strength." Then it seemed that his prayer was heard. A miracle happened. A dyed-in-the-wool, sheer, glorious miracle. The fair doll, about to perform yet another of her pretty little songs and pretty little dances, suddenly came to life. She started off by being a doll, a peculiarly tiresome doll with a black hat, and a shawl round her. She was singing, though remarkably badly. Then suddenly the stage had gone, artificiality had gone, and a living, blazing girl appeared in her place. There was no knowing what might be the trouble between herself and the good-looking pianist, but trouble there clearly was. Her eyes flamed, her fingers curved, ready to become claws and scratch, her body was electric, every moment it seemed she might pounce on the pianist and strangle him. As Dulcie danced off into the wings the guest lay back with a replete sigh. He dug Leonard in the ribs with his elbow.

"You're right, old boy, you're right. Haveweseen-somethin'! Oh, haveweseensomethin'?"

The guest was for going round behind the scenes in the interval to meet Dulcie. F. J. Higgs thought it would not be a bad idea to have a word with Tom Pollard. Leonard Barrow wanted to be sure the microphone was mended. Pinkie forestalled them all. Whatever they might think he had no illusions as to what was going on behind the scenes.

The day when Dulcie broke her grease paints would be nothing to it. He thought it was very unlikely she would appear in the second half, she was quite possibly half way to London by now. He had not heard his father's guest's pleased exclamations, and would not have believed them if he had. The evening was a fiasco, a bloody awful mess. There was going to be a hell of a row all round. The theatre was probably being torn to pieces even now behind the scenes. At all events the old man's party must be kept out of the way. He looked his father firmly in the eye.

"I've drinks, cigars and sandwiches waiting, Dad. They'll mend the microphone, they're far more conscious of what's gone wrong than we are."

It was seldom that Pinkie spoke so seriously or sternly to his father. It made the old man blink. There certainly was more in the boy than he had supposed. Evidently properly shocked by the mess-up there on the stage, and so he ought to be. All the same, Leonard Barrow wasn't too annoyed. Somehow or other Dulcie's atrocious performance in "She Danced in Piccadilly" was what his guest wanted to see.

"Well, lead the way then, Pinkie." He turned to his guests. "Anything we want to say to the company can wait until the end of the show."

The microphone cable had been mended, but the company had not recovered. John, Alfred, Dan, Dickie, Betty, Nella, Muriel and Alice were on the stage. They were not saying anything. They had gathered there officially to watch the microphone being mended. They were too shocked to talk. Nobody had the faintest illusion as to what had happened. Dulcie had taken a knife or a pair of scissors and deliberately hacked through the microphone lead, and ruined Nella's song. It was appalling. The Corners stood in one group, the Binns in the other. Suddenly Muriel could stand it no longer. Half crying she ran to Alice.

"Don't look like that, dear. You mustn't. It won't make any difference between us."

Alfred crossed to John.

"She's right, S'arnt. Not that you ever thought it would."

One of the two stage hands came over to John and Alfred.

"Did you know Mr. Barrow, Mr. F. J. Higgs and somebody else they say is very important was in front to-night?"

Alfred looked at John and John at Alfred. This was the end.

"Do you think she knew?" Alfred asked. John shook his head.

"Don't ask me, Corp, a jealous woman might do anything, even ruin her own show." He looked towards Dulcie's dressing-room door. "They're in there together having it out. It's a good thing or I'd be in there saying something to her that I'd probably be sorry for."

Dulcie's dressing-room door opened. Tom and Dulcie came out. The company on the stage gazed at them in silence. Dulcie threw up her chin and squared her shoulders. She marched straight across the stage to her father.

"Dad, I cut the microphone to spite Nella. Tom mucked up my song to spite me. We've given a lousy first half to the show, we want to give the best we've got in the second half. Can I go in front of the curtain, apologize to them, and tell them that we're opening with 'Poppies for England'?"

Nella gave a wail.

"Oh, no, Dulcie, I couldn't, not again to-night." Dulcie glanced at her over her shoulder.

"Oh, yes, you could, and you'll sing 'Mighty Like a Rose.' And you'll sing them well. F. J.'s in front. Tom wants him to hear you."

John had never liked his daughter more. He had to say something to break the nervous tension. He gave her an affectionate pat on the backside.

"Mr. Higgs to you, how often am I to tell you not to call him F. J.?"

Tom came forward.

"What about 'She Danced in Piccadilly' Dulcie? Are you doing that again?"

Dulcie shook her head.

"No, thank you. I wouldn't be seen dead doing that song again to-night, but I've got 'He Met Her at Waterloo' and 'Good night, George'." She looked at Tom. "I'm in the mood for 'Good night, George'." She turned to the others. "Let's give that crowd out there the best we've got. Thanks to me they've had a lousy first half."

Alfred put his arm round her.

"That's the girl! Tom, you'd better start your overture. Directly he's finished you go in front, Dulcie, and say your piece, then we'll dim out, and come up on Nella. Understood, everybody? Clear the stage."

* * *

The party in the dress circle were back in their seats, nourished with cheese sandwiches and whisky. The other side of the curtain Tom was playing the overture. Pinkie clasped his hands. "Bogles, bogeys and gremlins, hand out a miracle. Let the second half go well, and for goodness sake let Dulcie still be in the theatre." As if in answer the curtains parted, and Dulcie, collected, calm and smiling, stood in front of them. She spoke in a casual, intimate way.

"Ladies and gentlemen, we're so sorry about the microphone going wrong in the first half. Actually, it was my fault, so I've come to apologize. To-night we have with us Mr. Barrow and with him is Mr. F. J. Higgs." She was interrupted by a roar of applause. Everybody stared round, and told each other, "That's them in the front of the dress circle." Dulcie went on. "F. J. Higgs was my manager in London, and he released me to come here with my family, and he loaned us Tom Pollard, who has written most of the songs in this show. F. J. Higgs came down to-night especially to hear one song, 'Poppies for England' . . ." There was a light laugh, and she smiled back at the audience, "Yes, I know, it was funny as you heard it just now, but it isn't funny, it's a lovely song, and we don't want you to miss it, or Mr. Higgs to miss it, so we're putting it on again. You're going to hear it now." She moved to the side of the stage, "Nella Binns will sing 'Poppies for England' by Tom Pollard."

Behind the curtain Nella sat on the piano trembling. This was awful, she had been laughed off the stage once, she had spoilt Tom's lovely song, and now she was being made to do it again. She felt Tom's arms round her, Tom's face pressed to hers, Tom's lips against her mouth. At the end of the kiss he whispered, "Darling, I love you. Oh, darling!" As Dulcie's speech came to an end he was back on his music stool and, as the curtains rose, he said, "Not for the Monarch to-night, darling. Sing for me."

The audience sat back contentedly to listen. Dulcie's words had gone over well. It was fun that Mr. Barrow was in front. Every set of campers didn't meet Mr. Barrow. He was an almost legendary figure, flying from one of his camps to the other. It was nice to think they were going to see him in the flesh. Fancy F. J. Higgs in front, come all the way from London to hear this song. Must be worth hearing. They had not given it a fair chance when the mike went wrong.

Nella sat as if a lamp had been lit where her heart should be. "Darling," Tom had said, "I love you, darling." There was no audience, there was no F. J. Higgs, no Mr. Barrow, no microphone, she and Tom were the only people in the world, living in a tiny crimson glow made by a spotlight. It was a lovely song and he wanted to hear it. She leant forward, her brown hair falling straight each side of her face. Her queer, sexless voice, so much more like a wind instrument than a girl singing, slid into the theatre. The microphone carried it all over the house. Her happiness came through the whispered words and gave a magical quality to the evening. The older men in the audience were boys again, greasing their hair, putting a buttonhole in their coats to go out and meet their best girl, the older women forgot their grey hairs, and it was spring and they were prinking themselves up to dance with their best boy.

The boys and girls in the theatre drew closer together and held hands.

"He said, if it's the flowers you are wearing –
Will you please wear a poppy for me"

They were at the refrain. The sad little tune rose and fell. The words that had been said to a girl who now repeated them to herself,

"You ought to see the coast there
When the poppies are in bloom"

The audience were seeing it, crimson, flaming with poppies, not from a bomber as the boy had seen it and told his girl about it, but down on the ground in a holiday camp in the summer of 1946, when peace was creeping back into the world and into the heart. There were lumps in hundreds of throats and a mist before hundreds of eyes. When the song had finished Nella slipped off the piano. She was dancing for Tom, a ghost of a girl dancing through a field of poppies, stopping to pick an armful so that she could wear one for the boy who had said, "Will you please wear a poppy for me." The lights dimmed, Nella danced off the stage.

"Oh, boy! Has she got them," said Alfred, "has she got them!" He rushed on to the stage, he had the chorus on the card down, he was teaching the audience to sing, the roof was lifting, you could almost smell the poppies in the theatre.

"You ought to see the coast there
When the poppies are in bloom"

Old Barrow looked at F. J. Higgs. F. J. Higgs, hardened old theatrical producer, unashamedly cried. Leonard Barrow grinned at him.

"It's a winner. It's a winner. I spotted it was a winner first time I ever heard it."

F. J. mopped his eyes.

"It. You mean she."

It would have seemed impossible to catch the mood and the magic quality that Nella had created for the rest of the programme, but somehow it was done. John and Alfred had never been funnier, Dickie had never danced better, Muriel did not appear except for brief entrances in sketches, she had to be cut out of the second half to make room for "Poppies for England".

"Never mind," she said, "I'm part of it, and it's a wonderful evening that we shan't forget."

Dulcie had never been better than she was in "He Met Me at Waterloo", but her high spot was "Good night, George". She had known it. The passion, the torment, the jealousy, a silly girl's love affair. Tom did not want her, but he did not despise her. When he had kissed her she had seen the years ahead, when they would work together and respect each other. She would often have rows with him, but he was out of her system. Somehow, in going out of her system, he left room for the real Dulcie to come back. The honest Dulcie that John had known when he went away in 1940, but a Dulcie with added experience, artistry and charm. As she sat at the dressing-table holding the photograph of George, a queer smile came over her face, a bitter, amused smile. "Shouldn't be 'Good night, George'," she thought, "but 'Good-bye, George'. You've had it and you've earned it." There was no resemblance to Rose Reilly's performance of the number; it was pure Dulcie. She looked moving and childish in her dressing-gown. She knew what she was doing, there was no artifice about her. It was easy to imagine talking to the imaginary George, pretending to dance with him, pretending his arms were round her, that's what she had been doing with Tom. It hurt, it would always hurt perhaps, loving somebody who did not love you back. It was with a mixture of childishness and bitterness that she put the photograph down and whispered, "Good night, George."

Leonard Barrow looked at his guest, the guest nodded and rubbed his hands.

"I knew it when I saw her glaring at that chap at the piano. She'sgotsomethin', she'sgotsomethin'."

It was a risk, Alfred felt, to put Nella on again, she could never do it twice, but he did know what had happened. Nella sang "Mighty Like a Rose" for herself alone. Tom had said he loved her. If he loved her, presently they would be married, and after they had been married a little while they would have a baby who would look exactly like Tom.

"Sweetest little fellow,
Everybody knows,
Don't know what to call him,
But he's mighty like a rose."

At the end of the song F. J. Higgs looked round at the wildly applauding people behind him. He turned to Leonard Barrow.

"Curious quality."

Leonard Barrow nodded.

"What I'd call a collector's piece."

The curtain came down. Leonard Barrow had made his speech and the campers had gone off singing into the night. The company, with the exception of Dulcie, who was talking to Leonard Barrow's guest, were on the stage. F. J. Higgs sat down on the piano stool and beckoned to everybody to come round him.

"We'll be having a talk afterwards, I believe Mr. Barrow's arranging drinks and sandwiches for you all. I understand he's got great plans for you next year, but I have got plans which might suit you this winter." He smiled at John and Alfred. "There's a winter garden show I'm wanting for the north. Provided that a certain lady is willing to star and willing to sign a long contract, I think I can offer you an engagement which will keep you all together until you rejoin Mr. Barrow in the spring." He looked at Leonard Barrow. "We may have to come to some arrangement about that. I shall have other plans for the certain lady by then."

Alice was standing beside John. She slipped her hand into his. The whole winter doing another season, and the summer after that. Could the world hold so much happiness? Dulcie working with them, Dulcie starring. Dulcie would be pleased. Mr. Higgs wanting her for the winter and making it clear he had other plans for her in the spring.

Muriel was almost crying. Fancy her, with her funny old voice, working right through beside Alfred like that; so good for Dan, another year working all the time, he would soon be ready for any sort of engagement. Then, of course, Nella. She would be a star now. Funny to think of Nella being part, and an important part, of the family engagement.

Nella looked at Tom. Would he be coming to the winter garden? There had been nothing said about him. Tom caught her look and smiled at her, and her heart seemed to swell with warmth. "It's all right," his smile said, "if I don't go to the winter garden then I'll be somewhere else, but wherever I go you'll go." So lucky, thought Nella, that I'm not a star. I can go where Tom goes and it won't matter to anybody.

F. J. Higgs saw these glances and felt warm and fatherly. It was a nice thing this show with two families, nice being able to keep them together, a tiny bit of reconstruction, his bit towards putting the world straight for two families.

"We must go into details later," he said to Alfred and John, "but I don't suppose we shall quarrel about terms. That's fixed then. The winter garden up north November to March for the whole company, provided a certain young lady is agreeable."

Dulcie's dressing-room door had opened and she had heard the last words. Her eyes danced. This was the kind of situation she adored. This was the kind of moment she had always dreamed of. Pinkie was standing behind the company. He looked at her appraisingly. "Wait for it, Binns and Corners," he thought, "here comes the little fly in the ointment." Dulcie crossed to F. J. Higgs, smiling sweetly.

"But a certain lady isn't agreeable. A certain young lady agreed to oblige her family by coming to Comstock, but she has no intention of burying herself in a winter garden in some provincial town up north. She has had a very much better offer." There was a moan from Muriel, a sigh from Alfred, and a cry of real anguish from Alice. Dulcie disregarded them all. "I'm sorry, it's a shame you should be out of work for the winter, but I can't go on interfering with my career."

F. J. Higgs took Dulcie's chin between his thumb and first finger.

"You've got the picture wrong, Dulcie, my dear. The contract for the show to go to the north for the winter is not dependent on you. I hoped you would come, but if you've got something better to do we can manage without you." He let go of her chin and turned. "The girl I want, and the girl I hope to star in the spring, is Nella."

There was a stunned silence. After a moment Nella came to F. J. Higgs.

"But I don't want to be a star. As a matter of fact, I should simply hate it."

Alfred had to interrupt.

"It means a lot to us, Nella."

Muriel saw the little house in London, herself sitting alone by the fire, with Clemmie purring at her feet. Alfred would be on tour, he'd be sure to get something, perhaps Dan would get a panto, but there would be nothing for her.

To Alice it was as if a soap bubble, irridescent and lovely, had blown away, leaving nothing but a spot of moisture on the ground. The home must break up again, John and Alfred would probably go off into a pantomime somewhere together, Dickie would get a job somewhere else, Dulcie said she had a better offer so she would be away, too, there would only be herself and Betty. The home atmosphere, recreated this magic summer, would be gone again. It was too new, this new-found family happiness. It was too insecure to break up this winter. If F. J. Higgs had not made this miraculous offer, she would have accepted that was how things must be, but F. J. Higgs had made his offer, happiness had been within all their grasps, and it was being thrown away by Nella. She turned to her.

"You can't say no, Nella. It means so much to all of us. It's so long that your father and Uncle John have been away, it means everything our keeping together now."

Nella's eyes were on Alice's face.

"I know. I do know, but, you see, I want my happiness, too, just the sort of happiness that you want and have always had." She looked up at F. J. Higgs. "Is Tom coming to the winter garden? You see, we love each other, we want to get married."

F. J. Higgs found himself oddly moved. He had no intention that Tom should go to the winter garden. He wanted him in London, working on the new show for the spring which would star Nella. Surely he was a fairy godfather. If these two young things were in love with each other, wasn't he opening the gates of fame and fortune to them? Tom had his arm round Nella.

"That's right. We want to get married."

F. J. Higgs was worried, and because he was worried he

sounded cross.

"But you can marry and she can still be in the show. She'll be in London by the spring, I mean to star her, she's going to sing this song of yours, 'Poppies for England'. It's a wonderful chance for her."

Nella laid her hand on F. J.'s arm and stroked his sleeve.

"You've got the wrong idea. When I marry Tom I want to look after him, cook his meals, and see he doesn't lose his music, and very soon after we are married we'd like a baby."

F. J. Higgs looked down at her hand. He did not renounce his dream, but he saw it could not be fulfilled at the moment. Later on, perhaps, when she got the baby and the home she might see sense. He turned to Dulcie.

"What about you, young woman, when does this engagement start?"

Dulcie turned to Leonard Barrow's guest, who was smoking outside her dressing-room door.

"This is Mr. Pick. Cyril K. Pick."

The Binns, and even Tom, gaped. Cyril K. Pick was not merely part of, but almost, you might say, the whole of the British film industry. His was a name which was making film history. Mr. Pick came forward.

"She'sgotsomethin', she'scertainlygotsomethin'. Signing her up to-morrow for five years."

F. J. Higgs felt sorry for the families.

"Shall you be wanting her this winter? You've got all your productions planned, you don't want her till the spring. Couldn't you lend her to me for the winter garden for a few months?"

Mr. Pick shrugged his shoulders.

"Can't say for certain. I shall need her for tests and one thing and another, but it might be arranged."

F. J. Higgs smiled at the anxious faces round him.

"Mr. Pick and I are a couple of very old hands in the entertainment industry. When we say we think a thing can be arranged, it's the same as somebody else saying it's done." He winked at Leonard Barrow. "What about them all changing and those drinks? I'm getting thirsty."

*   *   *

Pinkie stood by Dulcie's dressing-table. She was so excited and talked so fast it was difficult for him to get a word in edgeways.

"As you're going to be a film star, you'll need a nice, unassuming husband, quiet about the house, humble, willing to be a doormat for the star to walk over, but with a nice eye to business. Always ready to hail the number eleven or the number thirty and say to the driver, 'Hi, why isn't my wife's name on your bus?' "

Dulcie powdered her face and got up to put on her frock. She looked at Pinkie with a puzzled frown.

"I can't think why you should want to marry me. You know all the worst about me, I never can hide anything from you."

He pulled her frock over her head and buttoned it up for her.

"It's just what you want. Even film stars must act natural sometimes. How relaxing for you to come home from the studio and lay all your lowest faults bare at my feet."

She pulled away from him.

"Come on, we ought to be going to the party. I still can't see why you want me."

He turned out the lights and led her through the stage door, into the night. It was dark out there; the wind was blowing, bringing with it the pleasant smell of seaweed. Pinkie put his arms round her and kissed her.

"Can't you, my sweet? Not even after I told you about Annabel? Men always fall for the same types. My fancy is for bitches."

In the office Leonard Barrow, seeing that all the glasses were full, rapped on the table for silence.

"Don't like a lot of toast drinkin', but here's to young Tom and Nella, and here's to the winter season in the north . . ." he broke off. The door had opened and Pinkie and Dulcie came in. He grinned. "I was going to say, 'Here's to the Barrow girl, our own film star.' But maybe I had better add to that. Here's to the Barrow girl, our own film star, and to my son, Pinkie. Are we drinking your healths together, boy?"

Pinkie looked at Dulcie.

"Can they?"

She nodded and took the glass that was offered to her. She gave her father an affectionate grin, then raised her glass to Nella.

"Here's fun!"